He Died of N

Shelley Smith

© Shelley Smith 1947

Shelley Smith has asserted her rights under the Copyright, Design and Patents Act, 1988, to be identified as the author of this work.

First published in 1947 by Collins Crime Club.

This edition published in 2017 by Endeavour Press Ltd.

TABLE OF CONTENTS

CHAPTER ONE - REQUIEM FOR A HOLY MAN   7

CHAPTER TWO - WHAT TIME HE DIED   21

CHAPTER THREE - ACQUAINTANCE WITH THE SEEKERS
    35

CHAPTER FOUR - THE SILENT BELL   56

CHAPTER FIVE - ONE FAIR DAUGHTER   72

CHAPTER SIX - ONE FOX TO ANOTHER   83

CHAPTER SEVEN - A PLEASANT WALK, A PLEASANT TALK...   97

CHAPTER EIGHT - THE GARRULOUS TAB   110

CHAPTER NINE - BROTHER AUDREY IS DISTURBED   130

CHAPTER TEN - MISS POST'S CURIOUS PHILOSOPHY   142

CHAPTER ELEVEN - SOMETHING IN THE CELLAR   154

CHAPTER TWELVE - OLD UMBRELLA'S LAPSE   167

CHAPTER THIRTEEN - ADDENDUM TO THE ABBOT'S BREACH DOSSIER   186

APPENDIX   202

For
ELIZABETH CROSS
To remind her of the happy hours we spent with The Seekers of Abbot's Breach.

CHAPTER ONE - REQUIEM FOR A HOLY MAN

SHAFTS of pale light cut across the layers of white perceptible air, creating unrealistic shadows, as though the sun was diffused through veils of chiffon. The incredible sky was as tender and far away as heaven. On the still air every sound carried beyond its normal destination, and you could hear the high invisible birds calling as they flew overhead; children shouting shrilly in a game; and the ominous rumble of cart wheels on a stony road.

Even on the station platform, keener than the curious compound smell of soot and engine-oil and trains, arose the odour of bonfires and decaying leaves, that heart-stirring and suggestive scent, presage of the death of the year. It was as though the year declared calmly, Good and bad, sweet and sorrowful, it's all one now; this is the end of spring's bright promise and summer's glory; now the cruel frost's spite matters no longer, and leaves cover the pits left by the drenching rains; the end of the year lies rotting on the earth, finished, forgotten ... Burn up its pitiful remains and *passons outre*.

The quiet solid gentleman on the platform, absently watching the little train cough its way round the bend and out of sight, was aware of this subtle aroma of decay, even found it press slightly on his spirits, though he would not have called himself a fanciful gentleman, not by any means, couldn't afford to be in his profession. And was it fair to say, Good or bad, sweet or sorrowful, it was all one in the end? There were certain mystics who held that evil was merely the other side of good, but wasn't that rather a flabby Hindu outlook? It did matter, he told himself staunchly, it was important, he said, as he picked up his suitcase and followed the only other passenger to alight from the train up the perilous steps of the overhead crossing.

The other passenger was a woman of perhaps thirty years of age, of medium height and slender, wearing putty-coloured tweeds of exquisite cut, with a brilliant violet shirt and a crazy little hat of the same shade swooping down at exactly the right angle over her sleek curls. The quiet gentleman noted approvingly her long elegant legs as she ran up the steps ahead of him.

He picked his way slowly across the bridge, looking about him at the fields beyond the fantastic yews, so absurdly out of place at the edge of the line, at the cluster of housetops behind the station roofs, at the paunchy ticket collector waiting at the barrier with a tall dark man in a raglan overcoat and a schoolgirl. The schoolgirl tossed her fair plaits over her shoulder and came uncertainly out of the shadows.

He heard the lady greet her coolly.

"Hallo, Ruby. How did you get on without me?" And handing her the pigskin suitcase she was carrying, she said, "Here, take this, will you? It's rather heavy. Everything all right at home?"

"Yes, Auntie," began the child in a surprisingly deep husky voice. "The baker came and I told him — "

"Any phone calls?" the lady interrupted. "Any letters?"

The girl shook her head.

The lady surveyed her with a kind of hopeless disgust.

"What a fright you look, my child! Why will you pull your hat down right over your nose?" she said in a low, impatient voice, jerking the round black beaver oft her forehead and tugging unavailingly at the navy nap coat strained across the child's narrow chest. "You simply can't go around looking like this any longer. I'm ashamed of you."

"It's been let down as far as it'll go," said Ruby apologetically.

"You can't wear it any more," she said flatly. "I'll have to find you something else." She turned away abruptly, and as she did so the tall dark man stepped forward and raised his hat. His brows ran together to form a black bar across his forehead, beneath which his black eyes were set obliquely. His sleek black hair was beginning to recede above his temples, leaving a mephistophelian peak in the centre. He had good features marred by an upper lip overhanging the lower, which gave him the saturnine expression of a shark.

"Hallo, Harold," said the young woman in a bright mocking voice. "How nice of you to come down to meet me."

He raised his brows and said, "But this is altogether an unexpected pleasure. I had no idea you were away." His voice was cultured, slightly affected, and pitched rather too high, as if he were accustomed to addressing a roomful of people. "I came down to collect a crate of apples

I'm expecting, but they haven't arrived yet," he added. The elaboration was a mistake, it gave him away, and the lady did not even pretend to believe it.

"Hardly the thing, I should have thought, for a headmaster to run errands of that kind. Very bad for your prestige, surely," she mocked. "However, since you have come you may run me into the village; there are some things I have to do."

He looked at his watch doubtfully and hesitated.

"I scarcely think — " he began.

"Oh, don't be such a stick," she said contemptuously.

For half a second it looked as though her teasing would make him lose his temper; and then he laughed; and she laughed; and together they moved through the barrier and climbed into his Lagonda coupé.

The schoolgirl, left behind without so much as a backward glance, dropped the suitcase with an indignant thud.

"Well, of all the dirty old cows!"

"My dear child!" ejaculated the quiet gentleman behind her. "What language! You really mustn't."

His dear child turned to face him hastily, little red paws pressed defensively to her chest like a squirrel. Her enormous innocent eyes were brilliant with sudden tears in her flaming face. Her rosy lips pouted defiantly. "Well, she is." But nothing could harden the naive curves of her baby face. "I gotta be sure 'n' come down 'n' meet her, she says, an' then she goes off 'n' leaves me flat."

"She met her friend and she forgot about you, that's all. It's nothing to get so angry about."

"Yes, 'n' he's a liar, too. I'm gointer tell the boys about him! Makin' out he never knew she was comin', 'n' when he rang up last night I partickler told him she was coming to-day. I think grown-ups tell shocking lies," she said crossly, "an' if I ever tell a whopper they don't half carry on." She kicked the suitcase sulkily with her shabby shoe.

"She could of took the case, couldn't she? She knows I wanted to go to the funeral. Ol' meanie!"

The gentleman's lips twitched slightly. What a quaint baby it was to be sure! With its hard-bitten language, its childish petulance and its morbid interest in funerals. He suggested pacifically that she might go to the funeral just the same. Ruby looked dubious. Could she? Like this?

Auntie said she looked awful. A funeral, the gentleman explained kindly, was not the same as a wedding, it was not necessary to dress up for it, it was a solemn occasion rather than a festive one.

She swung one leg back and forth, scraping the dust with her heel. She said at last: "Auntie was going wiv me. I don't like to go alone. I never bin to one before."

But now in the inconsequential way grown-ups had, the gentleman seemed to have lost interest. He said, almost impatiently, "Come. Give me the case, it's too heavy for you."

This unexpected courtesy alarmed and embarrassed Ruby to blushing pitch.

"You must show me the way," he warned her. "I'm a stranger."

"Where? Home?"

"You want to go to the funeral, don't you?"

She said, "Oh!" and again went pink with pleasure.

Together they strode up the road from the station, an oddly assorted pair, the solid square man and the shabby child stretching her thin black woollen legs like the points of a pair of dividers to keep up with him.

Frost still rimed the grasses edging the road. They passed the clump of yellow brick villas near the station and moved towards open fields. Cows loomed their heavy heads over gates and hedges to stare at them as they passed.

Her companion broke the silence to inquire the name of the headmaster. "The headmaster!" echoed Ruby, with round amazed eyes. "D'you mean Mr. Prescott, him what was at the station? How ever did you know he was the headmaster?"

"I heard your Aunt say so," said the gentleman, with a smile. "It wasn't magic."

"Soppy ol' Prescott!" Ruby chanted mechanically, and added sullenly in a different tone, with a sly upward glance at her companion, "Why don't she leave him alone? I know who he's gone on and it isn't her. I could tell her, but I won't. P'raps I will, though, one day, when I want to make her mad. Always thinks every one must be potty about her, she does." This, she thought, was something of a 'pick-up' (remembering with excited glee her 'Auntie's' warnings), and she felt the need to impress him with her sophistication.

"Ought you to talk about your Aunt like that — to a stranger?" said the gentleman in quiet reproof.

"Why?" said Ruby with devastating innocence. "Every one knows about her and the way she goes on. She don't care."

"That's not the point. It makes *you* sound nasty, you see."

She lapsed into a thoughtful silence, kicking a stone before her. A cat sitting neatly in an open doorway watched them pass with a flickering self-contained smile behind her whiskers. For a time they walked in silence.

Then Ruby burst out suddenly: "She isn't really my Auntie. I just call her that, see, cos she looks after me, sort of. I came to her as a 'vacuee when the war was on. All those years ago it was," she said dreamily. "Fancy! I was ever such a little tot when I came, 'n' now I'm turned fourteen 'n' I've left school."

"How is it that you are still with her, then?"

"Dad got blown up," she explained with the brutal casualness of childhood. "And after that Mum never came down no more, I don't know why, and the Government don't know where she's gorn 'n' they don't know what to do with me, so Auntie jus' keeps me."

"That's very kind of her, isn't it?"

"Oh, yes. I never said she wasn't kind, did I? She's kind as can be, sometimes. You can't help loving her. And you can't help hating her," the child said with impartial accuracy, and added candidly, "That's why I'm mad at her now. Cos she had to go to London and leave me alone in the house at night. She knows I hate that. I'm scared. Auntie says I'm a baby. So I try not to be. Cos it makes her wild."

"Ought you to go to funerals if you're scared of the dark?" said the gentleman quizzically.

"I dunno. I never bin before. But this is something special. I gotta go. He was my friend. Him they call the Master." She watched to see a glimmer of interest on his sad impassive face. "You know all about that, don't you?"

"About what?" he said.

"Go on," she urged. "You must have heard. It was in all the papers. Don't you read the papers? All about how 'e was shot, an' they were all there, an' nobody knows how it 'appened."

"No! " he said, and met her innocent gaze.

"They had to have a ninquest," she said proudly. Again the innocent glance appraised him. She licked her lips. "I was there," she announced daringly. "Coo!" she said, "it was awful! He banged on his desk with the hammer, the judge did, and they all came marching in. An' there was Mr. Titmarsh, 'im they called the Master, lying on a sort of table in the middle of the room, 'n' blood all over 'im, an' a great hole in the middle of 'is chest, 'n' his eyes all rolled up in the corner something horrible, like this — " Here she writhed her features into an appalling grimace. She grinned gleefully at her companion's expression and continued: "Some of 'em carried on something shocking when they saw 'im, fainting and screaming all over the shop. And the judge just as mad as could be banging away with his hammer. 'I order the contemp' of Court,' he says, 'clear 'em all out'"

They caught up and passed an old man lumbering slowly along with a barrowful of muck.

"Go on. What happened then?"

"Then?" Ruby frowned energetically. "Oh, well, then they talked a lot of stuff about who done it and how it could have happened. But it sort of went on and on then and I got a bit tired, I didn't listen much to that part."

"Well, what conclusion did they reach? What did they decide?"

Her brow cleared. "Oh yes, I'd forgotten that bit. All those jury people went away, and when they came back this old judge in his funny ol' wig sits up and says, 'Well, my twelve good men an' true, what is your vermin?' And the oldest one there got up and bowed and said, *'Your Lawship, our vermin is he died of murder!'*" With sure artistic instinct the child halted her narrative abruptly at the climax, and looked up at her companion with an artless smile.

"Thank you," he said gravely. "Thank you so much. It must have been a most interesting inquest, most unusual. How I wish I'd been there! So they say he died of murder, do they? What a neat verdict. They didn't chance to mention who they thought had done it, I suppose? No, that would be too much to hope for. Have you any ideas on the subject?"

Ruby looked astonished, as though the suggestion had never occurred to her before.

"Me?" she said. "Lumme, I don't know. Some ol' tramp, I s'pose."

"Not a local person at all, you think?"

"D'you mean it might have been someone who knew him?" Her ingenious face was troubled. She stuck a little cold red finger in her mouth thoughtfully. "Oh, I don't think it could be any one who knew him," she said at last. "Why ever should any one want to kill the Master?"

"Every one liked him, did they?" said her companion sympathetically.

"No," she said helplessly, with a puzzled frown. "Not that exactly, either. I can't quite explain."

"Never mind. Tell me instead why he was called the Master if his name was Mr. Titmarsh."

"I dunno. They just called him that."

"You've got to be Master of something. What was it — Foxhounds? "

"Foxhounds! " Ruby looked at him sideways and spluttered with laughter. "He wouldn't even let them go over his land! That was a shindy, if you like!" she added parenthetically. "No, he was the Head of them people called The Seekers. Haven't you ever heard of 'em? Honest? I don't know where you've been, you don't seem to know anything. Well, these Seekers, see, they're all Brothers."

"Brothers and sisters? Or Brothers like monks?"

"Like monks — sort of, only they're not Christians."

"Not Christians, indeed?" He was quietly amused. "What are they, pray? Mohammedans? Or Tibetan Lamas?"

"I dunno what they are, but everybody knows they're not Christians, I've heard the Reverend Foster say so, too, and he'd know, wouldn't he? Besides, they said it themselves."

"Then why is he having a Christian funeral?"

But that was taking Ruby beyond her depth, and she pointed to the church which became apparent round the bend. It was a low building with a pointed stone roof and an old Saxon tower. The vicarage, an ugly Victorian building with high windows, humped beside it. There was no one about. Presumably, they were either late or too early. Ruby hung back.

"He'll be covered up, won't he?" she inquired huskily. He assured her that the coffin would be closed, there would be nothing to see. Still she hesitated, glancing at him anxiously and running her tongue across her lips. If he was aware of these appealing looks he chose to ignore them, and bent forward to swing open the old lych-gate. Nervously she pulled her hat down over her nose, and then remembered her aunt's peevish protest and pushed it back again. She tugged at his sleeve.

"Before we go in," she mumbled, very red in the face, "I better tell you. All that stuff I tole you about the inquest was just gammon."

"You made it up?"

She nodded tearfully.

"Well, never mind, I didn't believe it."

"Didn't you?" she said, disappointed and relieved. "Wasn't it like a real inquest?"

"Not much, I'm afraid."

"Why didn't you stop me, then?"

"Why should I? I enjoyed it. It was a very vivid story."

"Then you're not wild with me?"

"My dear child, what do you take me for? A policeman?"

"A policeman!" Ruby wrinkled her nose. "No, I should jolly well say not. If it hadn't bin for that rotten ole p'liceman I could have got into the ninquest."

That curious repressive stillness which hangs about churchyards when a Service is in progress was noticeable now. As they walked up the wide pathway to the deep-set door their steps echoed hollowly on the stone flags.

" ... and our beloved brother ... " they heard the priest chanting as they gently pushed open the door. It was very dark in the church after the misted whiteness outside. They slipped furtively into a pew at the back. Considering it was a weekday and early morning, the church was surprisingly full. A lot of people had evidently come to pay their last respects to Mr. Titmarsh. Or was it only curiosity because 'he died of murder'?

The raising of Lazarus in the East window slid round the stone pillars in a distorted pattern of reds and yellows and disfigured the upturned faces of the congregation with patches of livid colour. The priest touched his forehead and breast: " ... *and* to the Holy Ghost," he said, and turned away.

As the priest disappeared, every one relaxed and began fidgeting with their hats and prayer-books, bending to whisper to their neighbour, or turning round to stare frankly and inquisitively about them.

And then suddenly the murmuring and restless movement faded away or was drowned in the greater sound that began to vibrate on the air. Four great pulsing chords on the organ startled the congregation to attention. The sound seemed to emanate from the walls themselves, seemed to fill the air ... The solemn, mournful statement died away into silence. And then, faintly, faintly — oh how pianissimo! — it stole upon the air again ... very gently ... very ominously ... little creeping arpeggios of despair. That four notes could sound so drear! It was saying, even as the gentleman imagined the year saying earlier (but in how different a tone!), We all die — however brave, however good; the end is the same for all; Death is the conqueror; effort is useless, Fate indifferent, "the paths of glory lead but to the grave." But at the last horror of desolation, there was a change of key, a note of gaiety and triumph developed, surrounded with tender chuckling little harmonies that stroked the mind soothingly to comfort once again. And before the mind could consent to smiling apathy, it reverted to the original theme, and ended with a thunderous and joyful paean that shook the sleeping echoes from the roof.

By this time they were all awake, emotionally as well as physically, startled, not quite certain whether to approve or be shocked. A decidedly unusual requiem, thought Ruby's new friend, very powerful, very interesting, very modern.

The organist descended from his loft and came through the vestry door. His appearance was as original and unexpected as the work he had so ably performed. He was a young man of medium height and build with limp yellow hair parted high almost in the middle and wide blue eyes in a round pink face. He was wearing a full-skirted robe like a monk's habit, with big loose sleeves and a cowl, and girt round the waist with a scarlet cord. The robe was of the dirty off-white colour of unbleached wool, coarse and heavy.

Ruby gave her friend a wicked spike with her elbow. "That's one of 'em," she muttered. "One of them Seekers."

As he came past the chancel rails three others joined him. They were the pall-bearers. The plain wooden coffin was carried slowly to the graveyard and lowered into the waiting grave. The rest of them trooped behind and stood patiently bareheaded in the chill air. Faint breezes stirred the priest's fine white hair into a silvery halo. "Man that is born of woman," he intoned piously.

One of the Brothers bent to pick up a lump of earth and crumbled it between his fingers, as it might be a farmer judging a bit of soil, before casting it down almost casually into the open grave.

"Forasmuch as it hath pleased Almighty God of His great mercy to take unto Himself the soul of our dear brother here departed ... " The priest's artificial tones struggled to rise above the cold rattle of falling clods.

The mist was dispersed now by little stinging winds which whipped the blood to the ears, reddened noses, and started involuntary tears to the eyes of those who could not weep. The pallid sun struck reflections brighter than itself from spectacles and purse-tops and buttons.

It was not the season for a graveside homily, but the vicar did his best. The uninspired platitudes were dully soothing to the inattentive ears of the congregation, but what consolation did they offer to the bereaved? Evidently, none at all. For after a few minutes there was an abrupt movement, a brief disturbance, and then the mourners gathered at the graveside swayed apart like a double curtain and the white-clad Brothers filed through.

They passed quite close to Ruby and her friend with stony or blazing faces. One spat out, "Hypocrisy!" as he passed, and another muttered disgustedly, "Lies, lies, lies; all lies!" Two of them, he noted with some surprise, were women; although they wore the same clumsy habits, their light swinging gait, was unmistakable. One of the women was dark and gaunt, with a profile rigid as a martyr's, and her black eyes burning straight ahead of her. The other, fair and lumpy, followed her unevenly, sometimes hurrying up against her and sometimes falling behind to let her incurious pale gaze wander over the people round about. The last one was a stoutish young man with fair hair tightly curling all over his head, but whose healthy ruddy face was marred now by red-rimmed eyes and a strained look. When he saw Ruby he hesitated and smiled.

She caught at his sleeve and whispered something.

He shook his head and bent down to her.

"She wouldn't come," he said. "Brother Audrey stayed with her. You shouldn't have come either, dear. You shouldn't listen to this old man's preaching, you don't need him to tell you what the Master was like, do you? Forget all this. It's all wrong, dear. This hasn't anything to do with the Master; it doesn't touch him really. Remember him as he is, as you knew him," he said softly, with a sad tender look at her. "I must go." He touched her cheek gently with the back of his finger and was gone.

"That's Brother William," said Ruby, gazing after him. "He's ever so nice. He made me a whistle once. And he can imitate birds and do all sorts of things."

Every one was moving off. As soon as they were as far from the grave as some unwritten sanctimonious law of decency required, they began stamping their feet with cold. "Look, I gotta go," said Ruby suddenly. But it was too late. She was marked down and pounced on by a vigorous elderly lady with a very brown face and white hair. She hailed Ruby in a robust stand-no-nonsense manner.

"Hallo," she said. "What are you doing here?"

Ruby was suddenly as bland as soap.

"'Morning, Miss," she said demurely.

"When's Miss Post coming back?"

"Back, Miss?" said Ruby, apparently uncomprehending.

"She's in London, isn't she?"

"Oh, no, Miss, she's here."

"Here? I don't see her."

"I mean, Market Keep."

"Ah! I made sure she'd be here if she were back. But I expect she had plenty to do at home. And that's where you ought to be, child, helping her, instead of running the streets."

"I'm not. She isn't," said Ruby hotly at this injustice. "She went off with — " She pulled herself up. "She had to go out," she amended.

"So you thought you might as well go out too, eh? While the cat's away ... " The elderly lady, forgetful of where she was, laughed mightily. "Well, you need have nothing to fear from me, Ruby. I promise not to tell." She glanced archly at the man beside her to see if he was appreciating the jest, but he was listening solemnly as though to some grave matter. She said determinedly, "And now, Ruby, I should like to meet your friend."

Poor Ruby flushed to the roots of her hair. It was this that she dreaded. Once let it get about that this was just a "pick-up," and before you could say "knife," Auntie would have heard of it and then there *would* be a dust-up. She stared painfully at her battered toecaps and mumbled something incoherent.

"Come, child! Speak up! There's nothing to be afraid of," she said with hateful brightness. The petrified silence prolonged itself. "The girl's an idiot! There remains nothing for it but to introduce myself," she said whimsically. She held out her hand with a great air of frankness and said, "I'm Miss Farrell."

The gentleman bowed. "My name is Chaos."

Just that. Chaos. An unusual name, she didn't remember ever hearing it before. He might be a solicitor. Or a doctor. Something professional undoubtedly in that dark suit and discreet tie.

"Cold," said Miss Farrell. "Very nice for a brisk tramp over the hills, but not exactly the weather for hanging about churchyards, eh? Are you just down for the funeral?"

"Oh, no. Actually, I came at this young lady's request. I understand the late lamented was a friend of hers."

So he was not the solicitor. "A friend, indeed!" Miss Farrell snorted. "I never could understand what Miss Post was about letting Ruby run in and out of that place whenever she wanted to."

"They never minded," Ruby protested huskily.

Miss Farrell ignored her. "I'd never have allowed any child in my charge to go there. I'd sooner give it prussic acid. You know what I mean, Mr. Chaos. It's not a fit place for a child." She halted and then added slyly: "But I dare say you know as much about them as I do."

"No, really. Nothing at all, I assure you," Mr. Chaos protested.

"They all live together," said Miss Farrell. "In this place they call The Sanctuary." She laughed sarcastically. "I should have said it would mean the same thing and be much nearer the mark if they called it The Asylum. So there they all live, men and women, openly professing love for one another and speaking the truth in all circumstances, and nobody asks any questions and nobody tells any lies — so they say." She arched her thick white brows ironically.

"You mean, they love one another too literally," said Mr. Chaos.

"Of course it is a free country," Miss Farrell acknowledged handsomely. " But, like all cranks, they have got hold of some perfectly obvious ideas and have become quite fanatical about them. Take this business of speaking the truth: I'm an ordinary God-fearing Englishwoman with plenty of faults I dare say, but I've managed to speak the truth for sixty-five years, without making a ridiculous spectacle of myself by eating nuts and generally dressing up like a circus clown in order to do so. It's such an unnatural life, that's what I've got against it. Seekers, they call themselves, you know, but as I say to Alice, I'll wager they've got something to hide too."

"And what is it they seek?"

"I tell you: Truth and Love. Honestly, it's hardly decent to my mind. I don't mind admitting that *I* wasn't surprised that Wesley Titmarsh got himself shot. If you ask me, he had only himself to thank for it."

"Meaning, he deserved it?"

"I speak no ill of the dead," she said smugly. "Pray don't misunderstand me, I had nothing against the man at all. I'm not saying he wasn't a good man, mind you, but you've got to admit he was responsible for all these goings on. And I suppose love-making and truth-seeking was a bit too much for somebody, and — poof! — a bullet through the brain. It's always the way, isn't it? Though a legal friend of mine tells me that we shall soon be getting to the point where we shall regard the passional crime as indulgently as they do in France."

Mr. Chaos said: "Ah, you favour the eternal triangle, do you?" and shifted the suitcases from one hand to the other. Miss Farrell smiled and refused to be drawn.

"I mustn't keep you hanging about in this weather," she said briskly. "Miss Post is putting you up, I suppose?" she suggested inquisitively. But it was no use. The gentleman was perfectly affable but definitely uncommunicative. She was an indomitable old girl, however, and she tried again, asking him this time how long he was staying in Market Keep. He said baldly and truthfully that he did not know. Still she was not ruffled. "I was merely going to say that if you are staying for any length of time and should find yourself ever in Bilberry Lane, you must be sure to drop in and see me. I can promise you a decent cup of tea, it comes to me straight from one of the finest gardens in Ceylon. A pet luxury of mine. Wee Holme is the name of my cot. Now, don't forget! " She wagged a finger at him roguishly, and strode off.

"Ooo, isn't she orful!" said Ruby indignantly, almost before she was out of earshot.

"Is she?" said Mr. Chaos innocently.

"She's a proper ol' cow! And nosy, you'd never believe!"

"Fancy that, now," said Mr. Chaos, quite forgetting to correct her language this time. "Why does that annoy you? I like nosy people; I'm rather nosy myself, as it happens. And I thought her very interesting."

"Well, you don't want to go believing all that stuff she says," said Ruby sulkily. "It was all lies. She's a norful liar!"

"Oh, I know," said Mr. Chaos simply. "That's what was so interesting, dear."

CHAPTER TWO - WHAT TIME HE DIED

Market Keep High Street was very ancient, and even the shop windows appeared traditional and musty, trailing the odour of antiquity. Having disposed of young Ruby, Mr. Chaos sought the local hostelry wherein he might deposit his own suitcase. The bosom of The Black Dog overhung the street with Tudor effrontery. Its mellow, quaint appearance had arrested the eye of many a hapless traveller, but once lured into the shadow of the upper storey a sort of gloom descended on the spirit. Mr. Chaos wondered anxiously if he was becoming fanciful after all. Black Dog was the right epithet for it; it was black, everywhere. One came from the bright street into the shadow, stumbling over the threshold, and stood blinking in inky darkness until one's eyes became adjusted to the gloom. By the dim light that filtered through the small leaded panes one perceived after a while that a calendar bearing last month's date stood out whitely against the panelled walls; the deep wavy beams that ran across the ceiling were varnished a heavy black; and the chairs and sofas were upholstered hideously in shiny black horsehair. There was no one about.

Mr. Chaos discovered a bell over by the fireplace and rang it sharply thrice. There was a fearful noise of tin trays and people falling downstairs and dropping brooms and boots — and then nothing. A poltergeist, decided Mr. Chaos, serenely. More thundering up and down stairs, and then a little grey wisp of a woman burst through a door at the back and said, "Bar's round the side!"

Mr. Chaos, incredulous that a woman of that size could have made so much noise, said slowly, patiently, that he did not want the bar. He wanted a room. He wanted service. Very likely he would want food. Was that possible?

The poltergeist woman looked astonished, as though no one had ever asked such a thing of her before, and said she really couldn't say, she was sure. Yes, they were open to receive visitors. Well, how long would the gentleman be requiring it for? She dare said they could do him, she agreed reluctantly.

"I dare say you can and I dare say you will," said Mr. Chaos glumly. "Let's see the room."

The room was not encouraging. It had a petulant wallpaper, and one light in the centre of the room with a shade of blue glass beads. The switch was by the door, so that even if one had been able to see to read in bed, one would have to get out to turn it off. There was a marble washstand with a ewer and basin embellished with peacock blue roses — or were they cabbages? The fierce turkey rug by the bed fought with the crimson eiderdown reposing voluptuously on the brass bedstead. Under the bed, as coyly as a solitary egg beneath a sitting hen, lurked a chamber-pot. The cosy old inns of Merry England! Mr. Chaos grimaced and resigned himself.

He regained the street just as Miss Post issued from the Private Bar with Mr. Prescott. She was laughing. This time she was coming towards him and he saw her face. It was a little disappointing. She was not pretty after all. But she was attractive; the kind of face that might prove very fascinating; a clownish face, a monkey face, with a wide scarlet mouth and sad brown eyes. As they passed, she glanced at him languidly, appraisingly, from the corner of her eye. He heard her say: "Who's the handsome stranger?" and the man answered in his high sarcastic voice: "My dear, you're forgetting our little tragedy ..."

Handsome stranger, indeed! Mr. Chaos, who had outgrown that particular childish vanity, grinned to himself.

The Police Station was hidden away in a far corner of the village and he might never have found it if he had not seen a notice, evidently placed there for the benefit of drunks, strayed persons and criminals, which obligingly informed the world that this was the way to the police station.

Inside, the office was warm, not to say stuffy. The sunlight touched the little fire with cold fingers that turned the flame to grey ash. There was a half-empty cup of cocoa on the desk; and the sergeant, with his jacket unbuttoned, was doing a crossword puzzle.

Mr. Chaos flicked his card on to the desk. The sergeant made out the name upside down. *Detective Inspector Chaos*, and in the corner, *Criminal Investigation De—* He had no need to read further. He sprang to his feet with a horrified expression, doing up his coat with one hand and turning the newspaper over with the other. He knew it was too late, of course, and it was not a bit of use trying to explain that it was the midmorning break. Mr. Chaos ignored his consternation and suggested pleasantly that they get down to business right away.

Sergeant Bean was a complacent, verbose soul, with a maddening habit of rolling his tongue lushly round his mouth. Now he launched into a long rigmarole about how on the day of the fatality he had had the misfortune to be on duty at the Petty Sessions and there was only a young constable left in charge who knew nothing — he'd only been in the Force six months. He wasn't saying the young lad hadn't done his best, far be it from him to say that, but of course it wasn't the same thing as having an experienced man on the job. He implied that if he had been there nothing would have gone wrong, it would never have been necessary to call in Scotland Yard at all. If Constable Lamb had even had the wit to ring Towchester Station for help, but he tried to manage everything alone. And here was the sergeant waiting all his life for a chance like that and just that very day he'd been called away. And they called him Lucky Bean! Of course, the moment he got back he took things in hand himself, but even so he had got a wigging from the Chief Constable. As though he was to blame! But if things were in a mess someone had to be held responsible, he knew that from his old days in the army. And that may have been why the Chief Constable called in the Yard as soon as it was a question of murder, instead of giving the local people a chance.

Mr. Chaos, instead of telling him to shut up or stick to the point, listened sympathetically and was sure that he could be very helpful in spite of that. With the result that Sergeant Bean stopped airing his grievances and began instead to tell the inspector about the inhabitants of The Sanctuary.

To begin with, if they called it The Sanctuary no one else did. It was known now, as it always had been, as Abbot's Breach. Long ago on the site where The Sanctuary now stood had once been a monastery, and there had been some kind of holy schism between the monks and the head abbot — hence the name of the place. The exact story was long forgotten and, anyway, the order had been dissolved later under Henry the Eighth. There were still the original lands, some five or six hundred acres, the sergeant thought. And these new people, The Seekers as they called themselves, farmed it. They had been there twelve years; but their number varied, they came and went, and sometimes there were more of them than at others. Just now — that is to say, up to the time of the crime — there were ten of them, six men and four women.

"Are they popular?" said Mr. Chaos. "I mean do the people round here like them?"

Sergeant Bean thought on the whole, no. Not that there was anything wrong with them, as far as he knew, but they dressed up, and that was like the blackshirts only worse, and they prayed too much. It didn't do. People didn't like that. Sunday was all right, and only respectful, but to carry on as if every day was Sunday was excessive and seemed faintly a mockery somehow, though how, he'd have been hard put to it to say. He didn't know anything else against them.

Then young Constable Lamb came in and was presented to the inspector. He looked very blond and innocent, and the blood came up under his fair skin in a way that reminded the inspector of Ruby. He looked scared now at the ordeal which lay ahead of him and busied himself collecting the files and various pieces of evidence neatly labelled. Then he began his report.

"At eleven thirty-five a.m. on the sixth of October I was called to the scene of the crime," he began, remembering how the door burst open and Mr. Carpenter came in with an ash-coloured face to say there had been an accident.

"Who is Mr. Carpenter?" interrupted the inspector. "You must give me more detail."

Mr. Carpenter, Mr. Rollo Carpenter, was a member of this Brotherhood of Seekers, a man of — it was hard to say just what age, but certainly no longer young. Lamb asked him for particulars of the accident: where it had happened, to whom, and the nature of it; all quite in order but it fretted Mr. Carpenter, who thought valuable time was being wasted and begged him to hurry. "It's the Master," he said, "he's been shot. For pity's sake, hurry. I'm off to get the doctor now. You go on. He's lying in Three Acre field."

Three Acre field, the constable explained, was part of the Abbot's Breach land. The garden of the house was on an incline and sloped downwards in a gentle gradient to a low stone wall boundary, and Three Acre field lay the other side of the wall and sloped upward till the top part of the field stood level with the house. The constable had photographs and diagrams to show the inspector. For the present he must explain that the field had been ploughed up recently and was lying fallow with piles of manure waiting to be dug in. It was here, in approximately the middle of the field, that Wesley Titmarsh was lying.

P.C. Lamb paused, remembering vividly those awful moments. He would not go through them again for anything. In some curious way he remembered the scene as if he were spectator as well as participant, and he saw his tall lanky figure hesitating on the edge of the field. There were The Seekers huddled in a group, praying or weeping, and one of them, Mr. McQueen it was, standing to one side sternly, shivering in his shirt sleeves, and still and solitary in the middle of the field, the body of their Master, as they called him. And he had to walk out, past the huddle of people kneeling on the bare earth, towards that lonely figure. It made his knees feel queer and weak, as if they were going to bend backwards, and it wasn't the lumps of soil clinging to his boots, he knew, that made them so heavy to lift. It was a raw chill morning, rags of mist were still caught in the branches of the trees, and it may have been the cold which made him shrink and shudder into his skin.

The Master lay so still that he thought he was dead. Only when he got up to him he could hear the noise he made trying to breathe through the blood bubbling up from the great hole in his chest just below his throat. It nearly made him sick; the sky and the trees and the earth all whirled round together. He had never seen anything like it before. The models and photographs you saw in the training college gave you no idea. Blood was upsetting anyway, and there was so much here, soaking into his robe, darker than the bright cord about his waist.

He almost lost his head, then. He hadn't the least idea what he was supposed to do. He only knew that he wanted to run away from it all and what it implied, anywhere, he didn't care where, so long as he might hide. He was ashamed of his unmanliness of course and had the guts to pull himself together and kneel down by the dying man. It was the being alone that made it so awful, if there had been even another constable with him it would not have been so terrifying; but he had no one to rely on but himself and somehow he had to see the thing through. He tried to remember helpful pieces out of the Police Code but nothing came.

And then like divine fire from heaven the first coherent thought settled in his empty tumbling brain, and he stopped feeling sick. Where is the weapon? he thought.

And there was no weapon. Mr. Carpenter had said an accident, but the fact that there was no weapon seemed to show that the wound was not self-inflicted. And that meant it had been done by someone else, either accidentally or on purpose.

Either way it was a serious business because it was plain that the man was dying. His pulse was just perceptible, dotting along unevenly. He was unconscious of course. It must have been a shot fired at very close range, P.C. Lamb decided. Bits of flesh were spattered about, and powder marks were visible here and there between the bloodstains. Someone, probably Mr. McQueen since he was in shirt-sleeves, had spread a habit on the ground beside the injured man. The constable called Mr. McQueen over and asked him if they had moved the body. He looked surprised and said, No, of course not. Everything had been left just as it was.

"It was here that he fell?" the constable insisted.

"Yes."

Mr. McQueen said it was his habit on the ground. He had had some idea of trying to make the wounded man more comfortable, but had then thought better of it. There was a spade lying on the ground a few inches from the dying man's outflung hand. And Lamb asked what it was doing there and to whom it belonged. It was there when he arrived, Mr. McQueen said, and he believed that was why the Master had crossed the field, in order to pick it up, seeing it lying there. Since they owned everything in common, he explained, the spade might be said to belong to them all equally. He did not know who had used it last.

In answer to further questions Mr. McQueen explained that the Master had entered the field from the gate at the top corner and crossed the field diagonally — there were his solitary footsteps in proof thereof — and when he reached the centre of the field he was shot.

Here Constable Lamb broke off to point out to the inspector that the right hand boundary of the field, looking towards the house, was a thickset hedge some ten feet high. Other side of the hedge was a path and that path chanced to be a *right of way*. Therefore any one might have been passing along there quite legitimately, and no one any the wiser. Some fool might have been doing a little careless shooting the other side of that hedge never thinking who might be behind it. That was one way of looking at it, anyhow. According to the measurements he had made at the time, while he was waiting for the doctor to arrive, the body was lying about three yards from the centre of the field, nearest the hedge. He had had just enough wit to send for the local photographer, who fortunately had some experience of criminal photography and knew what was wanted. There were ten plates, seven showing different aspects of the body in close-up, and the others long views showing plainly the position in relation to the rest of the field. In one of them was nicely visible the single file of footmarks leading from the gate to where the victim fell. The rest of the field of course was hopelessly trampled over by that time.

When the doctor came he seemed thoroughly put out that no one had attempted to help the injured man or stop the bleeding, though he must have known that amateur attempts were generally more harmful than good. By now the dying man's face had fallen in and was an earthen yellow, he looked ghastly, and the edges of the wound were turning blue. The doctor sent the constable running to phone for an ambulance, but with the waywardness of fate it had gone to collect a peritonitis case the other side of the county. The doctor said impatiently that in that case he would take him himself, and they must rig up a stretcher of some sort. Doctor Blake was always rather contemptuous of The Seekers, and now he spoke almost rudely, and told them to come and help him and he would show them what to do. In any case, he said, it would be helping their Master more than their prayers.

They got him down to the car and made him as comfortable as possible. He lay with his head in the constable's lap. His face was like clay. And he seemed to be breathing no more than twice a minute. When they were nearly there the constable leaned forward and said: "It's no use, sir. He's gone." It was then twelve fifty-three.

He had little more to tell Mr. Chaos on the matter, and the inspector began scanning the statements. These were as usual brief and disjointed, in a queer stilted style that approximated but did not resemble human speech. But Mr. Chaos was used to police reporting, and he knew that the words did not flow on evenly as a straight narrative, but were practically answers to adroit questioning, so that from habit he could supply the unseen questions.

The first on the file was Wesley Titmarsh's wife. It began:

"I am Lucy Titmarsh. I heard nothing. I was the other side of the house in the kitchen, baking. The first I knew of the accident was when one of them came in to tell me. Then I ran out. But they wouldn't let me go near him. Mr. McQueen said, 'There's nothing you can do, dear. Come away. We've sent for the doctor. Join us in prayer.' So I went over and knelt with the others. That's all I know. My husband had no enemies that I know of. My husband never had a gun, it was against his principles."

The next statement was Rollo Carpenter's.

"I was in my cell, meditating, since it was the hour of Meditation, when Brother William came in. I noticed he looked very white. He said, 'There's been an accident. Look!' I looked where he pointed, but I could only see what appeared to be the scarecrow leaning to one side. I said, 'What's happened?' And he said, 'It's the Master. You must come at once.' And we hurried down. Some of the others were there already and I could see Brother David was doing what he could. He asked me to fetch the police and a doctor. I went at once, I knew it must be serious if he wanted the doctor because we don't believe in materia medica; but of course in the event of a death the doctor has to be called in in accordance with the laws of the land. I didn't know why he wanted me to get the police. We have no guns. It is contrary to our beliefs to kill anything, either for the protection of our property or for food. I think it was an accident. I think someone passing through the grounds fired at a bird and shot the Master accidentally."

The next began:

"I am William Brown. I was in my cell. There was a terrific report. I was facing the window and I saw him fall. I ran out. I went next door to see if Brother Rollo had heard it too, but he had not. We ran down together. Then I thought of Mrs. Titmarsh, and I went to fetch her. I didn't think he was dead, I didn't know what had happened, I was just afraid."

"My name is David McQueen. I was in my cell when the accident occurred. I saw it happen. I was at the window and I watched him cross the field. And then just as he was going to pick up the spade, I think, the shot was fired, and he fell. I don't know where the shot came from. There was no one about. I rushed to him of course. I have done a little Red Cross work, and I could see he was too seriously injured to be moved. There did not seem to be anything I could do. When Carpenter appeared I asked him to go for a doctor at once. I waited by his side and saw that no one touched anything till the police arrived. Of course no one would want to shoot the Master. It was an accident."

"I am Brother Bernard," began the next. "I know nothing about it. I will gladly give you what assistance I can, but I was not informed of the fatality until after the Master had already passed beyond us. I was in my cell, and I dare say I might have seen what was happening but I was absorbed in meditation during the whole period, that is to say from eleven to one. They may have forgotten to call me or they may have thought I would be of no use. Very probably our dear Master had enemies, though I should not care to name them. From my experience a man incurs enemies in inverse ratio to his goodness."

"My name is Ella Slade. I don't know anything. I went down, but I don't remember what happened. I only know that I found myself suddenly lying on my bed. I can't tell you any more. I don't want to talk about it."

The last statement was Audrey Lewes's.

"I was in my cell, but I wasn't meditating. I tried to but I couldn't concentrate. It may sound absurd to say so now, but I had a premonition of catastrophe all the morning. It was horrible, but I somehow knew something like this was going to happen. So I was thunderstruck and appalled, if you like, when I saw him shot before my very eyes, but I was not surprised. I ran through the gardens but I couldn't see any one. Then I went into the field. When I saw him lying there all twisted up and all the blood and his poor dear face, I just burst into tears. David was attending to Ella some distance away. Then Rollo came. It seemed to me they were just standing around and talking while his precious life's blood soaked away. I asked where Lucy was and someone said William had gone to fetch her. Then Rollo went away. I can't remember any more, it all seems to dissolve into confusion and weeping."

Mr. Chaos said, "Well, well," and shuffled the papers together. Then he examined the exhibits. First the spade, old and much-used with a blade worn down as sharp as a razor, the long handle spliced with iron. The fingerprints on the grip were the deceased's. At the base of the handle where the spade was clamped on to the wooden upright was a ring of thin wire, the kind of thing that is used for fastening on a price tag. But it seemed a little unlikely that a spade should bear a price tag after some twenty years or more of usage, and Mr. Chaos scrutinising it more carefully with his pocket lens saw that the wire had been twisted together and the ends clipped off sharply with a pair of pliers quite recently, for the edges shone brightly new.

Among the few articles Mr. Titmarsh had been carrying at the time of his death was a hefty gardener's knife, a terrific affair, bearing among its implements a pair of clippers adequate to cut the wire. There was also his watch, a hunter, in a thin shabby gun-metal case with a bad dent one side. It had run down now, but P.C. Lamb assured him that it was going when he first had it and he had not omitted to check the time with the Station clock and noted that it was nearly a quarter of an hour slow. The regulator was pushed right up against the minus sign.

Then there was the typed report of the autopsy, and the "findings" in neatly labelled little boxes.

Stripped of its fancy terminology the doctor's report was blatantly simple. It described in nasty bald phrases the damage sustained by Wesley Titmarsh from the tearing, splattering soft-nosed bullet ripping its way impartially through vein and muscle, flesh and bone, as it pierced the thorax wall and opened arteries and windpipe, filling the injured man's lungs with blood. The bullet was lodged against the third spinal vertebra. It was a .22, and Chaos noted the six characteristic riflings marked on its small deadly surface. Among the fragments of bone and flesh the doctor found some minute pieces of cryptogamous matter which he carefully extracted and placed in one of the little boxes for the police to examine. Mr. Chaos was not particularly familiar with all the varieties of moss and this specimen was doubtless some local variety, but what puzzled him and gave him an uneasy sensation of dread that the case was not going to be altogether straightforward was why on earth moss should have been in the wound at all.

He began to whistle softly between his teeth. There was also the point that all these testimonies slightly differed. The Seekers were reputed to speak only the truth. Which of them was speaking the truth and which lying now? It was not easy to believe they were all telling the truth since none of their versions quite tallied one with another. It just showed you how unreliable facts were when they had to be sifted through the medium of another human's consciousness. Facts themselves could not lie, facts were the very purity of truth, but how they were interpreted depended on the individual with his particular history, constitution, beliefs, character and so on. He sighed. It was something of a wonder, when you came to think of it, that one ever arrived at the truth at all when one had to depend on human beings.

He broke off his musing to remark aloud that so far only eight of The Seekers had been accounted for and he understood there were ten. What had happened to the other two? The sergeant explained that he had not had occasion to mention them because they had both been away from Market Keep on the 6th. They were a Miss Miriam Fry and a Mr. Joshua Platt. It seemed that it was their custom to go up to Town once a week in the summer, once a fortnight in winter, to sell part of their produce so that in turn they might buy some of the necessary articles they could not supply themselves with.

*

When he left the Police Station Mr. Chaos returned to The Black Dog to get something to eat. The dingy dining-room with its stained cloths and grimy, dirt-smeared windows, was unutterably depressing. A plump not unattractive girl served him, her mouth ajar with anxiety. That and the way she tripped over her toes gave her a look of imbecility, doubtless quite unwarranted. Her nails were dirty and broken. Mr. Chaos, who expected little enough from life, ate and rose sadly from the table. There were evidently to be no compensations on this case.

A tubby little man came in at that moment and advanced towards him with folded hands to inquire earnestly whether everything was to his satisfaction. Mr. Chaos wondered sardonically what The Seekers would have answered to that inquiry. For his part, he was on a job and therefore the needs of the job came before his personal needs. His reply was modest and non-committal. What was the name of the proprietor, he inquired?

"Brewer's the name, sir," said the little man appropriately. "But I'm only the manager, I don't own the pub. It's a 'tied' house."

Ah, that accounted for it, thought Mr. Chaos gloomily, whose conviction it was that "tied" houses were the curse of the country. Nice for the trade no doubt but rotten for the customers. When a house was owned by a brewery you couldn't expect a chap to take the same interest in making it attractive as he would if the property were his own and its success depended on his own efforts.

"I understand you've been having a spot of trouble down here," he remarked genially.

"Trouble?" said Mr. Brewer vaguely. "Oh, I hope not."

"Murder," suggested Mr. Chaos. "Saw the results of the inquest in the paper. People calling themselves Seekers."

Mr. Brewer said, "Oh, that ..." and whisked some crumbs off a table on to the floor.

"Created a bit of excitement for you all, anyway, and it's good for trade. It's an ill wind ..." Mr. Chaos was bluffly affable.

"Unpleasantness never does any good that I can see," said the innkeeper unexpectedly. "People buzzing round like bluebottles, reporters, and such like. I don't hold with it."

"People will talk," Mr. Chaos agreed. "And a pub's the place for gossip. I gather they were rather a rum lot. Not altogether popular, eh?"

"I don't listen to that sort of thing. Too much to do. Got to have eyes everywhere in this game, back of your head and all over the shop, watching the glasses, the till, the clock, the counter. You haven't time to listen to all you hear ... And what's it all amount to, anyway? What do they know?"

"Somebody must know something."

"Lot of nasty-minded suspicions," said Mr. Brewer, "and all that happens is that it makes more bad blood than ever. Leave all that sort of thing to the police, I say. What do we pay 'em for?"

Mr. Chaos said yes of course but the police had to have something to work on. They couldn't be expected to drag the culprit out of a vacuum. He spoke of what he knew, he said, being in the profession himself.

With this bit of information, unexpectedly, just as Mr. Chaos was giving up hope, Mr. Brewer's attitude changed. His small plump hands flew out like wings. He spoke passionately:

"Whoever done it, hanging's too good for 'em." His guarded laconic phrases were gone. He said earnestly, "Only a lunatic would have shot Mr. Titmarsh. The best man that ever trod this earth!"

"I'm sorry I spoke as I did," said Mr. Chaos sympathetically. "How could I know he was a friend of yours! From the little I've heard he didn't sound the sort to be friendly with an innkeeper — too — too —"

"He was a friend to everybody who'd let him be. He was a good man. They don't understand that here, they're too ignorant. I won't hear a word against The Seekers, they all know that. I'm only an ordinary sinful chap and I've never bothered me head about religion, but I know enough to know they're all right, all of 'em. I'm not so stupid; you've not got to be silly in my line; and I reckon I know men pretty well, and women too for that matter, and I can tell the wrong 'uns from the good. There aren't so many good in my opinion that you can make much mistake about it."

"May I ask, were you a follower of theirs?"

Mr. Brewer patted his hair and stared at a point beyond the inspector. "I've never known to this day what it is that they're up to at Abbot's Breach. Some say one thing, some another. I don't pay any attention to it. All I know is that he saved my wife's life, Mr. Titmarsh did. I'll never forget that. How could I?" His sallow little face went pale as he remembered it. "Almost gone, she was," he said huskily. "A terrible time we'd had with her. The doctor said it was just a matter of hours. He'd promised to look in again later. The Reverend Foster was standing there," he made a vague gesture with his hand outflung. "The breath was rattling in her throat, I tell you. Do you think I could ever forget it?" His small plump hand was lifted to shield his eyes. "And then in comes Mr. Titmarsh. He never says a word, but goes straight to her and takes her hand in his, and just stands there looking down at her. I was too upset to think anything of it and the vicar was praying and never noticed." He sighed. "It got so quiet, I thought she'd gone; just slipped away like, as the doctor said she would. And I went over to her with a cry; and she opened her eyes and said, 'Hallo, Henry,' and smiled at me. And Mr. Titmarsh said, 'Perhaps you'd hke something to eat now, would you?' And she said she thought she would. Mr. Titmarsh said she was perfectly all right now; and so she was." The innkeeper stared at Mr. Chaos in a sort of blank astonishment. "You can believe it or not. And a moment before she'd been dying. I saw it with my own eyes."

"How long ago was this?"

"Seven ... eight years, must be."

"A really most unusual story. What did the doctor have to say when he came back?"

"What would you expect? Tried to make out she'd never been dying at all. But then why did he make out she was? And if he made a mistake and she never was dying, why then he's not the sort of doctor I've much use for. I wouldn't want to go through that again."

"I believe you," said Mr. Chaos. "And how did the vicar take it?"

"Tried to take it on himself," Mr. Brewer looked impish. "The wife won't have it, though, she says I'm not fair to him. She says he's as much right as Mr. Titmarsh to claim the miracle for his own. Of course she knows all right who called her back, but she allows Mr. Foster might think ... Oh, you know what women are!"

"And after?"

"After? Nothing. We wrote to him later to thank him as best we could and to tell him if there was anything we could do, any time — for they seem to be poor people, and in a manner of speaking you might say we owe him everything. But he never answered."

"And he never came back?"

Mr. Brewer shook his head.

"And you left it at that? You didn't try to pursue it? You didn't become disciples of his or anything like that?"

Mr. Brewer looked surprised.

"Oh, no. It's like I said, we're ordinary people. And I can't say I'm religious myself, though the wife goes to church of a Sunday. I've no objection to that, I think it's good for women. But the style of thing they go in for up there is right out of our line."

That was about as far as the subject took them and Mr. Chaos went on his way soon after, pondering the difference between the innkeeper's view of The Seekers and that which he had gathered earlier from Miss Farrell.

He walked beyond the village and turned up a pretty country lane. The air was more benign now. The sun had melted the late frost, and as he walked sprays of prisms scattered from the grass beneath his feet. From every branch flashed myriads of bright jewels. For an hour or so it would be a perfect crisp October day.

Death and resurrection, he thought, as he had thought on the station platform earlier ... The ever-recurrent mystery; but that was a problem beyond his ingenuity to solve.

CHAPTER THREE - ACQUAINTANCE WITH THE SEEKERS

The Abbot's Breach land spread outwards from the edge of the village, running over smooth low-lying hills tufted here and there with dark woodland. Barns and outbuildings dimpled the patched fields like shadows.

The house crouched secretively behind the original high monastic wall. Mr. Chaos opened the gate and stared down the broad shrub-bordered alley to the porch, centred with darkness from the open front door. He walked slowly down, watchfully. The open door was an invitation which the detective could not afford to ignore.

The hall was astonishingly, cruelly bare, bare as a barn. Just whitewashed walls and a plain wooden seat along one wall. And nothing else, not a rug, not a picture, not even a spray of autumn leaves. Funny how its bleakness conveyed at once the painful austerities of lives vowed to holiness and asceticism.

Mr. Chaos gently turned the handle of the first door he came to. It opened towards him with an ominous clatter. Unfortunately it chanced to be a cupboard, a regular glory-hole, all the higgledy-piggledy rubbish of years; not at all the sort of thing he had expected to find in this harsh neatness. A toppling pile compounded of worn-out sneakers, four rusty golf clubs, tangled balls of string, the rat-gnawed remnants of a straw palliasse, a ragged lonely Wellington, two ash sticks crook-handled, old gaping tin boxes full of "brads" and rusted nails. Somehow he heaped them up again and slammed the door hastily.

With that eerie unaccountable sense of being observed, he turned to find one of The Seekers standing beside him. He was a tall, gaunt, heavy-boned man with the great faraway eyes of a visionary. With his yearning eyes and furrowed jowl, he had the unspeakably tragic expression of a bloodhound. His head was feathered with grey. He wore, not the loose white robe of The Seekers, but a coarse linen shirt outside his breeches, something between a shepherd's smock and a Tolstoy blouse. He wore sandals on his bare feet.

Mr. Chaos held out his hand and said cordially:

"There seemed to be no one about so I came in. I take it the door is left open so that any one who wishes to may enter?"

The man, ignoring his hand, said gravely, in a deep slow voice that issued remotely from behind his teeth: "The door is also left open so that any one who wishes may leave. But it should not be open to-day. Not every one is welcome all the time. There are people without respect or discretion who disturb us." He broke off and added severely, "If you are a reporter you must go. We have nothing to say to the papers." He repeated more slowly still, "We ... have ... no ... in ... for ... ma ... tion ... to ... give."

Mr. Chaos was revolted at being taken for a newspaperman, but hiding the wound to his self-esteem, he reassured The Seeker. He presented his credentials.

"Detective Inspector Chaos of Scotland Yard," the other repeated, and it was evident that that was no less distasteful to him than popular journalism. "You'll want to see somebody, I suppose. I'll send Brother David ... If you'll be seated ..."

"But I am seeing somebody," said Mr. Chaos pleasantly. "I'm seeing you. One at a time. I'll interview Brother David later. I'd like to know your name, by the way."

He wandered back. "I'm Brother Rollo," he said. "Rollo Carpenter. I've already told the police all I know." He clasped his great bony hands in front of him.

"Oh, in this business," said Mr. Chaos cheerfully, "we have to go over the same ground again and again. We have to *see* what happened, you know, and some of us are very thickheaded and it's slow work making us see." He added blandly, "I often say it would try the patience of a saint."

Mr. Carpenter was not stupid. He got it at once.

"Oh, we're not saints," he said, and gave him a narrow mirthless smile, like a wolf's.

"Besides," said Mr. Chaos suavely, "things have altered quite a lot since you made your statement to the police. Then it was quite in order for you to say you thought it must be an accident. Now we know it was wilful murder."

"As a matter of fact, it appears to me just as much an accident now as it did then."

"Oh no, oh no," Mr. Chaos protested. "I can't allow that. The shot was fired at point-blank range, there were powder marks on his clothes, yet Titmarsh was found in the middle of a three acre field. Come, come! An accident?"

"I said, to me," Brother Rollo reproved him gently. "I know no more about it now than I did then."

"I wouldn't be so sure. It may seem so to you. It's for me to discover what you think you don't know. But I need your co-operation. It would be stupid and tiresome of you to be obstructive. I'm sure you can see that."

Brother Rollo said, "I don't know whether you are using the generic or the individual 'you.' Speaking for myself I shall do my best to be helpful: I have arrived at the conclusion that that is the right thing to do. I cannot speak for the others of course."

"Why should they not co-operate — if they are innocent? Do they not wish to see justice done?" asked Mr. Chaos in some surprise.

"Justice will be done — is done. Justice is a divine inexorable law." Brother Rollo held up a hand to avert the detective's sarcastic interruption, "*But* — God's justice is not man's. Our human sense of justice is too fallible, too uncertain. We make mistakes. Better to leave it to God."

"You would not have the murderer apprehended? You would not have your leader's murder avenged?"

Brother Rollo answered inevitably, "Vengeance is mine, saith the Lord, I will repay. You do err not knowing the Scriptures or the power of God," he said gently. "You see we need more than anything else to get away from the narrow personal viewpoint. There is no progress that way. Naturally, one has instincts of vindictiveness and self-pity, which we call self-righteousness; naturally, it would please our baser instincts to see the creature who murdered our dearest earthly friend punished. We — I want to rise above that kind of futile reprisal. What good does it do? Will it bring Wesley back? It is merely another evil deed adding to the sum total of evil in the world. We must never play evil's game. If we retaliate, evil has triumphed and we have lost, even thought we may seem to have gained. Evil can only be overcome by good."

"Meanwhile, the murderer is to go free!" Mr. Chaos tried not to sound bitterly shocked.

Brother Rollo answered with authority.

"The murderer is not free. Make no mistake about that. His crime hangs about his neck like the dead albatross. Wherever he goes he drags his guilt with him. Every step he takes betrays him, as clearly as if he left tracks in the snow. He cannot escape the inevitable consequences of his act."

"I wish I could agree with you. I have had very much more experience of crime and criminals than you, and I have not found it so. You would be astonished to know how soon the criminal sloughs off his crime, how soon even a murderer forgets his victim. If there is no punishment there is nothing for him to fear, you see."

"The punishment lies in the deed, my friend. You may be assured of that. You are the result of your thoughts and deeds. You cannot commit a crime and remain the same as you were before, whether you succeed in blotting out the memory of it or not. And what punishment is hanging, after all? That brief moment at the rope-end is probably respite from memory, don't you think? No, no, no," he cried positively, his eyes burning, "there is no physical punishment to equal the terror of God's voice, striking like lightning in the human soul."

"'And the voice of his brother's blood cried out from the ground,' you mean," interpolated the blond young organist, darkening the entrance to the hall. "Yes, but, Rollo, you assume that every one's conscience is as tender as your own." He put a hand on the older man's shoulder. "Take note of the flaw in your premise, dear," he said amiably, and smiled questioningly at the inspector.

He was of medium height — about half a head shorter than Chaos, and sturdily built. Near to it could be seen that he was not so young as his deceptively childish features and simple clear colouring led one to expect. The simplicity of the bright yellow hair falling limply over the wide brow, and the round blue eyes, were contradicted by the straight resolute mouth and small pugnacious jaw. He was in his early thirties perhaps.

Rollo Carpenter presented him to the inspector and then disappeared with surprising agility for one of his slow, dreamy appearance.

Mr. Chaos tried to frown and laugh at the same time. It was annoying, he wasn't getting anywhere, they were just playing with him. But it would not do to let himself get annoyed about it.

He turned to David McQueen.

"He's clever, isn't he?"

"Rollo?" said McQueen in amazement. "I shouldn't have said so. Not clever in a worldly sense, at least."

"Mmm! ... He contrived very artfully to inveigle me away from what I wanted to discuss with him, by means of a skilful red herring."

McQueen was amused. "Dear old Rollo! One of the best! But utterly guileless. I don't think it would ever occur to him to lead you astray intentionally; and if he did think of it he would think it beneath him to stoop to such a thing."

"I wonder," said Mr. Chaos, and left the subject there — momentarily.

Brother David, after a little silence, said, "Well?" For what did the man want of him, was it to question him or — ? It was absurd to stand there in the hall like two painted Indians outside a cigar store.

Mr. Chaos came out of his brown musing to say what he really needed was to get the hang of the place before he went any further. He must learn how they lived and what they did, the plan of the house, the extent of the land, so that he might not be lured through ignorance into making false prejudgments. A fatally easy thing to do. As one gathered together details of the unseen surroundings to a crime one instinctively and unavoidably made a picture of them in the mind, often creating thereby all sorts of future difficulties. For if one pictured a road running the wrong side of a house, or grasped the distances wrongly, frightful confusion ensued. If a wood has been placed in one's imagination behind a house instead of in front of it we shall not understand how the criminal was able to approach the front of the house unseen. Mr. Chaos liked to assure himself of these important details as early as possible on a case.

Brother David opened double doors at the end of the hall and said with a gesture, "The Refectory." It was a long high-ceilinged room with a big refectory table running across one end, a kind of low dresser carrying pottery plates and wooden platters, and to one side a high plain wooden armchair with a reading desk before it. A bookshelf ran the length of one wall. Yet even that provided no touch of enlivening colour, for all the books seemed to be in the sombre harmonious browns and greens of old bindings. There was a big open brick fireplace the other end of the room. The floor was bare. There, were no chairs or cushions, no small tables bearing ornaments or vases of flowers. The only softness to the eye were the heavy curtains of some dull blue material draping the big windows. It was here, in these surroundings of tolerable discomfort, that they ate and relaxed after toil.

McQueen led him through another door into the big old-fashioned kitchens, part of the original building. It was a pleasant place that gave Mr. Chaos sentimental memories of his childhood, with its wavy red brick floor and sturdy deal table, scrubbed into soft white ridges. It was all scrupulously clean. In the open black range the fire shone as if the flames had been polished too. Two women were peeling and grating mounds of vegetables. Carrots, leeks and onions lay chopped together on a board with an effect of swirling coherence, a brilliant little ballet of red, white and green. The two women wore the same kind of shepherd's blouse that Carpenter wore. McQueen presented the inspector. There was something protective, something guarded in his manner, Mr. Chaos thought. The two women he introduced as Ella Slade — Brother Ella and Mrs. Titmarsh. Miss Slade was the pale lumpy woman he had seen at the funeral staring about her with a vacant eye. She made a jerky indecisive little bow, unsmiling. She put down the turnip and knife she was using, as though to shake hands, then she hesitated, picked them up again and went on with her work. Her eyes flickered from one to the other. A look of nervous strain lined her face. She pushed a strand of fading hair off her forehead with the back of her wrist.

Mrs. Titmarsh was an elderly little woman with a gentle tired face. She greeted the detective gravely, sincerely, almost, he thought, with relief — or did it only seem so by way of contrast with the wary attitude of the others? And she was kind, too. A motherly womanly-woman. She was not the sort to be impressed with uniforms or decorations, he could see; she looked clean through them to the fellow creature underneath. He could not but be touched by her immediate concern for him. What time had he arrived? Had he had anything to eat yet? Would he like anything to take now? Where was he staying? At The Black Dog? Oh, that would never do. So dirty and inconvenient. Would he not prefer to stay here with them? They would be so pleased to have him.

Mr. Chaos felt rather than saw McQueen's dismay. Miss Slade said, "Oh, Lucy! Where?"

"Where, dear? He can sleep in Wesley's room. Don't be victimised by sentimentality; you are, dear, you know. The living must come before the dead, because the needs of the living must be met, and the dead have no needs." If she saw Ella Slade's eyes fill with tears she took no notice. "Come and see," she said to the inspector, and led him into a room off the hall with a door into the garden.

It was a bleak room, Heaven knows. A camp-bed against the wall. A chair. A kitchen table covered with papers weighed down with curiously shaped stones, and an oil lamp in the centre. There were shelves with a few books, neat piles of garments, and the few indispensible odds and ends. His other clothes hung from hooks behind the door. They did not require much room. In one corner leant a still muddy garden fork — pathetic relic of past industry, and a pair of dirty boots toppled drunkenly to one side.

Mrs. Titmarsh eyeing it dispassionately felt bound to apologise for it. She couldn't pretend it was very comfortable, perhaps not even as comfortable as The Black Dog, but it was clean, and — and — the fact was she wanted to have him near, wanted to get this wretched business cleared up as soon as possible. She turned her head away unhappily.

Mr. Chaos quite agreed. He liked the room very well, he assured her. It was hard but not cheerless, it was the hardness of a soldier's room, the hardness of discipline.

"You understand," cried Mrs. Titmarsh in pleasure and surprise. "He *was* a kind of soldier."

"So you want this business cleared up, do you? You're not afraid of the murderer being punished. You are not like Mr. Carpenter who prefers to leave punishment in God's hands?"

She looked him full in the face.

"I don't follow all they say. I'm not a clever woman. I'm very ordinary. And I take life rather as it comes. But I think we have certain duties to perform; and I think that God can act only through His creatures. Even human justice demands full penalty, and is mortal man more just than his Maker? You can't simply dismiss a thing like murder, can you? It's a beastly corroding stain," she muttered.

"Did your husband always sleep here, Mrs. Titmarsh?" She nodded. "You did not share a room?"

"No. David will explain that to you." She looked upset. "If you'll excuse me I must return to the kitchen." She ran her work-worn hand over the back of the chair and smiled tenderly. "This was the first piece of furniture he ever made. He was so proud of it."

He found McQueen in a big room that ran parallel with the Refectory. It had big square uncurtained windows all along one wall. Here were great bins overflowing with raw wool, and coppers for washing it, and spinning wheels for spinning it, and machines for carding it, and six-foot looms for weaving it, and vats for dyeing it. For not only did they spin and weave and make their own clothes, but their surplus material was sold (or else, and too often, given away).

"From beginning to end," said Brother David proudly. "The wool is home-grown, from our own sheep; and the final result — " he touched his neutral baggy gown with the suave gesture of a London tailor.

"Very nice," said Mr. Chaos absently. "So you aren't all of one mind here?"

McQueen did not pretend to misunderstand. "Mrs. Titmarsh has never been quite one of us. She goes with us part of the way, I think more for Wesley's sake than because the life really appealed to her, and the rest of it she either could not or would not accept. We don't think any the less of her on that account, you know," he added ingenuously. "I think this kind of life is hard on a woman."

"But there are other women here."

"Yes. But not married, you see. I think that must make a difference. They say what you've never had you never miss. There is nothing in this for Lucy. You can see she's the sort of woman who should have had masses of kids of her own: that's the way her thoughts run. Instead of which she gets masses of strange adults and has to make do with them. I can see her point of view, although it seems to me infinitely pathetic and unworthwhile. But then I'm not a woman — thank God! She never had a proper home-life with Wesley. I don't just mean the celibacy."

"Celibacy?" Shades of Miss Farrell!

"We are all celibates here. Didn't you know? What we have done before we came or what we intend to do when we leave doesn't matter. While we are here we observe strict celibacy. That is part of the routine of emancipation of course."

Emancipation? What was this? Mr. Chaos felt his head spinning.

"Emancipation from the tyranny of the body," Brother David explained patiently. "The Titmarshes were the only ones who were married. But not in that sense, not any longer."

Upstairs, either side of the corridor, were the doors leading to identical little cells, scarcely more genial than a monk's. Each one contained the same narrow bunks, the deal table, the chair, the shelves and hooks to hold their most personal, most intimate, cherished belongings. The rooms varied so slightly that it was not possible to tell for certain in which dwelt a man, in which dwelt a woman. There was not even a strip of matting to cover the boards, not even a gay cover for the bed, not even a curtain to hide the naked window.

What sort of people are they, thought. Mr. Chaos uneasily, who can live so comfortlessly? He could contemplate living among them with equanimity because it was only for a few days; because it was part of the job to get among these people and learn to know them, and the more he was with them the more quickly would that end be achieved; and because he knew darn well that however it would be materially it was bound to prove an interesting experience. But they undertook it in cold blood, and that required a stauncher philosophy than he possessed.

The rooms (or cells, as he could not but think them) on the south side overlooked the garden, and beyond that spread Three Acre field a warm light brown striped with blue shadow and bare now as the palm of your hand save for the heaps of muck standing at intervals, waiting to be dug in.

Yes, you couldn't hope to have a better view of a murder, it was practically a ringside seat. Murder committed in full view of six people. That was nerve for you! Or had the murderer been unaware of his audience?

"I suppose you must work to some sort of routine?" said the detective. "I wish you'd run through it for me."

Brother David said, "At this time of year the Rising Bell goes at four-thirty; that's an hour later than in the summer. At five we all meet in the Refectory for Prayers and Meditation. That lasts an hour, and then we all disperse to our various first duties of the day — feeding the animals, milking, cleaning the house, all the multitudinous daily tasks. At seven-thirty we congregate in the Refectory for Pittance, the meal with which we break our fast. After that we work from eight till eleven. Then comes

Solitary Meditation, for which we retire to our rooms, from eleven till one. Then we have Refection till one-thirty, and from then till half-past six is spent in work again. At six-thirty we stop work for our last meal of the day, Collation. And then from seven to about nine-thirty we have Discussion, Recreation and Prayers. And so to bed."

"But unlike Mr. Pepys, alone."

Brother David gazed at him expressionlessly from his round blue eyes, unamused by this jest, like the dear Queen. There was a little not uncomfortable silence. It was funny really how easy it was to be silent with these people without any sense of awkwardness. They were evidently not given to meaningless civil chatter, they were used to solitude, silence, and the company of their own thoughts. And Mr. Chaos thought it gave them a kind of dignity and made of them restful companions.

Brother David broke the silence to observe that, unless the inspector wished to see the cellars where the packing was done, they had best get out to the farm if they were to see it all before the fight went. Mr. Chaos concurred readily, and as they went Brother David explained his surroundings to him.

They passed through the midden with the cow byres on either side. They had seventeen cows; more than enough for their own needs but their butter was rather a speciality and they sold it in the town, and there were plenty of children in the village to drink up the surplus milk.

"Is this farm a modern experiment?" asked Mr. Chaos. Brother David looked blank and Mr. Chaos had to explain that he meant, were the latest agricultural ideas and appliances tried out here?

"No, said Brother David simply, "this isn't a factory, it's a farm. We don't have to grind every ounce of goodness out of the earth, we treat it fairly and what we take out we try to put back."

"And does it pay?"

"Pay! Of course it pays. It's not a profit-making concern, you know, nor do we have to bother about competition."

"I was thinking of — Education Farm, wasn't it called? Run by the intellectuals of New Hampshire, Bronson Alcott and that lot. They couldn't manage it, remember?"

"I seem to remember dimly something about it. America, in the nineteenth century, wasn't it? Well, why their experiment failed I can't say. Perhaps because they only regarded it as an experiment, perhaps they didn't go into it heart and soul. And then you've got to give more than heart and soul, you've got to put in your body too. We're not intellectuals here. We're very ordinary men and women, from all walks of life. We're not afraid of labour and our needs are few. It would be a wonder, I think, if we weren't self-supporting. As it is we are very nearly independent." He pointed to the low greyish-yellow stubble spreading from their feet into the distance. "Last year we grew thirty acres of flax. It was a marvellous sight when it was in flower, first thing in the morning, it looked as if heaven itself had fallen out of the sky. So you see, even our linen is literally home-grown."

You could tell from the expression on his face as he said this that he felt a proud satisfaction in this achievement, and Mr. Chaos with an effort of the imagination could sense the fullness of life there must be in winning the necessities of existence out of the bare earth. Directly eating the fruits of your toil; not selling your labour and changing the price of it into commodities, but putting your head down and digging what you needed bit by bit out of the hard ground. Not turning on taps and switches and letting the light and water stream God knows how from God knows where, not buying your bread at the baker's, but baking it from the wheat you have grown and ground yourself.

Mr. Chaos said:

"I don't know whether my question's taboo, as it is in the Foreign Legion, but what were you before you came here? And by the way, how long have you been here?"

McQueen smiled, for the first time, and he had a nice smile, there was something sweet about it though it did not reach his eyes, which remained the soft opaque blue they had been before.

"It's not taboo, I assure you. I've been here four years, I suppose. I'm a comparative newcomer. As for what I was before ... It's not easy to say. Looking back at myself I am tempted to say scornfully, nothing, I was nothing, nothing of any importance, a bladder of wind, an emptiness waiting to be filled. Or, if I see myself as others saw me, I was simply a rolling stone, a sort of waster, grasping with weak feverish fingers at unattainable success. Or, to see myself as I saw myself then, eaten up with self-pity, as a frustrated composer of cruelly-unrecognised brilliance."

He spoke extravagantly and Mr. Chaos divined that it was a sore point with him, perhaps a humiliation that he had never been able to wipe out entirely.

"David McQueen?" he mused aloud. "I believe I know the name."

"I believe you don't," said Brother David good-humouredly. "True, I've had one or two little pieces of mine performed in the States, but I wouldn't say they were exactly familiar with my name over there, and I've never had the least hint of recognition from my own, my native land."

"Come now!" Mr. Chaos pointed an accusing finger at him. "What about that requiem? I believe you wrote that."

Brother David went pink.

"Where did you hear it? Were you at the funeral?" Association of ideas caused him to add: "Wasn't it disgusting! That outrageous old man!"

"What old man?"

"The Reverend Edward Foster," Brother David showed his teeth in something ridiculously akin to a snarl. "Daring to praise Wesley, a man whose goodness he could never even begin to comprehend! Odious hypocrisy!"

Mr. Chaos remembered Brother Rollo spitting out 'Hypocrisy!' and this one crying, 'Lies, lies, lies!' He said quietly, "So your heaven is exclusive too. Not every one is allowed in, eh? It's a curious constant of every religion, it seems to me, this fact that not every one is fit to enter your particular heaven."

"No, no, no," cried Brother David vehemently. "That's not true! Only those who shut themselves out!"

Mr. Chaos smiled.

"In any case, I thought the requiem a grand bit of work, most interesting and original."

But Brother David refused to be drawn by praise, he only smiled secretively and pointed to a distant figure herding a flock of sheep down the hillside towards the house in the valley below. "That's William," he said.

Mr. Chaos observed William and the white balls of fluff that rolled down the hill before him, absently, and asked how McQueen had met Wesley.

"It was in the States. I reckon I was at rock-bottom then. Man's extremity was God's opportunity. Wesley just about saved me. I was playing jive in an Illinois hot-spot, and was glad of the job. That's what makes me know how low I had sunk. Up till then self-confidence and pride had kept me in such a state of anger when I had to take jobs I detested that I was able to carry on more or less cheerfully; but now I had been hungry too long and I hadn't any hope left, for I was thirty and I hadn't succeeded despite my inward vows; and I was beginning to be afraid of the future. So I was glad of the job and because of that I think I was at my lowest ebb, though I'd been in tougher nastier corners than that by a long way ... In between the numbers Wesley used to come and talk to me about God and the meaning of life (dear soul!)." He laughed abruptly. "It must have been rather funny when you come to think of it, talking about God in a night-club and then going off and hammering up and down the piano and shouting, 'Biddidy, biddidy, blah! mah floosie woosie blooh!'" he shouted, with the blood-red look and bolting eyes of an imbecile. He resumed his normal demeanour and shook his head. "My God, what a life!"

"You prefer this?" A question which McQueen took to be purely rhetorical it was so obviously absurd. "And yet, you know," Mr. Chaos continued mildly, "this seems to me actually a much queerer way of life for a young man than the other, so very hard and so meagrely satisfying. This is comfortless, if you like, and what of the future now?"

Brother David said seriously, "This is the future. All the future we have is in the present, just as all the past we have is in the present. The eternal now, that's the only rational way of looking at it, that I can see. As for comfort, as for satisfaction, there is a kind of spiritual ease which far surpasses any merely material comfort, you may believe me. I can't describe to you the transcendent satisfaction this life gives me."

"And transcendental satisfactions are enough? You don't miss the cruder bodily sort?"

"I get those too, inevitably. I know how to use all my muscles. I know just what my body can do; it is my trained servant. I'm always hungry, so I enjoy my food. I have the beauties of the countryside under my eyes all day long," he twinkled discreetly, "and if you are worrying because I live celibate, you can take it from me that one has not the energy for that form of exercise after ten hours hard physical labour. I sleep dreamlessly."

"Glad to hear it," said Mr. Chaos. "Apparently you get the best of both worlds," he grinned. And McQueen grinned amiably back. "I know what I wanted to ask you. How was it that Mr. Titmarsh was walking about in the fields when you were all supposed to be at Solitary Meditation? One had to be in one's own cell for that, I presume, and not roaming about at will out of doors."

"Of course. But by a curious mischance something had gone wrong with the bell and he may have been unaware of the time."

"Whose business was that?"

"The bell? Brother William's. He had to scurry round and tell us, individually. I suppose he couldn't find Wesley."

"Curious coincidence, wasn't it? Or had the bell gone wrong before?"

Brother David went pale.

"Coincidence? I don't know what you mean. There was nothing the matter with the bell at all, it had just got hitched up, I was able to put it right in a minute. Only, William couldn't manage it because he'd hurt his hand the day before."

"All right. Don't lose your temper," said Mr. Chaos easily. "It only occurred to me to wonder who would have been killed if the bell had sounded and Mr. Titmarsh had been safely in his room at eleven o'clock."

The young man frowned. "I don't get it." And then, "Dear God! You mean that bullet was meant for someone else, but because Wesley was late, he got it?"

"Well, doesn't that seem more reasonable to you? You say he had no enemies and you know of no reason why he should be killed."

They were standing in a beechwood copse at the top of the hill from which ran the little path that was a right-of-way. The leaves were metallic where the sun touched them, bronze and copper and gold. After a while Brother David said quietly, "Yes, it might be so. At first when you said that my heart lifted, I felt as if Wesley were in some way freed from the horror. But that's nonsense. He's gone, and we shall never see him again here. I find I don't like that suggestion at all. For if it was intended that someone else should die, we have to ask, Who? Wesley is dead, but the murderer isn't satisfied. He may be going to strike again."

Mr. Chaos agreed calmly enough that this might be so. His eyes were fixed on a figure advancing up the pathway. A tall upright man in a tweed hat, with a gun under his arm and a dog at his heels.

"'Day," he said, as he passed, and raised a finger to his hat. The retriever eyed them slobberingly and then padded on behind his master.

"Lord of the manor?" asked Chaos, when he was beyond earshot.

"Thinks he is. Owns the big house over there, The Grange. Percival Menzies, the overlord of Market Keep. Only, you can't do that with money and nothing else."

"You don't like him."

Brother David grimaced ruefully.

"The man himself is all right; must be; each one of us is made in the divine image. It's the things he stands for, the things he believes in. Just the opposite, you see, of all we stand for, so we can't help being opponents in some degree. He carries to excess the very things we most hate and despise — like blood-sports and — and," he corrected himself and ended, "that sort of thing."

As they came out of the copse a man in the unbleached linen smock of The Seekers looked up from the fence he was mending. The sunlight glinted on his pince-nez. He had a florid face oddly concave like a spade. He greeted them cheerfully.

"Inspector, this is Brother Joshua," said McQueen. "He was away the day the Master — "

"Ay," said Brother Joshua agreeably. But his smile was grim, and his eyes behind their glass defences were hard and piercing in their glance.

"So he's got nothing to tell you of course," pursued McQueen smoothly.

"Oh, I expect he'll have plenty to tell me when the time comes," said Mr. Chaos lightly. He was wondering where he could possibly have seen the man before. Where and when had he seen and taken note of that thin nose with its slight concave curve before the pointed tip; and those almost lobeless ears with the rims flattened at the top.

Conscious of his scrutiny, Brother Joshua stroked his grizzled hair, as if wishing to conceal his face from the detective's inquisitive stare. "That's raight, loov," said Brother Joshua approvingly. "We've all to do what we can to dis-close the perpetrator of this foul cri-ime, 'aven't we?"

McQueen agreed emphatically. He only meant, he explained —

"Quite, quite. We understood." Mr. Chaos waved him away impatiently and turned to Brother Joshua. "The difficulty is to find any adequate motive. Why should such a good man be killed? Who would want him out of the way? You — all of you who knew him best — say he had no enemies."

Brother Joshua shook his head. "I wouldn't say that."

"Wouldn't you?"

"It stands to reason that a chap as 'oly as the Master is bound to have enemies."

How did he make that out? asked Mr. Chaos.

"The 'oly suffer for the sins of the wicked," croaked Brother Joshua blandly. "The evil are only at peace with the evil, but goodness stirreth them oop, it rouses the evil in them to mischief. The innocent 'ave to be sacrificed for the guilty. Look at our Saviour! The Lamb of God —"

David put a hand on his shoulder. "Not now, dear," he said gently. "Some other time. Now we have to go round the place before dark."

Brother Joshua was not the least put out.

"My time's the Lord's time," he said benignly. He returned imperturbably to his broken fence. The two men walked on in silence.

"You don't agree with him about enemies, do you?" said Chaos.

"To the point of murdering him, no. It's too absurd. Naturally, there were people who disliked him bitterly, hated him perhaps, but good heavens, you don't go and murder a man just because you don't like him. Or do you?"

"It has been done. Why, should you say, does a person commit murder?"

Brother David pondered the question. "Perhaps if the victim was very much in your way," he ventured at last; "if you were in love and wanted to marry again and you knew of no other way to get rid of your husband. Something like that, perhaps. Something that seems desperately urgent." He looked anxious, troubled, his eyes intensely blue in his face beaten pink by the cold October air.

"At any rate," continued Mr. Chaos, "unlike Brother Joshua you must have plenty to tell me. Because you were right on the spot. You were the first to reach the victim, weren't you? How was that?"

"Oh, I don't know," said David deprecatingly. "I suppose I happen to be a bit quicker off the mark than the others. You see, they were all more or less absorbed in meditation, and the deeper your concentration the longer it takes for external things to penetrate your consciousness. That's how it is that people who are habitually absorbed in abstruse thought learn to perform certain acts mechanically or *absent-mindedly*. It works all right provided it's a routine action, like putting on socks before shoes, or overcoats before you go out. Anything a bit out of the way, though, stumps you completely. You either have to ignore it — as old Bernard did, or come out of your thoughts — as the others tried to, with more or less success."

"And you weren't lost in thought?"

"Perhaps. But not so much. I saw him, you see. I had watched him cross the field and pick up the spade."

"You recognised him?"

"Oh yes."

"Weren't you surprised to see him when you must have supposed him to be in his room meditating?"

"Yes, of course I was. That's why I watched. Otherwise I don't suppose I should have noticed him."

"And then the report went. What direction did the sound seem to come from?"

David looked perplexed. "Honestly, I couldn't say. I was thunderstruck. I saw him crumple, and I rushed to see what I could do. I didn't stop to analyse."

"Did you realise what had happened?"

"No, no, I didn't. But I'm the sort of person who can act without thinking in an emergency. It's instinctive."

"Were you surprised when you got down there and saw him shot — with no weapon near him and no one apparently within sight?"

"Surprised is hardly the word I'd use," McQueen rebuked him mildly. "There was no time for wonder. I had to act and quickly; the man was dying before my eyes. It was horrible! But by the time the others arrived I had got over the first ghastly shock of it."

"Yes, you didn't lose your head," said Mr. Chaos. "That was very commendable. You were able to take charge."

"It is what the Master would have wanted," said David humbly.

Someone was scurrying towards them, stooping and bending every minute, busy as an ant.

"Brother Ella," said McQueen. "You met her just now."

"Brother?" exclaimed Mr. Chaos. "I thought you called her Brother before. You mean Sister, don't you?"

Brother David sucked in his cheeks as at an anticipated joke.

"No. Brother is correct. We are all Brothers, you see, we make no distinction of sex. The minute we call a woman Mother or Sister we are stressing the sexual difference between us. The ideal is complete sexlessness, and we can best foster this by behaving to one another as if we were all brothers."

Her arms full of firewood, Brother Ella called to them as they passed. "We're going to have a fire." Her strained deadness was gone, she looked alive, almost excited. Brother David waved to her.

They came presently to a shed where an old man, looking remarkably like Tolstoy with his venerable white beard and Russian blouse, was hammering a boot-sole, his pursed mouth full of nails. This was Brother Bernard. The one who had been so deep in trance-like meditation that he had not seen his friend and master being murdered under his nose. He had an aura of great calm and benignity. You could not but feel that here was a man who had successfully divorced himself from all material considerations, for whom the spiritual life was completely satisfying. He greeted them with a kindly nod but did not stop tapping the nails rhythmically into the thick stiff leather sole.

Under the window sat the dark gaunt woman who had been at the funeral. She was stitching sandals, and it seemed to Mr. Chaos that she acknowledged the introduction sullenly. This was Miriam Fry. She had been with the Titmarshes since the beginning of their venture, altogether about fifteen years, because she had been with them three years in Cornwall before they decided that it was necessary to move to a larger place in order to be self-supporting. She was Cornish and evidently had her share of the Cornishwoman's suspiciousness. It was like dragging stones from the bed of the sea to get the plainest bit of information from her. She was tormented, lean and fiery, like John the Baptist. No aura of tranquillity surrounded her as it did the old man by the door. And yet it was not, after all, unnatural that she should feel disturbed since their leader was dead, and in such a dreadful manner. In the circumstances it was stranger to see Brother Bernard's supernal calm, the lofty indifference of one who has passed beyond the bitter conflict of human relationships into the Shekinah of impersonal benevolence and goodwill to all creation.

McQueen hurried him away from there. They were almost back at the house again now.

In the poultry yard a fragile-looking creature with a wild mass of curly dark brown hair and enormous misty grey eyes was tossing grain to the clamouring peevish fowl. She held a bowl in the crook of her arm and scattered the grain with easy gestures. Her stance was erect and her movements free, and Mr. Chaos decided that she was of the female type that hid a tough wiriness beneath a dangerously deceptive appearance of frailty.

By a process of elimination Mr. Chaos guessed this to be Audrey Lewes. Her voice was soft and musical. She had a small straight nose and a small straight mouth: a vertical line with a horizontal line beneath it — so! She was almost pretty.

When McQueen told her who Mr. Chaos was she clasped his great paw in her two tiny ones (Mr. Chaos to his bewilderment found himself mentally describing her in these winsome clichés: bear-like paws and little helpless ones; he found himself noticing the gallant poise of her head, the mutinous angle of her little chin, her bell-like laugh; and he anxiously took his emotional temperature. This didn't seem natural), anyway, there were her bear-like little paws gripping his great helpless hand, while she breathed very earnestly, her face turned up to him like a pansy, "Oh, I'm glad, so very glad you've come at last. We have much to say to one another, you and I."

Mr. Chaos said bravely, Yes there were several questions he wanted to ask her. She would see him at the house later. They moved away and Mr. Chaos inquired of McQueen how long Audrey Lewes had been with the Brotherhood. It seemed she had been with them in Cornwall and then had gone away, to return for a period a year or so before David arrived, and she had come for this visit about six months ago. Was that quite in order? asked Mr. Chaos. It appeared it was quite usual. People were entirely free to come or go as they pleased. Some people, for instance, felt the need of the moral toning-up of discipline now and again. Others required the solace of spiritual refreshment. Not every one was able to cast off his or her responsibilities entirely, though they might contrive to put them on one side for a few months. Some, after a few years, having found whatever it was they came for, were able to go back to the world satisfied, never needing to return. There were also the faithful few who wished for no other life, and stayed. Of these were Rollo Carpenter, Bernard Drag, Miriam Fry and, he believed, himself.

"Not William Brown?"

"Oh, William!" Brother David looked amused. "I don't know. William is an enigma. The sweetest man on earth. But ... but ... but — " He shrugged the rest away.

So far Mr. Chaos had had but a glimpse of William Brown, when he spoke so gently and charmingly to Ruby on his way out of the churchyard, but it seemed to him that of them all William was the least odd, the most normal; and McQueen's hesitation made a queer impression on him.

As they walked back towards the house, tinted a warm rose from the afterglow already fading from the sky, Mr. Chaos asked him what was the basis of the antagonism between the vicar and Wesley Titmarsh.

"Obviously, surely," said McQueen with a slight bitterness of contempt. "Wesley's innate goodness was continually exposing him. Even the people who did not care for Wesley's ideals could not but recognise that. To Foster, as to so many others of his ilk, religion was merely a career, as it might be medicine or law — except that those two require a certain amount of brains and sincerity. Apparently you don't need either for divinity." He had the grace to look a little ashamed of his heat, and to explain it added frankly, "It's not anger because he loathed and feared Wesley, but beastly self-righteous anger over the thousands of helpless souls in his keeping who have to struggle through this mortal coil unaided. All of them spiritually lost; and uncaring, because unknowing."

Emotion had made him quite pale. But rage and fear as well as grief could drive the blood from one's cheeks, and unfortunately, thought Mr. Chaos regretfully, there was no way of knowing which it was; blushes, tears, pallor and smiles could each be caused by several different emotions. One could but note the fact, and leave it at that.

"How many a death-bed has Wesley comforted when Foster has not been there! His parishoners may go hang for all he cares. All he wants from them is the money to carry out his futile schemes for improving the church. He's mad about the church, archaeology is his passion, and part of St. Chives is Saxon — or he thinks it is. The joke is that Wesley knew far more about archaeology than Foster, as he did about most things, and he said it wasn't old at all, it was a clever restoration."

"Did he ever tell the vicar that?"

"I don't know. I shouldn't think so. The occasion was hardly likely to arise; and Wesley was less given to malice than any one on God's earth."

The dusk rose up in dark pools from the ground, and overhead starlings flew voicelessly homeward. A few faint ghost-pale clouds hovered above the violet hills and vanished. The blue glass sky splintered to a star-shaped bullet-hole of white flame as the evening star appeared. Through the tall grasses a black shadow ran sleekly. A man and a woman stood outlined against the dimly lit doorway of The Sanctuary. The woman was Mrs. Titmarsh. She put her hand on the man's arm and for a second or so he blocked her completely from their view. Then he turned away. As he passed them on the path, something — the poise of his head as he raised his hat and his long hesitant stride, perhaps, told Mr. Chaos that this was Harold Prescott the schoolmaster.

CHAPTER FOUR - THE SILENT BELL

Now that he had the layout of the place in his mind was time enough for Mr. Chaos to begin his first questioning. He found Brother Ella laying sticks in the big open fireplace in the Refectory and rolling paper into hard neat screws. From the match-end flame licked up the edges of paper and crackled along the twigs. Brother Ella squatted back on her heels and watched it with an absorbed expression. She jumped when he spoke behind her.

He said, "Miss Slade, I want to ask you a few questions, if you please." She looked alarmed and he tried to reassure her. "There's nothing to be alarmed about. I only want to know where you were on the morning that Mr. Titmarsh was assassinated ... You were in your room, eh? Good. Good. Excellent. It's all quite straightforward, you see," he said bluffly. "And what were you doing there? ... Thinking? Ah, yes ... You weren't by any chance looking out of the window?"

She made no direct answer. She flushed absurdly and began messing with the fire.

"Were you not supposed to be looking out of the window, then?" asked Mr. Chaos gently. "It doesn't matter telling me, you know. I'm not concerned with the niceties of your spiritual life."

"I was kneeling at the window, praying. I like to see it," she mumbled, "like to watch what I'm praying to. That's not Pantheism, is it? Nature is the Mind of Eternal Being revealed, isn't it?" she said earnestly.

Mr. Chaos agreed obligingly, and asked her whether she had seen Mr. Titmarsh enter the field.

She shook her head and fumbled with the untidy bun at the back of her neck. "I was looking up," she said simply. "Then I heard a bang, and the birds flew up out of the trees," — she sketched a gesture with her big hands, palms up — "like a torn-up letter tossed into the wind. They made a fearful noise. They startled me. And then some huge black birds came flapping out of the mist towards my window. They were enormous, and somehow ominous, like vultures or something. I felt very frightened. I don't know why they frightened me so — I love birds. But these — they didn't look real, somehow. I wanted to get out of there quickly, and I ran down ..." Her face twitched and her voice died into silence.

"Yes?" said Mr. Chaos encouragingly.

She fumbled with the red cord at her waist.

"I don't remember any more," she said helplessly.

"Can't you remember anything? Not even arriving in the field? Or what you saw?" She winced away. "Well, never mind," he said kindly. "Don't trouble your head about it." The fire was roaring up now and she tended it carefully, crouching down guardedly, like a child, willing him to go away. He sighed and left her to it.

Brother William came down the corridor whistling cheerfully. He stopped with a look of surprise when he saw Mr. Chaos. "I say, can I help you?" he called politely.

"A few questions," said Mr. Chaos, and explained his identity. William's cheerful round face lengthened gloomily. But common sense told him this had to be. And it was stupid to dislike the poor chap for what he couldn't help, and very likely he detested his job too. After all, he was not the Public Hangman, William conceded, though he was closely related to him. It was on such sordid brutalities as these that civilisation was founded, and it was because of them that it was unendurable. Civilised barbarities, he muttered inside his head indignantly. But the detective was speaking, and he shook the thoughts from his mind as one shakes off drops of water, and tried to concentrate on the question.

"The bell? No, I can't say I remember it getting out of order before, it's generally pretty reliable. Brother David put it right very easily; it was only troublesome for a couple of periods. Shall we go to my room?"

"By all means," said Mr. Chaos, and as they strolled along, remarked conversationally: "Of course you realise that if the bell had rung Mr. Titmarsh would probably be alive now."

Brother William said nothing. He leant against the detective's arm. His rubicund cheerful face looked ghastly. After a long silence he said quietly that he hadn't realised it. He sat down on the edge of his bunk heavily and indicated the chair to the inspector.

"So it was my fault," he said at last, grinding out the words with difficulty. "It was something quite simple; if I had fixed it there and then ..."

"You'd hurt your wrist, I believe."

"Yes," he said inattentively. "I fell down in the muck by the shippon and broke it or dislocated it ... any way, something cracked, something gave."

"Wasn't it rather awkward having to pull the bell with an injured wrist?"

"Oh yes," said William drearily. "But I took a pride in carrying on and not letting down the troupe." There was a wealth of self-contempt in his tone. "But if I had climbed the bell-tower and seen for myself ... Only, I told myself it was dangerous with my gammy wrist. I might fall. Just imagine!" he laughed scornfully.

"Well, that sounds sensible. I expect it would have been risky."

"Don't you believe it! I was afraid. I was kidding myself, making excuses. May as well admit it now. I've no head for heights. Never been able to conquer that. I knew I was being cowardly and I meant to go up later, I swear I did. Well ..."

"And how is your wrist now? You have no bandage, I see."

"Oh, it's all right. It's better. I suppose I'm just as responsible for his death as the murderer," he shuddered. "Who would have thought — "

"Who would, indeed? Certainly, you were not to know. But is your hand really better? It got well amazingly quickly, surely? When did the accident happen?"

"To my wrist? The day before — that is, on the fifth."

Mr. Chaos looked openly incredulous. "A broken wrist healed in something less than a week! Oh, come! Mr. Brown, it's not reasonable to expect me to swallow that."

Brother William roused himself from his desolation in amazement. "Why ever not? There's nothing remarkable about it ... Oh, I see. You aren't familiar with mental healing. It's so much simpler really. It goes straight to the root of the trouble, and instead of struggling to heal the effect, as you do in pathological healing, you heal the cause of the trouble." He gave his wide affable smile.

"Oh, yes," said Mr. Chaos politely, too civil to leave it as Oh yeah! And at a sudden recollection, added: "Was that how Mr. Titmarsh cured Mrs. Brewer?"

"Mrs. Brewer?" Brother William looked blank.

"The innkeeper's wife. Don't you remember? It must have caused a lot of talk at the time."

"Oh, that!" he said indifferently. "Yes. Wesley was a great healer, it was as natural to him as breathing and as effortless. He must have healed countless villagers these last years. But whether it caused much talk ... "

"This mental healing, as you call it, how is it done? Suggestion, I suppose, and hypnotism? I know the sort of thing."

Brother William looked horrified.

"Good heavens, no. Not the result of self-will but of utter selflessness, self-abnegation. It is the divine afflatus of Spirit that heals."

Again Mr. Chaos could think of no other comment than, Oh! An illuminating idea swept into his mind unexpectedly. "You were trying to heal him," he cried in sudden comprehension. "When you all knelt there praying, while he lay on the ground and slowly bled to death."

Brother William stared. "Yes. Of course we were. Why?"

"Couldn't make out what you were all up to, but now I see. Only, you couldn't bring it off, eh?"

"It was impossible," said Brother William quietly. "I knew that from the start. Fear was among us. There was no serenity, no confidence, and our spiritual energies were taken up in combating panic and despair. How the others prayed I don't know, but as for me my mind was in a turmoil, I don't know what I was thinking. And when Doctor Blake came brutally to disperse us I was almost glad." He shuddered.

"In your statement you said you heard the shot and saw him fall, didn't you?"

"No, I didn't. I mean I said that, but I realised afterwards it wasn't quite accurate ... Only, at the time I was so dazed ... I heard the shot all right. A fearful report! It startled me out of my wits. I was completely wrapped up in the subject of meditation and this dreadful noise almost shattered me, it did almost literally shock me out of my skin. You know how the slightest noise can startle you when you are utterly concentrated and remote. And it seemed to me I'd never heard such a bang in my life. I thought my head was split open and my ears burst. For a moment I couldn't even remember who I was. You know, like that chap who was caught up into the third heaven, in the body or out of the body, Paul wasn't sure. Well, you can understand I was too confused, too scared to have seen him fall. But I did, after a moment, see him lying there, and it must have been some spiritual sense which told me who it was for I couldn't see. Anyway, I ran into Brother Rollo's room — an unpardonable thing to do except in special circumstances — and to my amazement he said he had noticed nothing. I said, 'Well, something awful has happened. There's been an accident. I think it's the Master. Do come and see, Rollo,' So we went down together. But I was still feeling oddly shaken and I was obscurely afraid of what we were going to see." He looked up from his abstracted self-communing to say very simply, "You see, I'm a coward. I have to tell you that, because I'm ashamed of it," he said gently. "So I made an excuse not to go on. I said that Mrs. Titmarsh ought to be told and I volunteered to go and fetch her. By the time I'd broken the news to poor Lucy, I'd got control of myself again. We went out. David was being wonderful. He said 'No, no. Take her away. She mustn't see this, and there's nothing she can do.' He sent Rollo for the doctor. Audrey was stumbling around, poor dear, waving her arms and crying. I can't remember who else was there."

"Brother Ella?" suggested Mr. Chaos.

"Oh, Ella. Yes, of course." He lapsed into silence.

"She's subject to fits, I gather," said Mr. Chaos.

Brother William looked reproachful. "Not often. Not when she's with us. If she would stay with us always we know she would be perfectly well. But she won't. She has a beautiful character. There are her father and her brother, and she won't leave them, she regards it as her duty. She submits to their tyranny without a murmur. Women are easily tyrannised over because they have had to submit for so many centuries. But none could have done it with more grace than dear Ella. Only, now and again she breaks down and then she comes here to be mended. She's so happy with us, with no one to shout at or frighten her, and so she very rarely has an attack. That day was different. It was a shock for her."

"Epilepsy?"

"Yes," said Brother William. "She was lying in the shadow of the hedge and Lucy and I carried her into the house."

"And when she woke up she remembered nothing of what she had seen?"

"That's how it is," said Brother William.

When he left William the lamps were being lit. Brother Rollo was going the rounds with a long taper in his hand, and by its faint wavering light his grave visionary's face was somehow more awe-inspiring than ever. Voices rose from the hall below. Mr. Chaos stepped to the head of the stairs to listen.

A light cool voice he recognised was saying, "I'm sorry I bothered you, Mrs. Titmarsh. Little monkey! I just can't keep her at home these days. I don't know where she gets to. But she's so often here that I thought I'd run down and inquire." Mrs. Titmarsh evidently murmured something, for Miss Post laughed and added, "Oh, I'm only too happy for her to be with you, then I know at least she's out of mischief. I hope you don't find her a frightful nuisance. You must send her away at once if she bothers you. She's got quite a 'thing' about you, you know. She raves about you," she laughed. "Oh, yes, my nose is quite put out of joint. But don't make her into too much of a young prig, will you? You've no idea how I have to mind my P's and Q's."

And then Audrey's voice: "Oh, she's a darling. We love her."

"Well, if she comes down this way this evening — but I don't suppose for a minute that she will — we'll send her straight home," said Lucy Titmarsh in her agreeable soothing voice.

"That's so kind of you," said Miss Post. "Well, I must fly. Oh, by the way," her footsteps pattered back. "Since I am here. Is David anywhere about?"

"I don't believe he is. Rollo, David's not here, is he?"

Brother Rollo said, No, like a bell tolling.

"Damn!" said Miss Post. "He told me — I thought that at this time of day you all came back to the house for supper."

"I'm sorry, but he is not available," Brother Rollo's slow voice was relentlessly decisive.

"But, my dear Mr. Carpenter, it's so utterly trivial. It couldn't matter less," she said ultra-sweetly. "Don't trouble to explain. I know how you hate telling fibs. You might give him a message from me. Tell him that if he wants his music he'd better come and fetch it. Ruby lit the fire with it yesterday and I just rescued it in time." Her voice sharpened. "I won't be responsible for it any longer. Tell him so." Her heels tapped through the silence.

"Poor little Ruby," said Mrs. Titmarsh. "Every time I see that woman I feel more sorry for her."

"Mind your grammar, dear," said Audrey lightly. "Isn't that what they call a false relative, Rollo?"

Rollo said, "More sorry for the woman or for Ruby?"

"For Ruby, of course."

"No, no, for Valerie," insisted Audrey. "I'm much more sorry for her. I could weep for her. She's dreadfully unhappy, poor creature. She's love-starved."

Lucy demurred, laughing.

"But it's the truth," insisted Audrey. "I do genuinely feel sorry for her."

"But not *love* starved, Audrey, anything but that." But Audrey was adamant in her sympathy. She *knew*.

Somebody came running lightly up the stairs, and Mr. Chaos prudently retreated. It was Audrey. She almost stumbled on to him, drew back with a little cry, and then said, "Ah, you!" She peered at him intently in the dim light. "You were listening of course," she said disdainfully. "I suppose we have to put up with that sort of thing now, being spied on for our own good. Ugh! Well, if you're so madly keen to know, that was the guardian of a little girl, an evacuee, a sad case, who's not wanted by her mother and has been abandoned to the mercies of the Government, who in turn have abandoned her quite cheerfully to this really *rather* unsuitable person."

"She didn't sound the sort of person who'd care to be bothered much with children, I must say," said Mr. Chaos glibly. "Did she just keep her on out of kindness?"

"Perhaps. Valerie Post is incalculable. She is not incapable of good impulses, I know. I believe she is genuinely fond of the child underneath that rather heartless manner. After all, Ruby had already been with her six years or so. But of course that's only my opinion. Lucy, for instance, thinks Miss Post has cleverly got herself a household drudge, for the price of the child's keep and perhaps a little pocket money, at a time when it is almost impossible to get any one to do your house-labour."

"You mean, she's a servant."

"Practically, yes. Isn't it *rotten*? Of course you may say that a girl of her class could hardly hope for anything better. And if Lucy's right, I would have to admit that Valerie took advantage of her position. And the poor kid *adores* her."

Well, there you were, thought Mr. Chaos, one said one thing and one another. Audrey pulled at his sleeve.

"Come on now, while we are free," she urged. "I do want to talk to you, honestly. The others don't believe me. I don't know why. They say I'm mad. But I'm not. You've *got* to believe me," she said forcefully.

Her room at any rate had a certain gaiety, a touch of personality and colour. Among the theological works on the shelf were nine or ten novels with vivid covers and equally vivid and sentimental titles. Mr. Chaos caught a few from the corner of his eye: THE PASSIONATE PURITAN — SWEET ENEMY — APPLES OF DESIRE, and he smirked inwardly. A spray of spindleberries splashed their bright crimson, like drops of blood spattered on the white wall. It reminded him unpleasantly of the execution he had been forced to witness of a charming young man many years ago in Nicaragua. Above where he lay, the whitewashed wall was splashed with red, just like that.

Audrey was saying, "I'm terribly, terribly sensitive to atmosphere. I suppose *you* think that's absurd; men always laugh at women's intuitions, don't they? But all the same I trust my instinct. I'm a funny little creature, very elemental," she spread wide her arms in their graceful full sleeves and flung back her head, poised like the Winged Victory for flight. "Sometimes I feel absolutely at *one* with the wind and the rain and the trees."

I — I — I, groaned Mr. Chaos inwardly and possessed himself in patience till she should have exhausted temporarily her little store of egotism.

"I had a premonition of evil growing upon me for days. Oh, you'll think I'm making this up after the event, but I *swear* it's true. It was a sort of nightmare feeling, and all the absurd little trifles that no one else would notice mounted up and aggravated it. I tried to tell myself I was being silly, but it was no use."

"What sort of little trifles?" said Mr. Chaos.

"Oh, idiotic! I've only to go into a room, you know, and I can feel it in the air ... anger and jealousy and anxiety ... it's like physical blows."

"Painful for you," commented Mr. Chaos. "What happened?"

She crouched on the end of her bunk and tucked her feet up under her. "I wish I could put my finger on it for you. I've tried since, but I still can't decide who started that *enervating* little discussion about the train

Miriam and Joshua were to catch the next day. The whole thing got out of hand because my poor Wesley's watch was a quarter of an hour fast and no one could convince him of it."

"Quarter of an hour slow, you mean, don't you?"

"No, *fast*," she said positively. "My gracious, you would expect me to be certain after that argument, wouldn't you?" She gave a little laugh. "You're as bad as he is. The darling, he would insist that his watch never *had* gone wrong and therefore it could not be wrong now. Over little things like that he was sometimes — He'd had the watch about forty years and he thought it was going to last for ever, bless his heart!"

"And that worried you?"

"Oh, no. But there *was* a little unpleasantness — perhaps I shouldn't mention it — between Rollo and David. Ostensibly it was because William had hurt his wrist and wouldn't let any one near to look at it, although he was obviously in great pain. So they made that an excuse to quarrel. Periodically they have these little outbursts. I know it's not serious, it's simply jealousy, but it hurts me dreadfully at the time. I'm *too* sensitive, you know, I feel it all so *acutely*, even when strictly speaking it's nothing to do with me at all, but the mere sight of people quarrelling sends me all white and trembly. Aren't I a fool? I could cheerfully kill them when they rag about nothing like that, and yet I *adore* them both and I can't fairly say either is to blame. Of course you can understand how Rollo must feel about it with the best will in the world, he's always been closest to the Master. He was his spiritual heir. And yet David is a dear boy and really very clever, and has been — he was," she corrected herself sadly, "he was able to take so much off Wesley's shoulders. He's so very practical and Wesley never was except in a tempestuous inspirational way."

"So Mr. Titmarsh favoured McQueen. Is that it?"

"He didn't *mean* to; and I don't think he knew he did. I always felt in some queer way that Wesley looked on David as his son. I know it was a disappointment to him that he never had children of his own." For some reason Brother Audrey blushed and tossed the hair away from her face. "Of course there was never any question but that Rollo was the nearest to the Master spiritually, he followed him in everything and was absolutely devoted to him. He has the most extraordinary perception of the spiritual universe. He's *rather* a rare person. I suppose even an outsider can see his passionate devotion to the things of the spirit. I honestly believe they hadn't a thought apart, he and Wesley. If anything Rollo is the more idealistic of the two, certainly more impractical. And that was how David came into his own. He's been around enough to know what was what, and he's no fool. He's not a materialist but he very sensibly sees no reason why the children of this world should be wiser than the children of light, if we may call ourselves so. All those wretched business details, it can't be much *fun* to have to spend half your time coping with them when you really want to be communing with the Divine Being; to be laden with materiality when you want to soar into the realms of Spirit. But David was always so good about it. And naturally Wesley was only too glad to hand over to him. David was always left in charge if anything happened, if Wesley went away, or anything of that sort; he was the second-in-command. And we all accepted it as right and natural. Even though he was very much junior to most of us. I don't mean in *years* of course," she explained kindly.

"You felt he used undue influence."

"Oh, no. I wouldn't say *that*. Wesley wasn't *at all* the sort of person who allowed himself to be influenced. You have quite a wrong impression of him if you think that. No, he trained David to take command *quite* deliberately, because he wanted to shift off some of the responsibility now he was getting older, and David is young and has a clear head."

"So the only one who seemed to object was Mr. Carpenter?"

Audrey frowned. "No. That's not quite right *either*. If he minded so did we all. Except perhaps Ella; Ella is quite above such petty rancour."

"So McQueen isn't very popular?"

Audrey laughed nervously. "Oh, you don't understand *anything*. Never mind. It wasn't *his* fault that we felt like that, it was ours. Our sense of injury was self-inflicted, wasn't it? It was not of his doing. You can see *that*, can't you? We love him all the more, you might say, as a kind of expiation."

"Very well. May I take it that there was a sense of strain between McQueen and Carpenter?"

"Sometimes," Audrey qualified. The candle was making a shroud and Audrey rose to adjust it. She said: "Somehow you make it all sound wrong, too uncomfortable and nagging. I can't make you see it properly. We *love* one another."

Mr. Chaos sighed. At this rate they would never be done. All this hullabaloo of instinct and atmospherics boiled down to an argument about the time with a cranky old man and a jealous quarrel over superiority about a masochistic young man with a broken wrist.

As though she had read his thoughts, Audrey said: "Of course on the *surface* it was nothing. But judged by *our* standards of Truth and Love it was horrible. I had the feeling that it was all quite *deliberate* and that it meant something else really — as when lovers quarrel in public while apparently maintaining perfect civility towards one another." She put her little hands about her throat as though she were choking. "If I had acted on my feelings I might have saved him. I *knew* something was going to happen. Don't ask me how. But I didn't know what. *I* didn't know where the blow was going to fall. So I couldn't have saved him, could I? *Tell* me I couldn't help it," she pleaded, her hands clasped before her appealingly.

"I can't know until you tell me," said Mr. Chaos patiently.

"I was waiting for it all the morning. I thought I was going mad. It was utterly terrifying, as if I was behind glass, and if only I could scream or break the glass or wake myself up it would be all right. But I couldn't. I just had to sit there and watch it all happen under my eyes, like some sort of nightmare film."

"Watch what happen?" begged Mr. Chaos.

"I'm trying to tell you," she said reproachfully. "I thought detectives were so keen to hear every detail however trivial."

Hoist with my own petard, thought Mr. Chaos grimly.

"I was up here that morning for Solitary Meditation, but I was quite unable to concentrate. I was so *strung up*. I tried to read some of the precepts of Lao Tse to calm me, but the words never reached my mind. I paced up and down beating my hands together. I could hardly *breathe*. Terror was pressing in on me — "

Me too, thought Mr. Chaos dolefully, wondering how much more of this personal tosh he had to endure before she got to the point.

She crossed her hands over her breast and looked at him abstractedly with an expression of anguish. "Through the window something, a movement, caught my eye as I turned. I leant against the pane peering out to see who it was. The mist was still heavy. It wasn't a steady pervasive mist that penetrates evenly everywhere, but the patchy kind that drifts and clings in veils. Whoever it was moving through the fields he looked like a ghost, a sort of central whiteness moving through white films. Then I saw the red rope like a dark line round his waist. At that I pushed my forehead against the window and thought, *Whatever* is he doing out there during Meditation? And then, without being particularly aware of it, I remembered that Wesley's watch was wrong, and the bell was out of order. Then I couldn't see him. Then I saw him again, the mist blew away a little just there and I saw Wesley digging." She paused and swallowed convulsively.

"Were you surprised?" asked Mr. Chaos to keep the pot boiling.

"I hadn't time to be surprised. I saw something *else*, you see." She began to gabble. "It was just as he lifted the spade, just as the shot was fired, I saw this *man* standing beside him. Perhaps a yard away, not more. It was only a second or two that he loomed out, but I saw him quite clearly. It was so unexpected it sort of *fixed* it in my mind. *They* don't believe me. He was thin and tall, *much* taller than Wesley, and in black from head to foot. He looked — *menacing*, is the only word for it. Wesley never saw him. At least, he wasn't looking at him. And then the pistol cracked. And Wesley fell." She stopped breathlessly and raised her eyes to stare in his.

But Mr. Chaos fancifully picked on a detail. He said sharply, "Who told you it was a pistol?"

Audrey stammered. "I don't know. No one told me. I just *said* it. I don't know what the weapon was. How should I?"

"Never mind. I thought perhaps you'd seen a pistol in this man's hand."

"No. I couldn't make out details like that."

"But you think he was the man who shot Mr. Titmarsh?"

She glanced at him furtively from the edge of her long grey eyes and then said defiantly, "Yes, I do think so. You'll think it absurd of me ... at that distance ... but the way he stood ..." She was silent for a moment and then said, with triumph that she had found the words she wanted: "He stood like a duellist. Like this, do you see?" She took the pose, standing sideways on, slimly, head slightly bent, eyes slanting down the outstretched forearm, in the classical attitude.

An exclamation broke involuntarily from the detective's lips. Audrey looked gratified.

"Well, go on. What happened next?" said Mr. Chaos impatiently.

Audrey stuck out her sandalled foot and stared at it gloomily, wiggling her toes. "Wesley fell. He tumbled over very slowly; as if he was going to pray; he sort of *leant* on the air. I couldn't believe my eyes. Frightened half out of my wits, I *flew* down, simply flew. The man must be *somewhere*, I thought. I ran up and down madly, looking for him. Stupidly, I called and shouted. I suppose I was warning him off really, but I was too hysterical just then to think sensibly, and the silence frightened me. I hunted through the garden. But of course there was no one. I saw David in the field and called to him, "Did you see him?" But he said he had seen no one, and then I saw *poor darling* Wesley with his face like a crumpled sheet of paper and blood, blood, blood everywhere, And *poor* little David looking quite *dumb* with horror. I began to cry, and he put his arms round me, sweetly. He said, "Don't look, dear, don't look." I said "We must do something." I said, "Darling, please, *please*, do something. Don't just stand there and let him die. It's too horrible!" And as we both stood there crying" — the tears were running down her face as she remembered it and unheeding she let them fall in dark spots on her habit "— Ella came up, out of nowhere it seemed. She startled us. She was looking at David. I thought she hadn't seen the still figure at her feet because she never looked at him. But all her features were twitching horribly, the way they do just before, and I had time to call to David a warning before she fell." Audrey drew in her breath in a great shuddering gasp. She was struggling for self-control. But in vain. Reliving it unsealed the source of horror again, and Audrey put her head down on her arms and wept.

Mr. Chaos as much as most men disliked to see women weep, but in the course of his professional duties he had become somewhat inured to it, had acquired a surface hardness. Waiting for the spasm of grief to pass, he whistled softly between his teeth, a habit of his when emotionally disturbed.

Audrey sat up and blew her nose on a man-size khaki handkerchief. "I'm sorry," she gulped. "Hateful to cry like that, but anything seems to set me off now. Shock, I suppose. Same as Ella only in a different way. You'll say, Why weep if there is no death? And of course I *know* that's true. I do feel it:" She babbled earnestly, gulping back sobs, "I think of Lazarus and I know that if Jesus were on earth to-day But even so, he lives. It's only losing him in that shocking way! If he had passed on — if he had died in the normal way of things ... but to be *murdered*! You see, I loved Wesley, Mr. Chaos. He was like a — like a father to me." Her voice broke again, but she recovered herself bravely, and bit her trembling lip.

Mr. Chaos made suitable murmurations. Then he coughed warningly to show he was getting back to the business in hand and asked if this enigmatic figure had been mentioned at all at the inquest. Brother Audrey said no. So far as she knew she was the only one to have seen him. She had not mentioned it to the coroner because — well, because the opportunity simply never arose.

Mr. Chaps said a trifle peevishly, "I can't understand why no one has mentioned this to me before."

"Oh God!" Audrey ran her fingers through her hair. "I keep telling you they don't *believe* me. They think I'm mad or suffering from hallucinations or something. They just don't believe me because there were no footprints in the earth to *prove* he was there. What of it? How stupid they are. I never said the creature was flesh and blood, did I? He may have come from somewhere *beyond* space and time. How do I know? He may have been a vision even. But I saw someone there, that I'll swear to, as plainly as I see you. *That* was why I wanted to see you and wanted to see you alone. They would have prevented me saying this if they could. Let them laugh or scorn me, that's totally unimportant, so long as you hear it, so long as whatever scrap of useful information I have gets to the right quarters and Wesley's murderer is discovered."

"Even if it's a ghost?"

Audrey lengthened her thin straight lips ironically. "I very much doubt if a ghost could fire off a ghostly rifle with a real bullet, don't you?"

A rifle this time, Mr. Chaos noted. But he only remarked that he thought she should know more of the capabilities of ghosts than he would. He didn't believe in them, as it happened.

"Nor do I," said Audrey frankly. "But you do believe *me*, don't you? You don't think I made it up or imagined it, do you?" Her little pointed face was drawn with anxiety.

Mr. Chaos patted her shoulder. "Oh, I believe you. It's so dashed improbable, I can't help it," he said with crushing geniality. Still he had yet to ask her a few questions. Had she not recognised the mysterious figure? No? Could it have been for instance McQueen? She looked horrified at the mere suggestion, and the detective had hastily to assure her that he was not implying McQueen was the murderer, it was more a question of build and possibility that he was concerned with at the moment. Then, if not McQueen, not William either presumably. Or Joshua Platt? Old Brother Bernard? If he held himself upright perhaps, she said doubtfully. Or the lean dark woman, what was her name? Miriam was the figure, she smiled, but not tall enough. And Carpenter? She said, Yes, she thought so, but of course it *wasnt* him? Mr. Chaos said, Of course not, and perhaps she knew of someone more likely in the village. The constable now was a tall man. Yes, the constable was well over six foot. Or the vicar? The vicar in his *black clothes*! Audrey went suddenly white.

Mr. Chaos said quickly, "I won't bother you any more with that. Tell me instead ... I want to know what you all did before you came here, and I forgot to ask William Brown when I was with him just now. Do you know what he did? Farming, something like that?"

Audrey smiled wanly, uncurled her legs and relaxed against the wall. "Bad guess," she said. "He was an actor."

"An actor, eh?" said Mr. Chaos. "Quite a little artist's colony. With McQueen composing and Brown acting and you writing — you do write, don't you?"

Audrey gave a little deprecating laugh. "You're never going to pretend that you've *heard* of me, I'm not that good. 'Fess up now, you saw my books in the corner there and guessed they must be mine. I scribble for a living some sort of trash. But highly moral trash. If trash ever can be moral." She had on her intense little face now. "Perhaps artistically trash is immoral but — but I do the best I can. My books do uplift, and I'd rather give some little girl from Woolworths a glimpse of the truth, a hint of the great universe of Spirit — " Her eyes were fixed on the inspector wistfully.

Mr. Chaos murmured unveraciously that he saw what she meant.

"They write me such sweet little letters to tell me how I've helped them, you know. It makes me feel very humble, and proud at the same time. I suppose you think I'm incredibly foolish. And yet, I feel, if that's the only way to reach them ... I am doing *some* good. It's better for them anyway than those horribly sordid crime stories. I do feel with the stuff I write that I'm of some *use*. Only a humble instrument maybe, but —

" 'My work is mine,
And heresy or not, if my hand slacked
I should rob God — '

"You know the thing, don't you? I often think of it. How does it go on?
" ' 'Tis God gives skill,
But not without men's hands: He could not make
Antonio Stradivari's violins
Without Antonio — '

"I do so believe that we *all* have a purpose here below," she said earnestly.

"Including those who write crime stories perhaps," suggested Mr. Chaos meanly.

"I don't know," she said seriously. "I think one can mistake one's vocation."

He let her patter on though she had nothing else to say. At last, between one breathless pause and the next, he managed to slide away.

CHAPTER FIVE - ONE FAIR DAUGHTER

The bell sounded for Collation, the last meal of the day. The Seekers trooped in and seated themselves about the long table in their accustomed places. The meal was already spread over the table. There were wooden platters piled high with crisp vegetables, sliced and grated. Dishes of apples and pears in beautiful green shapes; from the crannies of whose unyielding contours tumbled nuts in their neat brown polished cases. A great yellow mound of butter stood in a dull red dish. There were long, uncut, home-baked loaves. There was a cheese as smooth and pale as ivory. By each place stood a beaker of fruit juice.

They sat there silently, tired after their labours, meekly waiting. In his dark clothes and formal collar and tie Mr. Chaos looked as much out of place as a piece of solid, pompous unelegant Victorian furniture in the white innocence of a young miss's bedroom.

Brother Rollo in his slow echoing voice began to utter a grace. The others stared before them, listening intently (Mr. Chaos observed them from under his lids), and when it was finished joined in slow Amens. Then they relaxed, heaping one another's plates generously with food; careful not to neglect their guest, either. But all performed in silence.

When they were ready, David selected a volume from the bookcase on the wall and, seating himself a little away from them in a high wooden armchair, began to read aloud in a clear monotonous voice from the book propped open on the reading-desk before him. Out of deference to their guest perhaps, he had chosen some simple, charming prose extracts from the works of Sri Ramakrishna ...

"'The sunlight is one and the same wherever it falls, but only bright surfaces like water, mirrors and polished metals can reflect it fully. So is the divine light. It falls equally and impartially on all hearts, but only the pure and clean hearts of the good and holy can fully reflect it ... '

"'People partition off their lands by means of boundaries, but no one can partition off the all-embracing sky overhead. The indivisible sky surrounds all and includes all. So common man in ignorance says, "My religion is the only one, my religion is the best." But when his heart is illumined by true knowledge, he knows that above all these wars of sects and sectarians presides the one indivisible, eternal, all-knowing bliss ... '

"'Worldly men repeat the name of Hari and perform various pious and charitable deeds with the hope of worldly rewards, but when misfortune, sorrow, poverty, death approach them, they forget them all. They are like the parrot that repeats by rote the divine name, "Radha Krishna, Radha Krishna" the livelong day, but cries "Kaw, Kaw" when caught by a cat, forgetting the divine name.'"

They ate voraciously but quietly, listening to the honey-sweet words falling in slow clusters through the air. The warm amber glow of the lamps flattered the room. The blue curtains were drawn in twilit folds across the windows, shutting out the night. On the dark background of time-polished wood David's head looked as young and fair as an angel's. The light caught Brother Joshua's pince-nez, turning them to flat gold pennies. He champed methodically through his food, his square head with its grizzled hair bent over his plate. Suddenly Mr. Chaos remembered where he had seen him before. It hardly seemed possible that it should be the same man, and yet he did not see how he could be mistaken. He wanted to lean forward mischievously and say, "Mushrooms!" just to see what Platt's reaction would be.

Miss Fry was not eating. Elbows on the table, chin propped on her hands, she stared at him blankly, abstractedly. He felt rather than saw Audrey kick her under the table, and saw Miriam's head turn sharply towards her, saw Audrey faintly shake her head.

They clattered the plates together and pushed the dishes of fruit to and fro. Brother Rollo cracked a handful of nuts effortlessly, his great bony fingers as crushing as nutcrackers, and offered the kernels to the inspector. Mr. Chaos took them with a smile, remembering vaguely the incident in one of the Sherlock Holmes' stories (was it *The Speckled Band*?) where an outraged client tied the poker into a knot in an attempt to intimidate Holmes, whereupon Holmes languidly straightened it out again. A more difficult feat one presumes. Pity he, Chaos, couldn't show off to Carpenter like that, but you couldn't very well pop the kernels back into their shells.

The reading stopped and David closed the book and joined them at the table. At once Mrs. Titmarsh called down the table: "Mr. Chaos, have you everything you need?" He bowed, thanking her. Two or three sentences were started either side of the table. Conversation became general.

Rollo's deep voice boomed across the table to David impressively.

"I've had five loads of soil dropped on Screw Acres, David. I thought you'd like to know."

David looked annoyed, though his tone was pleasant enough. "Oh, why did you do that?"

"I thought it advisable," pronounced Rollo solemnly.

The eyes of the two men met in a strangely piercing stare.

"I think you might have consulted me first. After all, it is my business," said David mildly.

"It is the business of us all, separately and together, to safeguard the property," said Rollo, emphasising the words unduly in his queer hollow voice.

David flushed and was silent.

Mr. Chaos said, leaning across to Audrey, "Did any one give McQueen Miss Post's message?"

Audrey frowned. "Message?" she said vaguely. She might have forgotten all about it. She said, "Oh yes. Valerie wanted to see you, David. We said, No can do. She didn't like it but we thought we'd save you. She left a 'massage,' dear. She said would you please come and take away your rubbish as she was sick of seeing it lying around. Or words to that effect," Audrey smiled.

"Oh, did she? Thanks." David poker-faced. "I'll see about it. But if she came down why on earth didn't she bring the stuff with her?"

Rollo turned his head inquiringly. "Didn't she say she'd looked in on her way home from the Menzies'. I think she'd had tea there with them she said."

Brother Miriam said drily, speaking for the first time, "Clever of her. Mrs. Menzies is away. Gone to her sister's for a fortnight."

McQueen flushed, or perhaps the candles flickered.

In the silence Brother Rollo began the thanksgiving grace ...

Mr. Chaos slipped away to get his bags from the inn. The saloon was thick with smoke. The radio was rapping out *Itma's* machine-pun-fire. Three men were playing darts. One of them, Mr. Chaos recognised with a sinking heart. He was a reporter. There were two more in the bar-parlour. He found Mr. Brewer, explained, paid, and slipped quietly away with his case. Heaven knew he didn't want this queer affair further complicated by the crudities of reporters. And it was the least he could do for these people to keep them out of the press. This was not the kind of case to be helped by publicity.

When he got back to Abbot's Breach they were all seated about the bright leaping fire. From the words he caught it seemed that they were discussing time philosophically, but they broke off when they saw him to welcome him into the circle. He liked that. It was nice of them to try and make him, the impossible intruder, feel at home.

Mrs. Titmarsh was knitting a stocking. The firelight flickered pleasantly over her gentle fatigued face. He leant forward and in his mild sympathetic voice asked whether she had been informed of the contents of her husband's will.

She said, Oh yes. That had all been settled long ago. It was simple enough.

"Who benefits?" asked Mr. Chaos.

She smiled at him, her patient understanding smile, and laid down her work. "None of us. That is to say, we all do," she corrected herself. "Abbot's Breach and everything pertaining to it is left to the Brotherhood of the Seekers with David as the what do you call it? — sort of executor."

Mr. Chaos raised his eyebrows. "David?"

"Easiest to leave it like that. For one thing he's still young, for another he's got a head on his shoulders (haven't you, dear?), and he's been my husband's secretary for some years now and is familiar with all the details of the economy of the place."

"Just that and nothing more? No personal bequests? Nothing for you?"

"For me? Yes, I suppose you might say ... There was something, wasn't there, David, about his works going to his next of kin?"

Audrey said in an odd voice, "I've been meaning to ask what was going to happen to his works. So he left them to his next of kin, did he? A curious phrase, that, surely. Why not leave them to 'his wife' if he meant to leave them to you?"

"What are his works?" asked William. "His books and manuscripts?"

"I suppose so" said Mrs. Titmarsh more vaguely than ever. "Isn't that what they call 'personal effects?'"

"Oh no," said Audrey decisively, in a tone quite unlike her usual wistful gabble. "It doesn't mean personal effects at all. Make no mistake about that. It means, as William said, his books and manuscripts and the absolute right to do what you like with them. Understand?" There was something so sharp in her voice that Lucy looked up in mild surprise.

"Well, what should I want to do with them, dear? I'd always preserve them. I love them; though of course I don't understand them."

Audrey put her hand to her mouth and laughed like an urchin. "As who should wish to keep the Haffner Symphony in a drawer! Lucy *dear*, the manuscripts should be published, the books republished. They are something the world *needs*. You can't ... It's so *terribly* important, so much more important than anything he did *here* ... *This* was for himself: the other is for the world ... It's his whole life — it's what he lived for ... Oh, can't *any* one make her see ... They mustn't just be wasted!"

"Oh yes, I must try. I will, Audrey. How sweet of you to think of it. It will make a kind of memorial for him, won't it? I think he would have liked that."

Audrey shook her head helplessly, impatiently. That was not what she meant at all.

David said, "As a matter of fact I was looking through some of his manuscripts the other day, and it occurred to me then ... I always thought it a pity we haven't a little press here. We might get one. Or we could get it done at Towchester, a private printing ... " He saw her face and stopped. "No, darling," he said. "You can't do anything else. All that stuff has been the rounds. No one'll look at it. He had the utmost difficulty to find a publisher for the stuff he did get printed. It's very ... " He hesitated. "Have you read any of it?"

"Yes."

"Well, could you understand it? Honestly?"

"No. But then I don't expect to, I'm uneducated and I've only a narrow female brain. I can't grasp ... But I had glimpses ... *enough* to know it mustn't be wasted. After all, just because the average man can't understand it, is no criterion. How many people understood Einstein's Theory of Relativity?" She looked down at the small muscular hands on her knees. "I could get them published," she said in a low reluctant voice.

"Well, there you are, Lucy."

Lucy, absorbed in slipping the third needle through the cable stitches, said vaguely, "That would be lovely, dear."

She tightened her thin lips angrily. "No, *not* like that, Lucy. I wish I could make you see ... I wish (oh, this sounds a funny thing to say!)" — she rushed the words out quickly, "I wish you'd let *me* have them — altogether. I think you might. I mean, you don't really *want* them, do you?"

There was a strangely shocked silence. Memory winked up a shutter, and Mr. Chaos saw small children, lights and colours, adults hovering as huge and archaic as dinosaurs, and a table dazzling with jellies and a cake ... some sort of party. Settling at the table ... the breathless hush before one begins ... and then a little girl announcing clearly, dogmatically: "I'll have that one!" pointing ... And the same shocked silence. It wasn't done to ask for what you wanted. It wasn't done to grab. Rude little girl! ... The shutter fell.

"I'd pay for them, of course," she said hurriedly.

"It isn't quite that, dear," Lucy said quietly.

Audrey pressed her hair off her face with both her hands.

"You think I shouldn't ... I don't want to hurt you ... but Wesley *meant* me to have them," she gasped.

"Why, Audrey!" in a tone of simple surprise.

William got up and moved over to her.

"We don't have to discuss it now, do we?" he said, with his big friendly smile. "No one can do anything to-night, and almost any other time would be more suitable."

David edged in from the other side. She looked very frail and pathetic somehow between the two sturdy blond young men. He murmured to her that Wesley had intended it as a provision for Lucy if she ever wanted to leave the Brotherhood.

Audrey stamped her foot. "Then why didn't he say so?"

"He said, next of kin. What more do you want?"

Lucy said hurriedly, "Oh, never mind it. Let her have them if she wants them."

"I've a *right* to them. I'm not going to make trouble. Why do you all look at me like that? If he wanted her to have them he should have left them to her. I've as much right to them as she has. More. I'm his next of kin, too. He never did a thing for me in all my life. I'm entitled to something now. It's his way of making it up to me." She sucked in her breath gaspingly and stared blindly round at them. "I tell you he *wanted* me to have them ... Don't you *see*! ... *I'm his daughter*," she cried through her tears and pushed past them out of the room. They could hear her running, stumbling up the stairs, sobbing ...

A nasty scene. Nobody looked at Mrs. Titmarsh — except Mr. Chaos of course. She had pushed her chair back, deep into the shadow, but her hands she had forgotten; they lay in her lap, exposed and trembling. The steel pins tumbled to the floor in sharp flashes of light. She let them lie.

Brother Rollo bent over her protectively.

"Lucy, dear Lucy, it isn't true."

In her soft tired voice she answered him, clearly enough for all the others to hear.

"Oh, yes it is. Don't deceive yourselves; she would never have said it unless it were true. You mustn't mind for me, Rollo." She got up. "You see, I knew. Wesley told me about her long ago. Naturally ... If you don't mind, I think I'll go to my room now. Good-night. One of you look to the inspector and see he has everything he wants." Only the sound of her footsteps trailing softly away broke the silence.

They looked from one to another uncomfortably. If it had not been for the presence of a stranger, and a police detective too, they would not have felt so awkward.

Brother Rollo broke the silence to say: "Ought someone to go to Audrey?"

"What for, pray?"

"Oh ... Just to make sure she's all right. She was dreadfully upset, wasn't she?"

Miriam, her face like stone, said, "Serve her right. Little bitch!"

No one said anything. It was an evening of horrid revelations, and dismay had gone too far for protest. Ella said tentatively, "I think I'll just —" and slipped away.

Brother Rollo said, "Let us pray ... " and bowed his head.

An odd evening, thought Mr. Chaos as he got into the hard narrow bed some hours later. The house was still. They were all abed and probably asleep long ago. But Mr. Chaos had had work to do. Now he was in bed where he could relax and mull over the facts and impressions of the day.

What were the facts? Wesley Titmarsh, man of sixty-two, Master of a Brotherhood he had formed himself, was found shot with a .22 bullet at point-blank range in the middle of a three acre field. That was the broad outline of the scheme. And with half a dozen eye-witnesses watching from the windows upstairs — or at least, he corrected himself, potential eyewitnesses. When it came down to it they were none of them much good, so vague and contradictory. The untrained observer was the very devil, however truthful he was. In fact it was not so much a question of truth as of clarity of mental vision. People saw things without realising the significance of what they saw. All the facts you got were filtered through the idiosyncrasies of the individual mind. And when the mind was disorganised by shock, things happened in their wrong sequence, were absurdly exaggerated or, contrariwise, overlooked. Or there were more curious results still, as the strange spectral figure who came and went without footprints, that Audrey was prepared to swear to. Why had she been so insistent he should hear her story, so eager he should believe it? What a funny little exhibitionist she was! You could see her acting everything out, kidding herself all along the line. Being terribly sincere, and gallant, and wistful, because that was the way it was in the story-books always. And doubtless if you fooled yourself hard enough you could even get away with blackmail and make it sound simply a sweet earnest tale. Or was he being unfair?

Of them all, the most practical and level-headed was undoubtedly David McQueen. Where the others were vague, he was clear. He had acted with decision. He had gumption. His testimony was the only one that had been properly observed. Beside his, the other testimonies were muddled and uncertain.

And then there was William, so genial, such a restful agreeable personality, who was in charge of the bell which had by such a mysterious coincidence gone wrong just before the vital period. Nothing to do with William of course, because he had no head for heights, suffered from vertigo, and could hardly be induced to make that fearsome journey. He made no bones about that, wanted it to be quite clear that he was a coward. Hardly the sort of thing a person would ordinarily mention; but he had gone so far as to point out the excuses he had made not to run down and see for himself the horrors of the accident. And it was not to be forgotten that his wrist was broken, or badly injured (there were two or three witnesses to that, weren't there? Though no one had seen it happen), so that he could not possibly fire a gun, could he? Yes, there was a lot there that needed explaining. Mr. Chaos wondered just how good an actor he had been in the old unregenerate days.

And Rollo, the aloof, the spiritual, who believed that murderers should go unhung, unpunished. There were some queer ones among them and no mistake. Not least, dear old Joshua Platt, as he called himself. Mr. Chaos chuckled. It was a queer set-up. And yet he liked them; you couldn't help it. There was something about them, fresh, original, uncluttered-up with conventions, that appealed.

As yet no weapon had been found. The house had been searched of course. Not a difficult job in a place as bare as the palm of your hand. To-morrow the grounds ... his heart sank at the thought; five hundred acres, or whatever it was. A nice routine job for the constable and Sergeant Bean.

He saw again, with his inward eye this time, the pattern of cryptogamous matter on the microscope slide, with blurred edges first of all and then sharply precise as it came into focus. What the devil was it doing in the wound? he thought savagely for the fiftieth time. The improbability and meaninglessness of it nagged at the back of his mind all day. He had known from the start, he thought irritably, that this was not going to be a lucky case; everything that could go wrong would go wrong. And this nuisance of the moss was exactly the sort of thing that never got cleared up properly. Again and again, he knew, there would come the temptation to ignore it because it did not fit in with any of the known facts. It was these kind of moral struggles that made a case so tiring, Mr. Chaos found. You couldn't just discard a fact as irrelevant. Once again his old teacher regarded his class severely over the top of his glasses, his eyes like jewels in his sallow, whiskery, wrinkled face: "Gentlemen, in the solution every fact is accounted for. If anything, however trivial, has been overlooked or discarded the solution is not correct, is no true solution, but merely a theory, more or less tenable, more or less sound. The completed picture, gentlemen, is your standard of integrity." Yes, the damned moss particles would have to be accounted for; but not now, not yet.

What he wanted more than anything just now was to have a three-dimensional portrait of the murdered man. What character, what personality, what kind of a stumbling-block was it that had been so ruthlessly brushed aside into eternity? Nine times out of ten the reason for murder lay in the soul or body of the victim, forming some barrier to thwart the murderer's keenest desire. Often it was here one found the clearest indication of motive. Despite his long years of police training, Mr. Chaos was inclined to mistrust merely circumstantial evidence. Not that facts in themselves were unreliable; facts cannot lie; facts indeed say nothing one way or another; it is our interpretation of them that is so sadly fallible.

Find therefore the meaning of Wesley Titmarsh. From this person and from that gather the unguarded impressions, pick up the hints and contrive to understand the unspoken! Tentatively he laid the first strokes on the blank canvas that was called "Portrait of Wesley Titmarsh." There emerged suggestions ... a vague design ... an elderly man, strong and purposeful ... grizzled hair and red beard faintly flecked with white. A passionate man. A sweet and saintly man. A fiery-tempered man. Definitely a man who knew his own mind and had transcendental ideas of right and wrong. Was he, despite that, tolerant? Did he demand from others the same high standards of behaviour he insisted on for himself? And — this was important — which was stronger, his will or his love? Was he obstinate or yielding? What was the true relationship between him and his wife? Here were high-lights and shadows that Mr. Choas could not touch in.

But here in his room was the shell of his personality, the cast-off remnant of his mind, as it were. There were all those papers on the table and in those stuffed drawers to be gone through. A wearisome but profitable business that.

Mr. Chaos turned his head sideways and squinted at the books by his head. Swedenborg's *The Animal Kingdom*; *The Rig Vedas*; Emerson's *The Conduct of Life*; *The Kabbala*; *The Talmud*; *The Bhagavad Gita*; *The Koran*; more Swedenborg — *Conjugal Love* this time; Gandhi's *Satyagraha*; three books by Wesley Titmarsh himself, *Metaphysical Healing*, *The Fourth Dimension of Spirit*, and *Divine Metaphysics*.

Well, that was a clear enough indication, heaven knew. Not like most people's books, a jumble of novels and unread collected editions.

And there on the table was his mass of correspondence and MSS., weighed down with random stones, and even a lump of coal — of all unsuitable paper weights! but typical of the man that a common stone was better, truer, 'realler' than a manufactured article. Those papers should tell him much. Beside the oil lamp, was a volume of Plato and another book, left there as though they were often read, or as if they were the last books read. Mr. Chaos turned over the top book. It was a nice little copy of Emerson's Essays. It fell open to his hand at the essay on Compensation. It had been read and reread. You could tell not only from the way it opened but the elaborate underscorings down the page. The underlined words stood out sharply. Mr. Chaos read:

"Material good has its tax, and if it come without desert or sweat, has no root in me and the next wind will blow it away."

And next to it in the margin was pencilled in a small scholarly hand: See Luke 12: 15.

Mr. Chaos sat up and reached to the shelf above for a New Testament. Fluttered the pages. Ah! ... "And he said unto them, Take heed, and beware of covetousness; for a man's life consisteth not in the abundance of the things which he possesseth ..." and, "Thou fool, this night thy soul shall be required of thee: then whose shall those things be?" Mr. Chaos closed the Gospel thoughtfully and turned back to *Compensation.*

"I no longer wish to meet a good I do not earn, for example, to find a pot of buried gold, knowing that it brings with it new burdens ... The gain is apparent; the tax is certain. But there is no tax on the knowledge that the compensation exists and that it is not desirable to dig up treasure."

And then an underlined quotation from St. Bernard:

"Nothing can work me damage except myself; the harm that I sustain I carry about with me, and never am a real sufferer but by my own fault."

Mr. Chaos closed the books and put them away. He turned down the lamp. "The harm that I sustain I carry about with me." What did he mean by that? Mr. Chaos watched the moonlight shift round the room. Through the white hours he pondered it. Till at last he sighed and fell asleep, to dream that a great stone angel flew towards him with towering wings. He cringed in terror before it. And then, Oh, it's not real, he thought, relieved, it's Epstein's Lucifer. But the smiling face that rushed down on him he knew, and the recognition awoke him. He did not go to sleep again.

CHAPTER SIX - ONE FOX TO ANOTHER

Mr. Chaos on his hard cot heard the Rising Bell, the Bell summoning them to prayers, the Bell that dismissed them to work, and the Bell that called them together again for Pittance. Mr. Chaos was there in time for that. Pittance consisted of mugs of milk, huge bowls of steaming porridge with salt and hunks of crusty bread. Once again the meal was partaken in silence, but this time the reader in the big chair was Rollo Carpenter. He chose some verses of a psalm of exaltation, an extract on death from the *Vishnu Puranas*, and part of what appeared to be the memoirs of a Bhuddist monk of the 7th century. He read very slowly and without expression and his remote hollow voice resounded dolefully in the big silent room.

When the rudimentary meal was over the group dispersed to their duties. Mr. Chaos intercepted Mrs. Titmarsh and carried her away to his room for an interrogation. She did not look any the worse, he considered, for Audrey's painful disclosures of the night before, her expression was as peaceful, as dimly tired, her smile as placatory as before.

"What sort of a man was your husband, Mrs. Titmarsh? I'm getting the most confused impression of him from one person and another. You knew him best; you've known him longest. What was he really like?"

Lucy Titmarsh spread her work-shapen hands against her rough dun-coloured skirt and stared at them before she answered. Then she looked up at the inspector almost fiercely and said with an odd kind of determination: "He was a *good* man. It isn't easy to describe him in a way that'll make you see, partly because he's too familiar to me, and partly because Wesley was such an unusual person. Some of them will tell you that he was a saint, people like Miriam who'd given up everything to be with him, who simply adored him. I don't know whether he was or not. I should have said he was too impatient and had too wild a temper for that. Though of course I'm no judge of saintliness and perhaps the Miriam Frys are better qualified to speak on that point than I. But saint or not, there was no mistaking his goodness, it burnt in him like a flame; goodness was a passion with him.

"It was always the same, though when I first knew him he had not begun his search for the road to perfection. But the inward desire was there, making him restless because he did not know what it was he wanted, or what it was that drove him from one country to another — ceaselessly searching. He was a strange young man in those days. He always had a strong, mysterious, spiritual attraction; and in those days he was physically very beautiful as well. He was irresistible. Every one warned me against marrying him. It seems funny and almost blasphemous now, but he wasn't considered good enough for me. They told me he was probably crazy; they said he was a rolling stone; they prophesied it would end in disaster. But when you're in love ... They might have spared their breath, we just laughed at them."

She gave a little smiling sigh and went on: "Not that they weren't right, of course. Often it was not easy. He could never seem to settle to anything. I suppose he was roving after a better, after the ideal way of life. It was as if he had to try every kind of life, to live among every kind of people. Till he found God. Then he became focused, as it were."

"Was that when he founded this place?"

"Well, no. It took some years for him to develop to this point. And then it evolved more or less accidentally. He always had people who were interested in his theories staying with us. They came from all over. Sometimes they got into touch with him after reading something he had written somewhere, or would drift down casually for a visit, the way Miriam did. She was so captivated that she chucked everything to become one of his first disciples. Others came to him because they felt he had the words of eternal life. Or he healed them, like Ella. Or he saved them from despair and death, like Rollo. Be that as it may, there they all were (though not quite the same ones as are here now), and there were the seeds of a little colony, a community of Truth-seekers, vowed to simplicity and a kind of unpretentious poverty. We learnt to be self-supporting, and after a few years we came on here." Here she stopped as though that were the end of what she had to say.

Mr. Chaos knitted his brows above his kindly sorrowful eyes. These people were really extraordinarily difficult to keep to the point; to get out of them what you wanted to know required the guile of a Jew and the patience of a camel.

Mr. Chaos said, "But what was it your husband believed?"

Mrs. Titmarsh frowned energetically. It was so hard to describe when one had never followed it very clearly in the first instance. "I don't understand it all but I can tell you what he used to say. He used to say, We are in and of Spirit, all facets of one Spirit. He tried to explain to me once that the body is no more than a piece of seaweed you hang outside the window to tell the weather, just a sensitive media for gathering impressions, and you are much greater than that, your body is only part of you — the least part. And then he'd say. Truth is the centre and circumference of the universe. And Love, of course. Love, he said, is the supreme power of the universe. Love is God. They make out that Love and Truth are the same thing. And what they are striving for, I think, is a keener perception of Truth, a purer apprehension of Love. And for that naturally you have to give up your human sense of love and the uncertain truth of the senses. Oh, it is so difficult to explain! But they say you can't have both, you can't have this world, which they call mythical and private, and the other world, the world of divine Spirit, which they say is real and universal. I don't see why not. But since all the seers and prophets through the ages seem to agree about that, I suppose they're right and I'm just being dull and womanish. Wesley said the mistake the desert fathers made was in shutting themselves away from humanity, moping about sin, and weaving a few palm-leaf baskets to keep the pot boiling. It was unreal in the wrong sense, Wesley said. So here we all worked. Head in the clouds but feet on the earth, said Wesley. What is that phrase? 'Having all things but possessing nothing.' That's the idea. Like Rollo, who Heaven knows had everything on this earth that money could buy. He was frightfully rich, positively rolling. Rolling Rollo," she repeated with a smile. "But what good did it do him? His child died under his eyes between one moment and the next, and his wife whom he adored ran away from him. He nearly went mad, I believe. He couldn't understand how such a thing could have happened to *him*. Rich people are like that, aren't they? They feel money gives them immunity from common disasters, and, I suppose, to a certain extent it does. He was like the young nobleman in the Gospel who had kept all the commandments all his life and couldn't understand why it wasn't enough. It seems so unfair to be punished when you haven't done anything wrong. But unlike the young nobleman Rollo was only too ready to sell all he had and give to the poor. He fairly chucked his money away, he couldn't get rid of it fast enough. Possessions are burdens, he says, they're chains fastening you down to earth and no good to you at all. He won't own a thing. He's like St. Francis of Assisi. I believe he'd go stark naked if the climate were only more suitable — like the holy men do in India, the Sannyasin, as they call them."

"You seem to know so much about it that it seems a little odd, if I may say so, that you don't count yourself as one of the Brotherhood."

"Do you think so? No. It just isn't my style, that's all. I'm a very ordinary sort of person, I'm not at all clever, and that rather mystical side of life doesn't seem terribly important to me. I can see it may be awfully important in the long run, but just now other things seem to matter more. I can't help feeling that it's better to do some of the things that need doing, some of the ordinary ephemeral day to day things. It seems to me wiser not to think so much, not to ask so many unanswerable questions. I don't see that it makes for happiness. At least it doesn't make me happy. But then I get my happiness in trying to make other people happy and comfortable. I believe that is the real religion of the average woman, if you got down to it. And I'm a very average woman; I like to have people depending on me and coming to me to be cheered and comforted. I like to warm them and soothe them and send them out again renewed."

"As you say, someone has to do it. Tell me, why, should you say, Miss Lewes really joined the group? I should have said all hard living and high thinking was quite out of her line of country."

"Or do you only think that since last night?" asked Lucy drily.

"Not altogether. Before last night she seemed out of place here. She's the sort of little person you'd expect to find in Chelsea, not living quite out of the world and roughing it without any glamour. I thought then, she must have some motive. Last night only simplified it a bit. And we know now, or we can make a shrewd guess, what it was she was after."

"Oh, she's welcome to the manuscripts," said Lucy. And then, "I shouldn't mind about it, it's so long ago," she burst out through narrowed lips. "But I do. I hated the humiliating way she came out with it last night, turning it into a sordid scandal, blackening his name! Why didn't she come to us straight away? We should have acknowledged her. I longed for children, even not my own." She was as indignant as if she had been done out of something.

Having got her reaction, he turned her gently from it. Now he wanted to learn something of Wesley's relations with the inhabitants of Market Keep. At first the villagers had been barbarous, she told him. They used to follow them in the street when they went out, and throw stones at them and call them names. Sometimes a few drunken louts would come up and break the windows or set a hayrick on fire. But gradually the bouts of hooliganism lessened, and after a few years they ceased altogether. The villagers had got used to them, though it would not be true to say they had accepted them. And of course the Brotherhood had done a lot of good one way and another. Healing a crippled child, curing some supposedly hopeless disease, helping the poor, succouring the widow and orphan. Presumably that had been taken into account.

"And the gentry?" inquired Mr Chaos. "They were rather more friendly, perhaps?"

"You would think, wouldn't you, that people of breeding and education …"

"People like Menzies, you mean?"

"Oh!" She looked uncomfortable. "Have you heard about that already? In a village they make gossip out of anything. There was nothing to it really. Except that it was characteristic of the man. Characteristic of both of them, I suppose."

"I'd like to hear your version of it, though," said Mr. Chaos.

It seemed that Percy Menzies could afford to fancy himself as a nob and made himself M.F.H. of his own pack. That gave him something to throw his weight about on, undoubtedly. And then, the first hunt of the season, about three weeks ago, they had "viewed" on Abbot's Breach land and Wesley had stopped them.

"He stood there with his arms outstretched. He looked very fragile and dauntless standing there defying Menzies on his great bay. 'Not on my land,' he said. 'Never. Thou shalt not kill, Menzies.' After all, he was perfectly within his rights to forbid him. And besides, we don't kill anything ourselves, not even for food. Wesley felt very strongly indeed about that. To kill creatures inferior to ourselves he regarded as a breach of trust. He believed that God had put them in our care. But you couldn't expect a man like Menzies to see that. He was beside himself with rage, prancing up and down and swearing.

'Damn you, will you let me pass!' He hated being made to look a fool in front of so many people, with all the villagers gawping round. And it was spoiling his day's fun, too. The hounds were running back and forth along the fence whimpering, trying to break through. Menzies was stupid, he lost control of himself — his ungovernable tempers have been his undoing before now — and slashed at Wesley with his whip. There was a hush, a sort of noisy hush, if you know what I mean. People hereabouts don't like that sort of thing. However much they might dislike Wesley and side with Menzies with ingratiating snobbery, that was going too far, even for them. Wesley took his hand away from his face. The cut stood out in a long red welt. It made his skin look very white, his eyes very blue: they were blazing, and his beard glinted like fire in the sunlight. He looked terrifying: like Jonah about to pronounce doom on Nineveh. My heart turned over. He said very clearly, so that each word must have hit Menzies like a stone, "It's no good, Menzies. You can't kill a defenceless man in this country in order to get your own way." She twisted her mouth into a cynical smile. "That was enough for Menzies, he wasn't going to stay and bandy words about that. He never uttered another sound, but plunged his horse through the crowd and trotted away."

"Why?" said Mr. Chaos. "I mean, why did your husband make that peculiar remark about killing a defenceless man to get his own way?"

Mrs. Titmarsh looked at him wryly.

"Yes, it has become a very peculiar remark indeed now, hasn't it? For, so short a while after having said it, here is this most defenceless and honourable of men killed." Tears choked her voice and she struggled to swallow the lump in her throat. Then she went on with eyes cast down, "You see, Wesley knew Menzies when he was a young man in Africa. He was a spoilt young man and something of a bad lot even then. When I say Wesley knew him, I'm not quite right, he knew *of* him but they didn't move in the same circles of course. It was only afterwards ... It happened that in a fit of temper, Menzies killed a native. In those days ..." she shrugged. "Besides, there were pots of money behind him. So the magistrate chose to regard it as a rather harmless undergraduate spree — you know the sort of thing. A nigger beaten to death once in a way didn't really signify. The case was dismissed, with a fine or something. But not by Wesley. Even in those days he didn't take murder so lightly as that. The place became too uncomfortable to hold Menzies."

"In other words, he was run out of town."

"Actually, he had to — or he chose to — leave the country. A good thing too; he wasn't a coloniser. It was an unfortunate coincidence that he and Wesley should settle in the same village after all these years."

Unfortunate for whom, Mr. Chaos wondered. But aloud he asked whether it was in Africa that Mr. Titmarsh had learnt to farm.

"In Australia too," said Mrs. Titmarsh. "We worked my brother's sheep station for two years while he was ill."

"Mmmm! ... Had there been words between your husband and Mr. Menzies before this passage the other day?"

"Not that I know of. They weren't likely to meet much in the ordinary way of things, they had almost no points of contact. This was ..."

"You wanted me to know about it, anyway."

"I thought you should. Perhaps I've done wrong. The others wouldn't like it, I dare say, but then they have a different way of viewing things, and it isn't their husband who's been murdered. I thought, if I tell him it won't be on my conscience, and he can draw his own conclusions." She was the least bit aggressive about it, as though even now she had not quite decided if she was right to speak or not.

"Quite right. Very sensible," quoth Mr. Chaos. "And Mr. Menzies is married, I take it?"

"Oh yes. A funny little woman. Looks like a cook," said Mrs. Titmarsh abstractedly. "She was away when this happened, though. She's been ill." She was not really attending to her conversation; you could see her thoughts were elsewhere. Probably she was reliving that scene in the cold autumn sunlight, the greedy crowd surging about the two men, the brisk volley of words, the violent gesture, the taunting riposte: "You can't kill a defenceless man in this country in order to get your own way!" ... and now he lay dead, and perhaps Percy — But perhaps not, she corrected herself sharply.

Mr. Chaos broke in on her thoughts to ask if she had any idea why her husband was late for Solitary Meditation that morning.

"Well, for one thing, the bell didn't ring, you know. And then his watch had become very unreliable of late."

"Unreliable, was it? Do you know whether it was fast or slow or just what was the trouble?"

"Fast *and* slow." she said. "I suppose the truth of the matter was that it had had its day; but Wesley couldn't bear to think that. He loved it. It was the only watch he'd ever had. I think the only possession he cared for at all. And that was mainly sentiment. It saved his life once in Africa. It stopped a stray bullet; you can still see the dent it made in the case." She looked distracted, sad: thinking, Not this time. But the detective was asking more questions about its inaccuracy: She explained how first it had been fast by the house-time, and he had altered it, and then it had been slow, and he had altered it, and then it had been fast again, and so on. It irritated him, and at the last he didn't like to have it argued about.

A shadow fell across the room. They turned. "Ooo-hoo! Look at me!" shouted Ruby dumbly through the window, her pigtails flying up in the air, her face contorted with excitement as if she were under water.

Lucy smiled and shook her head. "Not now, darling." But Ruby couldn't hear through the glass and it vibrated with her impatient thumps till Lucy was forced to go across and slide the sash up. She began again to say, "Darling, I'm occupied. You mustn't interrupt. Run along now and I'll see you later." But Ruby was effervescing with greetings and kisses, as different as could be from the child of yesterday greeting her other "Auntie" defensively and sullen. The long black skinny legs scrambled over the sill. There was something she wanted to tell Auntie Lucy, some frightfully important childish nonsense. But she noticed Mr. Chaos. "Hallo," she said. She slid to the ground. "Didn't speck to see you here." She looked uneasy. She had muddled into one of these queer grown-up things again. In a minute one of them was going to tell her to go away, she knew it. She was never allowed any fun. But no, Mr. Chaos again proved more agreeable than the average grown-up. Now he strolled to the door and said, "It's all right, Mrs. Titmarsh. The rest of our conversation can be concluded any time. I'll trot along now. I've plenty to do. See you later, young lady." Nice of him. Young lady! A term she rated only a shade higher as a rule than "little girl," but somehow he made it sound different, he was so polite, he sounded as though he meant it and not as though he was laughing down on you. Funny him being here, though, when only yesterday he'd said he didn't know them ... Still, she couldn't be bothered with that now. There was Auntie Lucy ...

Mr. Chaos had advanced but a few yards down the corridor when McQueen came flying towards him, the skirts of his robe billowing behind him. He pulled up abruptly at sight of the detective. "Ah," he said, "I rather wanted to see you." And then he fell silent.

"Well, here I am," Mr. Chaos reminded him.

"Yes." He tucked his thumbs unhappily through the scarlet rope of his girdle. "I wish ... The fact is," he said with a nervous laugh, "I've an idiotic confession to make. When we were asked about weapons we all said, no, there was no such thing in the place. I suppose it must have slipped my mind. We have a weapon in the house — somewhere. It's an old shotgun." He rubbed his hands together as though they were sticky. "As a matter of fact it's mine."

Mr. Chaos said, Oh, that was rather interesting. "I'd rather like to see it," he said, in the sociable tone of one who suggests it more out of politeness than genuine interest.

McQueen appeared somewhat relieved by this mildness.

He said more cheerfully, "I was just going along to look for it when I bumped into you. I think I know where it ought to be; but I haven't seen it for years. I can't imagine now how I came to forget it, or why I suddenly remembered it again just now. It just happened to float into my mind the ways things do. And I thought it might be dreadfully serious and I'd better let you know at once; but I suppose it isn't really. It's not perjury or anything, is it? It's not very likely that any one knew about it, or that knowing about it would have used it. Still, I suppose there is just that chance. To tell the truth," he said, with a rather endearing sheepish smile, "it's not even an ordinary shotgun. Most people seeing it wouldn't suspect it was anything but what it pretended to be. It is one of those phony affairs got up to look like a walking-stick. A poacher's gun. I brought it back with me from the States. I bought it in my dizzier days when I lived in the Village, and it was up to every one of us to pack away something even if it was no more than a sword-stick or a stiletto — such a wild lot as we were! I hate to think what would have happened if I'd ever tried to use it; exploded it in my face, I expect. Still, it was the done thing, and I got it and used to carry it round with me and finally I brought it here, heaven alone knows why." He coughed and glanced at the detective from the edge of his eye, guardedly: "Of course I never had a licence for it," he said hopefully. "That would have spoiled the fun, wouldn't it?"

Mr. Chaos pursed his lips and smiled non-committally.

"It used to be in here, along with all the rest of the rubbish that 'might come in' one day," said McQueen advancing towards the cupboard by the entrance. "So with any luck ..." He pulled open the door, and the uneasy pyramid tottered and fell out against him. He tried to save them, laughing, as they skidded and thundered. He scrambled among the mess at the back of the cupboard. Mr. Chaos watched him but made no attempt to help. In a couple of minutes he emerged, tousled and abashed, to murmur that it was not there. "Now where could I — " he muttered. "It can hardly have got loose by itself, can it?" he smiled whimsically through the dishevelled fringe of yellow hair which fell into his eyes, giving him the pert, ingenuous air of a Skye terrier. "Well, if it's not here, I don't know where it can be. I wish now I had looked before mentioning the *verfluchte* thing to you. Let's shove the things back and forget all about it. Maybe someone found it and threw it out a couple of years ago."

Perhaps it was his exertions that made him so flushed. Perhaps. But Mr. Chaos divined that it was nervousness that made him suddenly so chatty. He had first to screw himself up a little for his silly confession, but it was not until he did not find it where he expected to that he became really apprehensive. It was that little extra effort to charm, in a character that was ruggedly honest, the sprightliness in one who was habitually cool and reserved, that gave him away. For a moment perhaps David McQueen doubted the essential rightness of objective truth; better to have left things as they were. His besetting sin of impatience constantly led him to interfere in things that were better left alone. The great difficulty for him always was to relax his will.

Mr. Chaos bent and picked up a bottomless wicker basket and a pair of rusty pliers. "How about that?" suggested Mr. Chaos, indicating with the toe of his shoe a stick propped in the corner behind the hinge of the door.

David said, "Ah!" in a tone of mingled relief and satisfaction.

"No!" cried Mr. Chaos. "Don't touch!" But it was too late.

Without thinking, McQueen had sprung toward eagerly to seize the stick. At a rough glance it might pass for a bamboo walking-stick with a crutch-shaped handle. But it was hardly necessary to take hold of it and feel its unwonted weight to know that it was painted steel and not the light and jointed bamboo.

"Interesting," said Mr. Chaos blandly, taking it from him. Indeed he found it more interesting than he allowed himself to show by so much as a glint of his eye; for Mr. Chaos remembered perfectly the contents of that cupboard the last time he had looked in it, and the bamboo walking-stick had not been there then. Now wasn't that surely very odd? Particularly when you called to mind that the deceased had been murdered with a .22 bullet from a rifle and not with shot from a shotgun. So why was it taken away? And why put back again, and his attention so ostentatiously drawn to it? Curiouser and curiouser.

"Well," said David awkwardly, swinging the red tassels on his girdle, uncertain whether he should go or stay till the detective dismissed him.

"Do you want to come and see if I can get it to tell me anything? You may if you want to," said Mr. Chaos, strolling across to his room. He wasn't going to examine it meticulously just then, but there were certain things he wanted to know about it at once. Fingerprints, he needn't bother himself with for the moment; there were not likely to be any except David's. Though he was careful to carry it in his handkerchief and did not touch it with bare fingers. There was a spring catch in the head and the handle clicked open, disclosing the simple mechanism. With his pocket lens he saw that the steel on the underside of the hammer appeared slightly scratched; but that might have been done at any time. The barrel was clean as a whistle, as the saying is. Mr. Chaos was hardly sensible of a feeling of disappointment, for he had really not expected anything from it, and he would have thought it odd if it had been otherwise. He did not expect the case to drop solved into his outstretched hands. His soft brown eyes rested curiously, sympathetically on the young man before him.

"Where did you say you got this? In the States, I know, but where?"

McQueen said pat: "I told you, when I was in the Village. I forget the number of the street. A little alley off Washington Square. A joint called Fuseli's."

"Did you buy it new?"

"Yes. At least, so far as I know it was."

"Ever used it yourself?"

McQueen shook his head.

"I never had any ammunition for it. I never meant to use it. It was just the stylish thing to do." He smiled tentatively, and brushed the limp yellow locks off his forehead.

Mr. Chaos leant forward confidentially.

"And now tell me, where did you find it?"

"Find it?" echoed McQueen with his wide blue stare.

"Exactly. Where did you find it before you hid it in the cupboard, before deciding, very sensibly, to see that it got safely into my hands?" he asked persuasively.

David said blankly, "I assure you, sir, I haven't the least idea — "

Mr. Chaos slotted a pencil through his fingers and tapped it edge and edge in rhythmic impatience on the table.

"My dear young man, the most idiotic thing you can do — *I* assure *you* — is to attempt to shield any one by tampering with the evidence. It's far more likely to result in a miscarriage of justice. To meddle your puddy fingers in a murder case is the sheerest damfoolery. Come now, out with it! Where did you find it?" That was about the nearest he was likely to get to losing his temper, and even that was deliberate.

McQueen folded his arms and tucked his hands inside his wide sleeves. Against the rough white wall the round head, round features, round blue eyes, pink complexion and yellow hair, were like a child's drawing of a child, touchingly simple in colour and form. He said with a trace of bewilderment in his tone, "I can't imagine why you should think I am deceiving you."

Mr. Chaos said patiently, "Long years of dreary experience have taught me what I have to expect. It's always the same old story. When it comes to anything dangerous and unusual people are as stupidly credulous and unreasoning as the foolish Moor who thought he understood the evidence of a stolen handkerchief. Mr. McQueen, only the trained mind is capable of fairly judging evidence. Don't try to cover up the mistake you believe someone to have made, I beg you. You don't know what harm you may be doing."

Somewhat to the detective's surprise, McQueen leant his hands on the table and bringing his face close peered at him intently, as though the detective's thoughts were inscribed minutely on the pupils of his eyes. He stood upright, again and mumbled unhappily.

"I don't like it. You seem to have the strangest ideas about us. You don't understand apparently what it means to seek the Truth. It means to seek the truth in all things, to look ceaselessly through the Appearance of things to the Reality behind. We are surely the least likely people to be taken in by the outward seeming of a thing. But even if we were so mistaken, why should we cover up truth? That in itself would be acting a lie. And lying is as much a negation of our principles as — "

"As killing," suggested Mr. Chaos.

McQueen gave him a look.

"If you like," he said, "though I was going to say, as much against our principles as hatred, which is the negation of Love, which is God." His voice rang out clearly. "But killing, too," he sighed, and his voice dropped to a mumble again. "I don't like it. If you think I'm shielding somebody, that means you've got it into your head that it's one of us who has committed this crime. And I wish I knew what had given you that notion."

Mr. Chaos smiled faintly.

"Thank you. That gives me a pretty good example of what I was saying a moment ago. The layman misreads the facts. The fact that I suspect you of knowing more than you tell does not necessarily mean that I therefore believe the criminal to be one of your friends, whom you are naturally trying to shield. The accurate deduction is simply that I think *you* suspect one of your friends — rightly or wrongly — and on that account are withholding information. Not at all the same thing, you see."

"I'm glad to hear it," he said suavely. "Then we were both mistaken." His eyes were like blue marbles. The bell rang, in a spiral of liquid sound, to mark another period. "If you'll excuse me ... " said McQueen. His tongue slid over his lips, "I shall be needed ... "

"By all means," said Mr. Chaos wearily. For what was the use of keeping him? You could argue at that rate all night and you'd never get anywhere. Slippery as eels, they were. Did they stick to the truth or did they not? If he could once catch them out, if he could point to one thing for certain ... What was the point of bringing him this silly toy unless it meant something, unless there was something behind it. What was it McQueen said? They looked for the Reality behind the Appearance of things. Mr. Chaos laughed to himself, Well, that was just what he had to do. Assemble the facts, discard the fake, and read the metaphysical significance of this jolly old shotgun.

There was a murmur of voices outside his door and suddenly Ruby's indignant husky tones rose high on the air. "Oh, I never, David! As if I would! Oh, she is a stinking liar!"

Mr. Chaos thrust his head round the door and said reproachfully, "Language! Language, Ruby!"

She jumped round, squirrel-eyed. Oh, it's you! Well, she is. Ask David. Makes me sick, she does."

"Talking about your Aunt again, I suppose," he said severely. "What's the trouble this time?"

"She told 'im I went and put his music on the fire. As if I would. I'm not such a fool. It's on the pyanner, same as always. Far as I know."

"It doesn't matter, dear. Very likely I misunderstood it. She didn't say it to me. Only, I thought that if she found them in her way she might have given them to you to bring down. Never mind, I'll collect them myself some time," said David, with a hand on her shoulder. "And don't speak like that about your Auntie, dear. It sounds horrible." He began walking away from her, as if he had no wish to waste any more time.

Ruby hopped up and down and shrugged her shoulders. "What are you doing here?" she said frowning suspiciously at Mr. Chaos. "You tol' me you didn't know them."

"So I did. And so I didn't," said Mr. Chaos cheerfully. "Want to come for a walk?"

"Okey doke," said Ruby, and slipped her cold velvet paw confidingly into her friend's capacious hand.

CHAPTER SEVEN - A PLEASANT WALK, A PLEASANT TALK...

The chill autumnal weather of the last few days was gone. The clammy mists were all blown away, leaving the atmosphere as clear and fresh as in a Dutch landscape, keyed in high flat colours like a poster. The sky was a penetrating Reckitt's blue, with low clouds like hysterical sheep chased by a sheep-dog helter-skelter across the sky. Trees and houses stood out sharply with a firm outline. Their black paper shadows clung to their sides. Brisk as a housewife, the wind puffed the dust out of her road and shook out the sleepy branches. The sun struck the falling leaves like jewels, like blood, as they tumbled through the air, fighting to the death. Ruby scuffled her feet heartlessly in the fallen thousands.

"Where are we going?"

"I'm going to call on Mr. Menzies. Know him?"

"The tall gentleman. He don't never come to our house. But he rings Auntie up sometimes, I've heard him." The child looked sly. "I can show you a quicker way from here."

"Up the right-of-way and through the beech copse, you mean. I know that way. I want to go the long way round, the usual way."

They walked along in silence, with Ruby giving a little chassée now and again to keep in step. Mr. Chaos was busily assimilating the topography, making a mental map of the roads, the relative positions of the houses, clumps of trees, hills, streams and so on. From sheer habit not so much as a piece of rag clinging to a hedge could escape his notice, and dogged curiosity would make him decipher any pencilled scrap of paper crumpled in the gutter. In the same way his training made him note the characteristics of the features of every one he met, and store them away in the files of his memory. That was how he had recognised Joshua Platt. Still it tended to spoil one's most innocent pleasures. Not that he expected to enjoy himself when he was on a job. But even when he was on holiday he could never simply enjoy the charms of nature. It was disgusting to sit in a theatre and find oneself mentally photographing the back of the head of the man in front.

He began to ask Ruby about her friends The Seekers. Whom did she like best?

"Oh, Aunt Lucy, of course." There was not a shade of hesitation. She was enthusiastic about the quiet little woman. She made you see in her place a kind of goddess, the personification of beauty, wisdom and love. "An' she never gets mad at you," Ruby adored.

"Do the others?"

"Oh, no." She looked shocked. "They don't get mad, not ever. But you do something wrong an' see what happens! It's *awful*! You wish you were *dead*!" she said passionately.

"My goodness!" Mr. Chaos was taken aback by her vehemence. "What is it they do, for heaven's sake? Beat you? Lock you up in a cupboard?"

"Nuffin' like that!" she said contemptuously. "Look! Once I told the Master a fib, like I did you that time about the ninquest. Well, what d'you think he did? He never said a word to me, he jus' looked at me as if he wanted to cry, and he went off and he wooden touch a drop of anything to eat or drink all day. Think of that! All because of me! I kep' telling him I was sorry," she said tearfully. "But he never took no notice; he only smiled. It did make me feel horrid."

"You don't like being punished that way? "

"It's not fair to punish someone else cos you've been naughty, is it? When I was little Dad used to tan my backside proper, and Auntie catches me a good clip when I'm bad; and I'd much rather, honest I would. It don't hurt much, and when it's done it's done. Their way you feel all sorry and sort of rough inside, and it goes on hurting in your chest for a long time." She pressed her little hands to her flat chest. "It hurts now when I think of it. He was so kind to every one, he didn't ought to 'ave punished hisself for me. If you know someone good is going to cop it when you do something bad — well, I dunno, it's not fair somehow, it doesn't give you a chance."

"No, it doesn't give you a chance," agreed Mr. Chaos. "They count on you feeling that. You see, they think it's not much use punishing you now if an hour later you're going to do the same thing again. This way they hope to put you off it altogether."

"Aunt Lucy never does it. She doesn't think children ought to be punished like that, I heard her talking about it to Mr. Prescott once."

It was then that the child took the wind completely out of his sails by asking him in a carefully flat little voice if he thought she was going to marry him now.

"Marry whom?" he gasped.

"Mr. Prescott of course," she said impatiently, and added irritably. "I tol' you the other day that it wasn't any use Auntie running after him, he was in love with someone else. Well, that's who the someone is."

"My dear child," protested Mr. Chaos mildly. "Are you sure? You ought not to make statements like that unless you are."

"Course I'm sure," she said indignantly. "What do you take me for? Time and time again I seen them."

Mr. Chaos felt bound to tell her that it was hardly probable. That Mrs. Titmarsh, though a charming, lady, was well on in middle age, certainly in her early fifties, and Mr. Prescott a good ten years younger. Also Mrs. Titmarsh was married.

Ruby squinted up at him through the dark frill of lashes.

"She's not married now," she reminded him.

"And just what do you mean by that?" asked Mr. Chaos pleasantly.

She didn't mean anything in perticuller, she assured him. Only he didn't seem to believe her. As though she didn't know about grown-ups and love, after living ail those years with Auntie. Not that she'd ever seen them spoony, she didn't mean that erzackly: though they were always going off together for long walks. Sometimes she'd followed them. Only for fun, like Lemmy Caution or someone. And she'd heard the things they said. Often and often she'd heard Mr. Prescott say that if only he was married to her how different everything would be. What did Aunt Lucy say to that? Oh, she sort of laughed and said it was too late now.

"Yes. A kind of grown-up joke, you see."

"Was it? Well, why did Auntie Lucy promise me that she'd have me to live with her when she married Mr. Prescott?" Tears trembled perilously on the long black lashes. Her lower lip quivered. "She wooden promise me that unless she meant it, would she? She didn't like me being with Auntie, an' she knew I wanted to live with her." To hide the sad tears trickling off the end of her nose, she busied herself untying the creased ribbon that fastened her plait and then retying it more securely. Through the tuft of hair clenched between her teeth, she muttered, "I never meant to tell any one, but once she said, 'You'll have to get rid of him, Harold. There's no other way.' I wasn't going to tell that."

"And what did you understand by that?"

"I dunno," she said, and hung her head.

"But, my charming infant, what are you dreaming of? They might have been discussing a — a sick dog or something of that sort."

The child said implacably. "No, Mr. Prescott hasn't gotta dog."

"Ruby, how many times a week do you go to the movies? Too often, anyway. Ladies do not casually ask their gentlemen friends to get rid of their husbands for them. You've got the wrong end of the stick somehow."

Ruby said, "They was speaking ever so soft. And he swung round and pointed his finger at me. 'Were you listening?' he said. I said I wasn't listening, but I couldn't help hearing. And he gave Aunt Lucy such a *look*. 'That's torn it,' he said. 'If that little gasbag ever breathes a word of it, I'll murder her.' That's why I wasn't going to say nothing. But I don't care now."

"And Aunt Lucy? What did she do?"

"She did look upset. She said, 'You mustn't talk like that, Harold, to your future step-child. She's not one of your boys.' And she knelt down and put her arms round me and made me promise not to talk of what I'd heard. Only, she spoke nicely. She said: 'Please don't, darling, or there might be trouble.' And so I never did."

"How long ago was that?" asked Mr. Chaos, and he could not prevent a note of sternness sounding in his voice.

She didn't remember erzackly. It was after term began, and term began on the sixteenth. Say about a fortnight ago. That was as near as she could remember it off-hand, and Mr. Chaos had not the opportunity then to coerce her to a closer search, for they had arrived within sight of The Grange, Mr. Menzies' little mansion.

"I'll meet you in the village for an ice in an hour's time," he said, and, puzzled, watched her skipping light-heartedly away.

A man-servant opened the door. Mr. Menzies was out. Would be back later. Couldn't say when. He obliged Mr. Chaos by taking his card and reading it. He then disdainfully dropped the information that Mr. Menzies was getting some target-practice up on the range.

"Where the deer and the antelope play," murmured Mr. Chaos as he turned away. The range, as indicated by the lordly gesture of the butler's hand, was somewhere on top of the big hill on the left, Beacon Hill as it was called. "And there seldom is heard a discouraging word," he hummed, as he advanced over the springy turf. There was some kind of a track, and on either side the ground slid away into dips and hollows, in which gorse bushes blazed their cold yellow flames. Indigo cloud-shapes raced across the fields and hesitated, caught for an instant in the chimney-pots of a house below. "And the skies are not cloudy all day," affirmed Mr. Chaos cheerfully.

The wind was keen now, sweeping through his hair and blowing his breath back smartly into his mouth. He turned round and leant his back against the wind to get a breather. He laughed to himself. Then he stared. Below him to the left a man was clambering out of the earth itself, heaving himself up by the crown of scrub. He stood there rocking on the edge for a moment and then bent to pick something up. It was when he stood upright again that Mr. Chaos recognised his silhouette and the drab garment in his hand that the wind blew out like a flag.

Mr. Chaos ran towards him, calling. The wind carried his voice. William turned round and waved energetically. At the same time he began struggling to put on his habit.

"It's a strayed sheep ... It's that man's fault. They ought to have this place wired off. He knows that, he's been warned time and again. It's a death-trap ... They ought to be compelled," William raged bitterly and incoherently. His face was streaked with dirt and sweat and his fair curls clung in dark tendrils to his temples.

"Have you been down there?" Mr. Chaos peered apprehensively into a sort of chasm half overgrown with bushes and weed, out of which stuck some stumps of rotten wood in a decayed grin. A dilapidated ironwork lopped brokenly over the edge. A notice-board with the word DANGER on it lay on its back in the furze.

"I heard the sheep bleating. And I went down." Brother William was having some difficulty with his other sleeve which the wind kept teasing out of his grasp.

"Doesn't this land belong to you?"

"No. That's our boundary, that line of birches down there. This is common ground." He knotted the red rope about his waist.

"Who were you talking about then, when you said *he* ought to be compelled to do something?"

"The Rural Council. Lord Tom Noddy runs that too. We've spoken to him about it often enough. We lost a heifer down there last year. He says, Don't let them stray. Nothing will be done for *us*; but if one of his precious hunters should break its neck," he grumbled, scrubbing the sweat from his forehead with his sleeve, "that would be a different story." His usual sunny humour was temporarily dissipated by this disaster.

Mr. Chaos knelt on the brink and stared down into the impenetrable dark. "I can't hear anything."

"The poor creature's probably dead. I saw it but I couldn't reach it. And even if I had been able to I could never have brought it up. I shall have to get help." He flashed him suddenly a replica of his radiant smile. "I'm sorry to be so surly, but it really is enough to make one curse, isn't it?"

"Oh lord, yes, I should think so — and worse," Mr. Chaos agreed. "What is this place used for?"

"It isn't used for anything now. That's what's so silly. It really should be filled up. It's a disused quarry; but it's been derelict now for hundreds of years. What's the use of it? Why don't they brick it in?" He made a sudden grimace. "Oh, what's the use! I must go," he said suddenly, and went, running easily downhill towards the distant farmhouse.

Mr. Chaos walked pensively on. Was there a sheep down there? Or had Brother William himself strayed — from the truth; had he gone down there for some other purpose? But what in the name of reason ... ? Bearing in mind always that Brother William suffered from vertigo, it was a pretty remarkable feat. To swarm down into that alarming blackness with its precarious occasional footholds was not a thing he would care to do himself, Mr. Chaos confessed. It was surely much worse than climbing into a bell-tower by however rickety a ladder. It would make a good schoolboyish hiding-place for a treasure, thought Mr. Chaos, lapsing idly into a sort of Nick Carter daydream. And if Brother William had really been the monk he was pretending to be it would not have seemed so unlikely. In fact though, there was no reason for him to risk his neck to conceal anything however precious; he was a perfectly free person and could come and go as he pleased. He was ruled by nothing higher or more tyrannical than his own conscience. If he chose to wear the Hope diamond slung round his neck on a string, there was no one to forbid him. Possibly he was intent on rescuing a sheep, after all.

There was a round red sign to warn him before the echoing crack of firing reached his ears. Here and there flags blew like giant poppies blossoming high above the faded turf.

Behind the target on either side were butts of sand. Menzies and another man were standing about five hundred yards away. The wind was too high for any accurate shooting, and the men had stopped firing and were talking.

Mr. Chaos made some ordinary social observations about the weather. He fancied they looked at him suspiciously but they answered him civilly enough. He inquired carelessly what they were using.

".22's," said Mr. Menzies.

"Oh, the same type that Mr. Titmarsh was shot with," said Mr. Chaos ingenuously: about as naïve as a fox.

Mr. Menzies surveyed him from beneath a drooping cynical lid and turned to his companion. "What do you think of that, Welkin?"

Welkin was a small dark man. He might be a groom or a keeper or something in that line; he had that typical hard, scrubbed, relentless look. Now he said stolidly that he didn't think it very surprising. The .22 was a very popular type of gun.

"Yes," said Mr. Chaos in a different tone. "It would be interesting to know how many .22's are in use round here."

"Well, the police would know. They've only to turn up the licences." Menzies turned away. Civility was all very well, but one didn't want to hold a damned *conversation* with the fellow; it wasn't a bar-parlour. He jerked his head to Welkin. Jerked his head in the other direction at the stranger and muttered a haughty "Good-day, sir." He moved away with the long confident strides of a man who owns the earth. Mr. Chaos stomped after him with the tread of one who doesn't give a damn who owns it. But duty is duty. He intimated as much to Mr. Menzies. It wasn't sensible to run away from him when he had toiled up here on purpose to see him.

"Running away!" sneered Menzdes. "Good God!" He hoped the man wasn't trying to sell him something.

Mr. Chaos sniggered. "Far from it." And introduced himself.

Mr. Menzies said, "Cut along, Welkin. Tell Farmer I'm coming down to the kennels later." Menzies took off his hat and wiped his face, pausing deliberately to give Welkin time to get out of earshot. He was a not unattractive specimen, height about six foot two, with a fine muscular torso, a light complexion and soft thinning fair hair. The expression of his face was not so pleasing, though his features were imposing; the long aristocratic nose, the curling mouth and keen blue eyes hidden behind their drooping lids, the high sloping forehead; features good in themselves but marred by their cold, sensual and self-complacent expression. He was a man of perhaps fifty, though his look of greedy vitality suggested that he might be less. When he spoke again his tone was more agreeable, less haughty.

He said, "It's to do with this Titmarsh affair, I suppose. An unsavoury business. How can I help you?"

Mr. Chaos looked as though help was the last thing he expected. Oh well, for instance, how well did Mr. Menzies know the dead man? Mr. Menzies thought that over for a bit and replied, "Not very well." Then he added, "We were neighbours, of course."

"Yes. Well, that doesn't always make for friendliness, does it? *Pourquoi les haïssez-vous? Payee qu'ils sont nos voisins.* Anatole France's fame rests on that crack; it's so wretchedly true. Or have you not found it so? Oh, I seem to remember someone else mentioning that there had been some fuss or other between you."

Mr. Menzies' eyes were as expressionless as two bits of paper torn from a sugar-bag. He watched a plover rise from the ground a little way ahead and flutter off. The tightened muscles at the corner of his lips made little dimples come and go. He said carelessly, "When was that? I dare say I wasn't always agreeable," he added, "but they were dashed awkward customers to deal with. The old man had a way of putting my back up. He was so damned autocratic you'd have thought he was the Lord of creation." He shut up, annoyed with himself for having said so much.

Mr. Chaos recounted his meeting with William earlier and his grievance.

"Oh, that!" said Menzies. "Good lord! Now that's typical of their mentality. *He* lets his sheep stray and then blames me. It isn't my property, but because I happen to be the one poor fool on the council whom they know, I have to be responsible for the council's decisions. Very likely the point doesn't arise, or there are other things more important to be settled first, or else I'm simply overruled. Why don't they get on the council themselves? It's open to every one. As a matter of fact I do think it ought to have better protection than it has, but as for their idea of bricking it up! Never mind that blokes who know come from all over the place to see it, it's an abomination to Titmarsh and Co. so brick it up. *They* ought to be bricked up, they're all batty," he said contemptuously.

"He said it was an old quarry."

"No, it's not a quarry. That shows you how much he knows. Titmarsh knew better than that. He looked it all up in the archives not so very long ago, he told me."

"And what was it, actually?"

"What? Oh, I don't know. I'm afraid I'm not very interested in antiquities. Not in my line of country, you know."

By this time they had passed through the park and had arrived at Mr. Menzies' house. The hall had a tessellated marble floor and antlers branched from the walls; it was that kind of place; tasteless, comfortless; about as homelike as the Natural History Museum. Menzies led the way to his "den."

"You'll have a drink. Sherry? Whisky?"

"Thank you, nothing."

Menzies helped himself to whisky. He drank half of it, and then, leaning against the mantelpiece, said: "Well, now, what is it all about?"

Mr. Chaos stood, his legs a trifle apart, his hands behind his back; the stolid policeman.

"Just routine inquiries, sir. Checking up. We thought you might have some information for us."

"You mean about this rotten business?"

"The murder of Mr. Titmarsh."

"Oh, no. No, I'm afraid not. Naturally, if I had I would have told your chaps before now."

"Oh yes, I'm sure, sir. But sometimes a little thing ... well, it seems so small you can't think it's very important; or sometimes it just slips the mind, doesn't it?"

"Perhaps." Menzies sighed, bored to tears, poor chap.

"We wondered, seeing the two estates adjoin, seeing the right-of-way runs directly past the site of the crime, whether you might have seen any one passing that way about the time the murder was committed."

Menzies shook his head.

"Definitely, I can't help you at all there. Sorry, and all that."

"When I say anybody I mean that quite literally. Did you see any one at all, however unlikely? We're not imputing them to be the murderer, you know, they may simply be another link in the chain of evidence. Even if it chanced to be one of The Seekers it's important."

"My dear Inspector, as I said before, if I had any information it would have found its way to you by now." There was a shade of irritation in his voice.

"Mmmm! Well, let us see where you were at that time, and then we shall be in a better position to judge what you might be expected to see."

"That time." Menzies frowned and groped for a cigarette, pushing the silver box towards the detective. "Have one? I don't even know what the crucial time was."

"Thank you. Say, eleven a.m. Near enough."

"Thursday, was it?" The murder of one's neighbour barely a week ago was too trifling to be remembered accurately. Or was he playing for time?

"The sixth," said Mr. Chaos shortly. "Come now, the morning of the sixth? Where were you?"

Mr. Menzies emptied his glass.

"Of course. That's why it doesn't seem very clear to me. I wasn't here. I was away, and so was Mrs. Menzies."

"I see. And when did you return?"

"Er — actually, on the sixth."

"What train?"

"Er — the four forty-eight."

"Did Mrs. Menzies come with you?"

"No. I think you've misunderstood me. I didn't go away with my wife. She's on holiday; she hasn't been too well lately."

"That's right. Staying with her sister, isn't she? I remember someone mentioned it to me."

"What for?" said Mr. Menzies, with the distaste that amounted to shrinking of the secretive conventional Englishman at hearing that himself or any of his possessions have been the subject of vulgar gossip. The less reason there was for gossip the more odious and suspicious it became.

"Miss Post had been here to tea — "

"Oh, that was nothing," exclaimed Menzies, tossing his fag-end into the grate. "Good God, how people talk! The fact is my wife had asked her weeks ago, and I forgot to cancel it when my wife went away, I forgot all about it, as it happened."

Mr. Chaos nodded vaguely.

"To get back to what we were talking about. When did you go away?"

"The day before. I had business in Town." He brought up his hand and stared at his finger-nails with weary contempt.

"Fine, fine!" said Mr. Chaos. "Then you can give me somebody who can confirm that."

Mr. Menzies transferred his stare to the detective.

"If I may say so," he drawled insolently, "I don't see that it's any damned business of yours."

Mr. Chaos with charming imperturbability assured him that it was of not the slightest concern to him personally, but it happened to be part — a rather tiresome part — of his job to verify facts.

Mr. Menzies said, "Damned prying! What is the country coming to? Is the liberty of the individual of no account any more? I've told you I wasn't here till after the crime was committed. That's all that can concern you legitimately." He jabbed his thumb at a button in the wall. "Ask my servants if you want to know about my private life. Isn't that your proper role? I thought detectives always snooped round back doors."

"So we do. Searching dustbins is our speciality," gibed Mr. Chaos mildly. "But just now I am not concerned with your private life. I only want to know what you were doing at eleven o'clock on the morning of the sixth."

"Do you imagine that I keep a something timetable of how I spend every minute of my day? I don't remember what I was doing at eleven o'clock on the sixth. Do you?" He squirted a measure of soda-water into his glass and drained it down. "I happen to have a shocking memory. Couldn't tell you even what I was doing this time yesterday," he said more peaceably. "Never can make out how these Johnnies can get up in

Court and reel off like a clock what they did on July the third 1943. Couldn't do it if my life depended on it."

"Surprising, too, how often one's life does depend on it," said Mr. Chaos gloomily. "I once knew a man hanged because he hadn't any way of proving where he was at a stated time."

"There's justice for you!" observed Mr. Menzies. His cynical, plausible face flushed. "It's just come to me ... I must have been on the train. I had to go to Towcester." He looked relieved. "I had an appointment at two-thirty. With my dentist. I'll give you his name."

"And you caught the four forty-eight home from Towcester, is that it?"

"That's the idea ... Oh, Johnson!"

"You rang, sir?"

"The inspector is just leaving. Will you give him the address of my dentist before he goes." He nodded cheerfully. "Glad to have been of some use to you. Good-bye, Inspector."

Mr. Chaos thought, My dear man, you can't say good-bye to me as easily as that. You're a silly fellow really, to think you could get rid of me with bluff. You're just the type I want to grapple to my soul with hoops of steel. He watched the man-servant stooping over an address book in a blue satin cover embroidered with a flaccid shepherdess. His grey hair was darkened with some heavy fixative to keep the sparse hairs plastered across the scalp.

Mr. Chaos said: "Where does your master usually stay when he's in Town?"

In a voice between obsequiousness and disdain, Johnson said: "Mr Menzies resides at his club — in Dover Street." And gave him the address of the dentist in Towcester.

But Mr. Chaos wanted something else before he left the premises and that was the rifle that fired a .22 bullet. The meagre little man, Welkin, had gone off with it under his arm. He had some little trouble to get it away from him, but authority — even detested authority — prevailed in the end.

Down at the Station it was tested. A bullet was fired from it into a sort of sand-pit they kept in the garden shed. Then it was unearthed, and examined under the microscope. There wasn't any doubt about it, there were the six identical characteristic riflings; experts could only confirm the fact that the two bullets were fired from the same rifle.

By the pricking in my thumbs, murmured Mr. Chaos to himself; and aloud, "Whitehall 1212." He was put through to the five-figure extension and asked that someone should go to the Bath Club and make an inquiry. He was to be rung back as soon as possible. He got on with his work while he waited. At last the bell shrilled excitedly. With the telephone jammed in the crook of his neck, his eyes upturned to the ceiling, he waited, listening.

"You're quite sure? ... He didn't sleep at his club the night of the fifth and sixth? ... He didn't go there at all, eh? ... Now, I call that really very interesting," he said softly, as he replaced the receiver in its cradle as tenderly as a spider hooking a strand of web about the body of a fly.

CHAPTER EIGHT - THE GARRULOUS TAB

The postman threaded the letters through the eye of the door. There was no light smack of sound when they hit the floor, for the simple reason that they never did hit the floor. They were arrested in mid-air, as it were, and fell into the waiting hand. In his stockinged feet, Mr. Chaos pattered back to his room with them. He sorted them through: bills, circulars, three pamphlets from three separate societies, one on New Life, another on New Thought, and the third on Contemplative Health; there was a copy of *The Aryan Path* with an article by R. Carpenter; there was a seed catalogue from a well-known nurseryman's; a letter for Audrey, obviously from her publishers, and a postcard for Ella presumably from her brother; nothing of any genuine interest to Mr. Chaos, except possibly a letter for Wesley Titmarsh.

With the point of a thin round silver pencil, Mr. Chaos rolled up one side of the upper flap of the envelope. Then he inserted the point in the little gap left at the edge of the corresponding half of the underneath flap, working that up in the same way. He pulled out the paper tongue and withdrew the letter.

It was a business letter written in the queer archaic jargon still used by some old firms who had respect for but no understanding of the English language. It was from a firm of Consulting Engineers called Blizzard & Lake. And stripped of its hideous latinisms and tortured phraseology, it was to advise Mr. Titmarsh that their representative would be in the neighbourhood on the thirteenth and, if convenient, would call then.

Mr. Chaos made a note of the address and folded the letter back into the envelope and resealed the flap. Then he went back to the hall and spread them out on the floor in a design of artistic carelessness, as they might be supposed to have fallen from the letterbox.

"Can I help yer, loov?" said a voice just above his head.

There is something peculiarly undignified in being caught without shoes on, particularly when you are grovelling on your hands and knees like an inquisitive bear, but Mr. Chaos with his customary presence of mind merely looked over his shoulder at the intruder and remarked with amiable melancholy, "Nothing here for me, I'm afraid."

Behind their little windows Brother Joshua's eyes were hard, the eyes of a man who knows a thing or two, the eyes of a man who wasn't "soft," nay, and who wasn't daft, neither. His mouth was an inviting trap. When he spoke his slow, harsh, northern voice was reproachful. The inspector had no right, he protested gently, to meddle with their correspondence.

Mr. Chaos sat down on the floor and folded his arms about his knees while he explained that in the ordinary way he would not dream of looking at their letters, naturally, but this was a case of murder, and murder

"Nay, loov," Joshua corrected him mildly. "I know t'law."

"Yes, you do, don't you, you wicked old sinner," chuckled Mr. Chaos. "So your name's Joshua Platt now, is it?"

"It always 'uz been," said Joshua.

"And how about your last little venture? A mushroom farm, I believe. And what were you offering? Eight per cent, wasn't it? Oh, Joshua, how could you! how could you!"

Brother Joshua said calmly, "Ah! many an evil 'ave I done on the face of the earth. There's 'ardly a crime I haven't committed. I've robbed widows and orphans. My 'ands are stained with blood. But He 'as washed me clean in the blood of the Lamb."

"Really?" said Mr. Chaos with a shade of incredulity. "Well, that's very nice for you, I'm sure. But not so gay for the widows and orphans perhaps. What about them?"

Brother Joshua took off his glasses and rubbed the tiny red marks at the side of his nose. Without them his eyes lost their hard and piercing look and instead looked helpless and confused. "I'm a changed man now," he said humbly. "I'm like Zacchaeus; what I have stole I will repay."

"I'm glad to hear it," said Mr. Chaos tartly. "What happened to the mushroom market? Did it become too hot to hold?"

"Nay," said Brother Joshua. "That's all done with, loov. The Lord 'as visited me. I 'ad a vision. I saw two angels with a mighty scroll and on it was written — "

Mr. Chaos nodded glumly and began to walk away. Visions were all very well, but he had work to do. Brother Joshua padded after him.

"Here," he cried. "Don't you want me to tell you 'ow I repented?" He could not believe that any one should not want to hear. His heart was bursting to rehearse the pangs and glory and struggles, as an invalid in convalescence longs to gloat over past agony and horrors.

After Pittance, Mr. Chaos went up to the Grange again. There was plenty for Mr. Menzies to explain away — if he could. The pity of it was that he seemed no more inclined to be reasonable than he had before. He was in a morose, hang-overish mood. Plainly, he was the sort of chap to whom bright words at breakfast are anathema. Besides, Mrs. Menzies had returned the night before from her visit. She sidled into the room while the inspector was there; a peaky little woman, dressed expensively without style, but to make up for it a surplus of fussy trimming. In contrast with the peaky face like a shrew mouse, she had a head full of lustrous curls dyed a rich auburn.

Mr. Menzies sulkily refused to tell the inspector where he had slept in London. He didn't see, wouldn't admit, that it was any of the inspector's damned business, he objected.

Mr. Chaos was patient. Some people were naturally rebellious and secretive. Perhaps if he understood how serious his position was he would become more sensible about it. "We know," he said, "we know you didn't sleep at your club that night."

"Damn it! I never said I did, did I?" he began to rage. But it seemed to Mr. Chaos that there was something artificial about his bluster, as though it was assumed to distract his attention from something else.

Mr. Chaos tucked in his lips slightly.

"I should tell you that the bullet which killed Wesley Titmarsh was fired from your gun."

Mr. Menzies' handsome sly face turned the sickly white of a toad's belly. The drawer of the Boulle-and-marquetry cabinet in which Mrs. Menzies was fumbling fell to the floor with a clatter.

Menzies' lips stammered flabbily.

"But — but — that's p-p-preposterous!" he got out feebly.

Mrs. Menzies ran across the room to him with a sort of decorous shuffle as though her knickers were coming down. She said, "Percy! what does he mean? Percy, say something!"

Mr. Menzies knocked her arms away without noticing her. Suddenly from yellowish-white he had flushed a deep and angry red. There was no pretence now about his feelings: they were outraged. He strode forward shouting. He demanded furiously what the bloody hell the inspector was insinuating. And without waiting for an answer he plunged on into an absurd tirade, mainly about his own importance. Someone should pay for this impertinence, as he chose to regard it; he would write to the papers, he would write to the Commissioner, he would communicate with his great friend Major Bellows, the Chief Constable; he would— Behind him, his wife echoed and approved in a shaky, indignant treble.

Now that ms features were transformed by passion, the indolent cynical expression habitual to them had vanished. Mr. Chaos recalled Lucy Titmarsh's comment about his ungovernable temper. He could believe it all right now. He must have looked like this the day of the hunt, when Wesley Titmarsh had proved an intolerable barrier. He had slashed at him uncontrollably with his whip. And Wesley's response had been to taunt him with the significant remark, "You can't kill a man this time to get your own way." Mr. Chaos thoughtfully recommended the incident to Mr. Menzies' attention.

For a moment a look of panic seemed to invade his eyes; they seemed to shrink and retreat under their lids like snails into their shells. He half-turned away and put out a hand with a blind involuntary gesture. Mrs. Menzies took it in hers, gazing up at him anxiously.

"Don't say anything, dear," she fluttered at him. "Don't say anything. Don't answer till you've seen your solicitor. That's quite in order. They can't make you. I'll go and ring up Rutherston now."

"Don't be such a fool, Elsie," he shouted savagely, quite restored to ill-humour by her ineptitude. "Do you think I'm going to allow this damned policeman to browbeat me? He's as good as accused me in front of witnesses of murdering someone. That's slander. He can't get away with that. I'll sue him. I'll — "

"You know," said Mr. Chaos wearily, "you're not doing yourself a ha'porth of good by this. Not a ha'porth. Can't you see that it puts the worst possible construction on it for you to carry on so? An innocent man has nothing to fear. I can't see that you've anything to get excited about. I admit it is not at all nice to be in such an equivocal position, but I've no doubt that you can explain it all quite easily if you choose. We can't compel you. But as a rule an innocent person only wants to serve the ends of justice. And unless you have something to hide, why can't you tell me the truth? Of course we can get the information we want in other ways, but we always like to approach people directly wherever possible. We think it's fairer. However, if you have nothing to say we'll leave it at that." He bowed to the shrew-mouse and turned on his heel.

"The Chief Constable will have something to say about this," complained Mr. Menzies. "I'm not going to let a thing like this pass. I think you'll find you've exceeded your powers, my man."

His rage was childish and absurd, like a little boy viciously, impotently, kicking his nurse's shins. Mr. Chaos with an inward smile mused on the fact that the personal friendship of the Chief Constable was so often taken to be a trump card. One knew the magistrate, therefore one would get away with a fine. Or one knew the local J.P., and he would see to it that the next time Ted Smith came up for poaching he got a proper sentence. Or one was well acquainted with a High Court Judge, and he would give one tickets for the new murder show at the Old Bailey. Mr. Chaos often fancied he would one day write a little monograph on popular fallacious legalities.

The latch failed to grip behind him — a careless habit of his. And as he moved away from the door it swung open an inch or so. He heard Mrs. Menzies' peevish voice say anxiously, "But Percy dear, I don't understand. Why did you tell him you were in London? You know you weren't. You phoned me from here that night, didn't you?"

"For Christ's sake!" snarled Menzies softly, and kicked the door shut.

The dentist in Towcester confirmed Mr. Menzies' appointment for two o'clock on the sixth. Yes, he had kept it. Yes, he *was* a little late. But it did not matter, because there was nothing much to be done, just a little filling in the right molar. Mr. Menzies came regularly twice a year.

Satisfied with that, Mr. Chaos next went into a public call-box, dialled Trunks with his left hand while he fluttered the pages of the London Directory A to K till he found the number he wanted. It did not take him long to get through. He gave his name, quoted a reference number and asked a question. But whether he was pleased with the answer or not it was impossible to tell, for when he came out of the glass-box he was frowning and his gentle face was set in hard lines.

Towcester was a cathedral town, the nearest big town to Market Keep. It was busy compared with Market Keep; it must seem quite lively and up to date, with its shops and traffic and one-way streets, to the women who came in once a week for their little bit of shopping and two and a half hours' romance at the flicks. Actually it was provincial and slightly decayed, living on faded glories like Chichester or Salisbury, or any other cathedral town.

In the Town Hall Mr. Chaos was directed to the Record Office. It took a long time to find what he wanted, much longer than he had reckoned, but it was worth it, for he found more than he bargained for. It meant searching the archives all the way back to the fifteenth century. He turned over old maps, parish records, skimmed through legal documents in a queer sort of Norman French, searched Ministers' account books, and came across a hundred and one curious transactions that were pages of history.

As for the piece he was looking for ...

In the records of the year 1487, the Steward of the Manorial Household mentioned the arrival of a Commission appointed in 1485 by His Gracious Majesty, King Henry VII., with "Liberty to dig and search for metals, except under the houses and castles of the king and his subjects." This band of worthy gentlemen, scientists, mathematicians, and metal-artificers, proposed to "delue after the Alleman manner" in Towcester and the environs and make "diverse experiments beneath the Earth."

Shafts were sunk in three places: two to the north of Towcester, which proved useless, and one to the west, "five furlongs from the Abbey land," in which carboniferous deposits were found. This mine was worked (according to a slip of paper pasted to the bottom of the page and written in a different hand) until 1514, and then abandoned because it was worked out.

Now Mr. Chaos — partly because hunting through old records is something like turning up a dictionary, you are led from one thing to another, and partly because he wished to verify the position of the third and last-mentioned excavation — looked back to see what abbey this was and where it was situated.

It seems that in those days, when Abbot's Breach was a flourishing monastery, what was now the church of St. Chives was then an abbey. In 1484 the abbey had caught on fire and much damage had been caused before it was put out. The pre-Norman tower and the nave had been gutted, of the central portion only the huge cross upholding the writhen drooping Christ, which legend maintained had been carved by St. Chives himself, remained miraculously unscathed. It was as a result of this disaster that the breach between the abbot and his monks had arisen. The abbot had evidently desired his monks to rebuild the abbey with their own hands; whether from motives of economy or piety the records did not relate, but it is to be presumed the former, for the monks rebelled, or the majority of them did. But of the struggles of the opposing factions, the disciplinary and punitive measures employed, and the startling denouement it is not necessary to write here, though Mr. Chaos gloated over every crabbed line of it. Enough, that it had not been rebuilt until 1533.

On his way back he got out of the bus at the cross-roads and visited the church for the second time. There was no drama this time. The church was empty, and the more interesting on that account. In the porch was a wooden box containing printed leaflets of the history of the church, beginning with the life of its founder, St. Chives. According to this quaint report extracted from a Chronicle of English Saints written in the thirteenth century, St. Chives flourished circa A.D. 650. To begin with, he was but a rude swineherd, as the saying is, so rude, in fact, that his fellow herdsmen refused to have anything to do with him and he was cast out from the common hut at night to couch with his swine. It is not known what the poor beasts thought of this intrusion, but the contemned swineherd appeared to live humbly and happily enough with his new companions. But St. Chives did not enjoy the universal approbation even of the animals. It is said that once, pursued by a wild boar (or bear), he turned on the animal and subdued it with the strength of his breath alone.

And so it went on, till the saintly and virtuous outcast had built a wooden church roughly in the form of a stable. From that time his life was attended by radiant miracles, and he died in the odour of sanctity. ... so much more pleasant than the aroma of onion he carried about with him during his lifetime, and which was the subject of the first of his miracles after death: for when they came to prepare the body for burial, in place of the strong exudations it habitually gave off, it breathed forth the holy scent of roses.

Soon after that his disciples pulled down the wooden edifice and built a more splendid and lasting monument in stone. Since then it had been altered and added to, but — the leaflet seemed clear enough on this point

— it was still in the main the original Saxon building. No mention was made of a fire in 1484 or at any other time.

Clearly it was rebuilt on exactly the same pattern as the original; the central part of the church was a copy, a replica of the old Saxon. And here was the vicar appealing for funds to restore the precious old tower ... the precious old tower! Obviously it was to this that Titmarsh had been alluding when he said Foster was an old fraud ... a precious old fraud!

How many people looked over those records, or, looking over them, would chance across that particular passage which mentioned the fire? Or, coming across it, would be familiar with the church of St. Chives, and so see its significance? As for the thousands of people interested in church architecture who came and stared lovingly at the old tower, not one in a hundred probably could claim to be an expert; and the expert hundredth would be dogmatic and fallible as all experts are. No, it would be easy enough for Foster to get away with it. The point was, *why* did he do it? Was he deceiving or self-deceived?

Mr. Chaos strolled across to the vicarage. The vicar, black as a crow, came down the path at right angles to meet him. No, not to meet him. For he was almost on the detective before he noticed him. Then he, so to speak, waved him away. Mr. Chaos said, "Ah, vicar! The very person ..." But the vicar waved him to one side nonchalantly: "Not now," he said. "Sorry. I'm engaged," passed the sanctuary of his threshold and slammed the front door in the detective's face.

For two seconds Mr. Chaos was taken aback by this calm rudeness. Then he sprang forward and stabbed at the bell with his finger. The vicar opened the door. Mr. Chaos apologised prettily for disturbing him, but as he was passing he had visited the church (such an interesting example!) and had noticed that the vicar was appealing for funds for the restoration of the tower.

At this point the reverend gentleman begged him to come in. He apologised for his apparent rudeness of a moment before but ... but ... but ... And it was all explained away. He led the visitor joyously into his little sanctum, wondering how much he intended to contribute to the fund.

It was a nasty shock to learn that nothing was to be contributed. He eyed him sideways suspiciously. He could not but consider the man had got in under false pretences. Probably it would end as he had thought in the first place: by the man *trying* to sell him something. He sighed, and hoped he would not be long in coming to the point.

Mr. Chaos came to the point at once. Did Mr. Foster know that the very part of the building he claimed funds for restoring as a fine example of Saxon architecture was actually not genuine at all?

The vicar looked unutterably blank.

"My dear sir," he said. "My dear sir, there must be some mistake."

"I think not," said Mr. Chaos. "Why should there be?"

The vicar smiled graciously. The late sun outlined his delicate spiritual profile against the dark spines of the books ranged against the wall. Here and there the sun picked out gilded titles, and suggestive words ... *The Past ... Tumuli ... Saxon Features ... Roman ... Old Burial ... Archi* ... It suited him as a background. He looked like some ancient coin himself, worn down, refined.

He was saying ... "Every stick and stone of it. I think I may say it has become my life's work." The long neurotic scholarly hands caressed a small volume. "You may have heard ... you may have read ..." He turned the book on end so that his visitor might see the title and author. "I think I am not quite unknown," he said with a kind of modest pride. "I think I may fairly claim to know as much as any one can know of this particular ... There are some people who even regard me as an authority on the subject, if you will allow me to say so," he added with a deprecating little laugh. "I think you'll admit that if any one should know the truth of available facts, it is I."

"'Who's denying of it?'" murmured Mr. Chaos. Aloud he said clearly, "But on the other hand, it is hardly likely that, unless I were sure of my facts, I would dare to come in here and accuse you of fraud."

The vicar smiled. "Oh, if you'll forgive my saying so, people are always coming to me with some crazy tale or another. If I allowed myself to become excited ... *Fraud*!" echoed the vicar wonderingly, interrupting himself, as it were, to remark this in a different tone, as though the word had only just sounded on his brain. He said with sudden dignity, "I must remind you, sir ... "

Chaos said gently, "You know, you haven't asked me what authority I have for speaking like this."

The reverend Mr. Foster slid his tongue across his lips.

"Well?" he said.

Mr. Chaos interlaced his fingers and said softly that he was a Scotland Yard detective.

Mr. Foster said, "You can't touch me. I haven't done anything wrong."

"You see, Mr. Titmarsh —"

Mr. Foster laughed brightly, without mirth. "Oh, if that's where you got it! Poor old Titmarsh — *de mortuis nihil nisi honum* — his head was choc-a-bloc with theories and cryptograms and mystic numbers!" He rose. "Let me set your mind at rest, sir ..."

"Ah, then Titmarsh did tell you about it," said Mr. Chaos. "I wasn't sure about that. Thank you. And now I should like you to tell me," he went on in his dangerously suave manner, "how you proposed to stop him making a scandal out of it."

The vicar smiled down his nose.

"There was never any question of him trying to make anything out of it. It was quite a simple matter — er — Inspector, to show him his error."

"Was it, Mr. Foster?" Mr. Chaos rose dreamily. "I think not. The evidence is so very unmistakable, isn't it? Mr. Titmarsh would have to be a fool indeed if he swallowed your cock and bull story after that. And even if he pretended to accept your story, it must have left you very uneasy. You could never be certain that it would not come out somehow or other, *so long as he was alive to tell the tale.*"

"Good God!" cried the vicar, white as a surplice. "You're not implying ... good God, man! Consider what you're saying! You can't honestly mean ... you don't really think ..." He couldn't make up his mind whether righteous indignation or scornful laughter were the proper reaction.

Before he could decide, before he could become coherent, Chaos said, "But you didn't like Titmarsh. I've heard that on all sides. They said the quarrel was parochial, theological, but —"

"There was no quarrel, sir. It was a mere difference of opinion. I'm afraid he had no respect for my cloth. But right or wrong —"

"Right or wrong doesn't signify at the moment. You —"

"Damn it, sir," shouted the vicar. "You're making a mountain out of a ridiculous molehill. Titmarsh had nothing to go on. The merest supposition. I didn't even pay any attention to it."

"Oh, yes, you did. Because it wasn't news to you when Titmarsh told you about it. You had already discovered it accidentally for yourself." Mr. Chaos smiled like a crocodile. "The clerk at the Town Hall remembered you, you see."

White-lipped, the vicar said, "You are imputing, sir ... you are imputing ..." The dull broken words stuck in the groove of his mind.

Mr. Chaos said very gravely, "I am imputing, sir, that you knew the truth and deliberately suppressed it to serve your own ends. And I am further suggesting that Mr. Titmarsh was aware of your defection and that you knew he knew."

His look of dignity and refinement was gone. With his shallow blue eyes staring and his fine white hair shocked in a halo round his head, he looked foolish, faintly clownish. He tried dimly to recoup himself. "You don't know what you're saying. It's too ... why should I, pray?"

"You can answer that better than I. It may have been part of a deliberate financial fraud. It should be quite a simple matter to find out what the money was used for. Or it may have been an inconvenient fact which ruined some theory or other you were working on. The scholar's conflict. It comes up again and again among historians. Some new vital interesting theory which holds water perfectly but for one tiny little fact. The chances are against any one else discovering that inconvenient little slip. After all, it may even be wrong. Or you may have misunderstood its significance. In any case, is not your theory of more value than that? The alternative is to suppress or destroy the results of years of work. It is heart-breaking, I know. It seems like part of oneself. On the other hand, if you succeed in palming off your work as the genuine article, why then you are leading future generations of students on to the wrong path. It may be very hard indeed for them to fight their way back to the truth." Mr. Chaos sighed. "Oh, yes, your reputation is ruined all right when once a thing like that comes out, even if it is never known that it was chicanery."

But the vicar wasn't paying any attention to Mr. Chaos now. He was kneeling by the desk, his face in his hands. "Oh, God," he was moaning. "Oh, my God, my God!"

The detective's sad brown eyes were sadder as he gazed at the thin black figure huddled there. He remembered Audrey's Man in Black, tall and thin. He remembered too how white she had gone at the realisation that it might be the vicar. From where he stood he had a wide uninterrupted view of the hills from the window of the study. If one cut across the fields in a straight fine one would come directly on The Sanctuary. From the window above one must be able to see the field where Titmarsh met his end.

It was on his way back to Abbot's Breach that he was startled from the world of his thoughts by a voice from heaven proclaiming triumphantly, "Aha! Caught you!" It gave a jolly laugh. "You thought you were going to sneak past, did you?" It laughed again. "Up here!" it commanded, as Mr. Chaos stared about him.

The top of the cottage peeped above the screen of trees, chimneys pricking. And on the sagging rusty tiles a head was stuck with horrid effect. It made him think absurdly of revolutions and decapitated heads on pikes, and cut-out turnips on broom-handles at All-Hallows E'en; but it was only Miss Farrell leaning out of her dormer window, with her mop of flossy white hair blowing about her healthy brown face split now by a wide porcelain beam. "You know you promised to come and have tea with me, you wicked man!" she cried, with the dangerous affability of a wolf.

Mr. Chaos waved back. "I know I did, and so I will ... some time."

"What's wrong with now?" she demanded. " There's no time like the present."

Mr. Chaos began to murmur that this was not the most convenient— But she cut him short. "Oh, nonsense!" she said. "How long will it take? The kettle's on the fire now. And I bet you're dying for a cup of tea. I know men. So lift up the latch and walk in. I'll be down directly."

Little Red Riding Hood grinned feebly and marched meekly down the little crooked crazy-paving path. It must be with some such mixture of inertia and masochistic curiosity that flies sidled to their doom in the spider's web. The knee-high gate was archly inscribed in Gothic characters: WEE HOLME. And wee it certainly was, a Wendy house, a fairy home, with two magic casements opening out of the faded roof on to perilous vistas of garden now forlorn. And though there scarcely seemed room enough for two floors, one slant-eyed window gazed out quizzically from beneath the eaves and next to it a door roof-high leading to the garden.

Mr. Chaos jerked up the latch by its leathern string and walked in, bumping his head.

"Mind your head!" Miss Farrell screamed warning as she clattered down the stairs. And seeing him ruefully rub the place, she added cheerfully, "Too late!" Inside it had the compact, faintly nostalgic charm of someone else's caravan, very bright and cosy and ingenious. "There's not room for a life-size man here. You'll crack your head again if you don't sit down quietly and watch me get the tea," chirped his hostess.

She gave him a good tea, too, with a new loaf, fresh butter and a pot of home-made quince preserve; none of your prankish wafers or sugary fallals. Like Miss Pole, her father was a man and she knew the sex pretty well. So the tea was brewed in an earthenware pot and the cups were decently capacious.

It was a major triumph for Miss Farrell to have got the detective into her house for tea; the detective, mark you! Not only a strange man, which would be a triumph in itself, but actually a Scotland Yard inspector. She savoured on her tongue, as sharply and sweetly as the quince preserve, the fury of Alice, the raging jealousy of Mrs. Hemming, and Connie's greedy curiosity, when they learnt of her adventure. But to round it off, to press the last drop of value from the event she needed to glean from him some ripe titbit about the case. To be able to say, I told you so! To be able to pass on something told her in confidence, that was what created glamour for an elderly spinster; to be in the know, to be of importance. And very likely, it occurred to her, she could be of use to him, too. There wasn't much that went on in Market Keep which didn't come to her ears. The private lives of most of the inhabitants were an open book to her. To be able to say afterwards, "I told him ..." and "If it were not for me ... "

It would be more tactful, she considered, to not ask him outright how the investigation was going. Although she felt she owed him something for what she regarded as a piece of dirty double-crossing at the funeral when he had skilfully concealed his professional identity from her. Better simply to talk about things she thought would be of interest to him.

She poured him a second cup and refilled the pot from the old black kettle on the hob. To start with, she mentioned the incident at the Meet. After all, that was pretty exciting, pretty important, if he did not know about it.

Mr. Chaos half-listened. That is to say, he listened for the emotional pitch in which the tale was recited, that indefinable tone which, if listened for, reveals more than the words used. He listened enough to notice any difference in the recital from the other versions he had heard. For the rest, he dreamily observed his surroundings. In the fight of the fire her eyes glistened like wet toffees. Dusk crept up to the windows. Microscopic flames danced in the witch-ball; on its bewitched surface the berries in the pottery jar on the sill looked like fireflies against the darkening pane; and Miss Farrell's face had shrunk to the size of a brown Dutch bean topped with a fluff of thistledown.

"And now every one's saying he killed Titmarsh," she concluded with an amused smile. "It's all nonsense, of course, and I don't believe it for a moment; but in a village, people haven't anything better to do than gossip. And I admit it doesn't look too good for him, coming when it did. It was an unfortunate remark, wasn't it? Besides, I think quite a lot of people would be glad to see him taken down a peg or two. He gives himself such ridiculous airs. People who really *know* simply laugh at him." Miss Farrell laughed dryly to show that she was one of the people who really knew. "It's all money, money, money nowadays, isn't it? Anybody with twopence to rub together can climb into society to-day — or what passes for society," she amended bitterly. "And to make it worse, if it wasn't for his wife he'd be nowhere. Have you seen her? She's a miserable little creature. We all know that he married her for her money; and he treats her abominably ... Another cup? It's rather brewed; do you mind? ... It makes me so dreadfully wild," she resumed, handing him his third cup, "the way that sort of thing is condoned and even thought rather 'clever' and 'naughty' because he happens to be a man, and a handsome one, what's more. It's so unfair, no one has a thought to spare for the wife. Any pity there is goes to the man. As though he deserves it! It's, 'Poor soul his wife nags him,' or 'She's cold,' or some other absurd excuse. Yes, I am a feminist, and I'm not ashamed of it. Not that I hold any brief for that little creeping thing, Elsie Menzies.; she has only herself to thank for marrying him in the first place. But that doesn't mean that I condone his behaviour to her. He makes her a laughingstock. It's the talk of the place the way he carries on. He's after anything in skirts.

"Of course Elsie Menzies can't keep a maid. Servants can't bear her. She doesn't know how to treat them. I've got one of her girls now. She's only been with me a few weeks but she's absolutely devoted to me already. And she told me that really she left because of him. She's very respectable, quite a superior type, and she didn't like it. He was always after her, she said. And she told me that her cousin who works in the newsagents has been carrying on with him for months. Isn't it disgusting! And of course there are others. The latest one I came across quite by accident myself." Her slippery eyes appraised him. Was this right off the track or would it draw him out?

"I was in Cotterley's — I don't know whether you know it? It's a very smart shop in Towcester, and I was buying, as a matter of fact I was buying some corsets," she confessed. " I couldn't see him because I was in one of those little cubicles, but I recognised his voice at once. The departments sort of run together there, and while the girl was searching for different models for me to try on I couldn't help hearing what he said. He was evidently buying a fur coat. There wasn't a woman with him; he was talking to the sales lady, I made sure of *that*. But believe it or not, he bought it, and paid cash for it, a hundred and ninety pounds!" She leaned back triumphantly. "What do you think of that?"

"Well?" said Mr. Chaos, amused despite himself by her vigorous malice.

She snorted. "I haven't seen Mrs. Menzies in a new fur coat this winter. But I have seen your little friend's guardian, Miss Post, in one. A very smart affair in mink. Quite the latest style."

Mr. Chaos raised his eyebrows almost imperceptibly to indicate his palpitating interest.

"Ah, you don't find that convincing enough! But wait! you haven't heard all. The other day — now when was it? Yes, the day before that poor wretch was murdered — that's right, because I remember thinking —" She pulled herself up abruptly. "But I mustn't ramble. What I want to tell you is, quite bluntly, that I had gone to Towcester in the afternoon to the pictures, and as I came out of the cinema I saw them coming out together just ahead of me. They didn't see me. Now then, Mr. Chaos, she and I had travelled into Towcester on the same train. I got into the same compartment as she did. She was carrying one of those very superior dressing-cases that wear a velour cover to protect the leather, and I asked, more out of politeness than anything else, if she were going away. She said no, she wasn't, she was taking the case in to be renovated; it needed relining, and so on and so forth. I don't remember the details because I wasn't particularly interested. I *believed* her, naturally. I mean, you don't expect to be told gratuitous lies."

"It was a lie?"

Miss Farrell smiled on one side of her face without exposing her fine white porcelain dentures. "She still had the case with her when they came out of the cinema, only now *he* was carrying it. Something held me back from calling to them —"

I bet it did, you inquisitive old tab, you, thought Mr. Chaos leniently, listening to her describe how she had followed them unseen to a small but luxurious hotel. Good God, he thought in mild dismay, it's a wonder that any one dares to go off the rails in the country with all the spinsters ready to pounce on you like the Vigilantes. It's a wonder the guilty don't all suffer from persecution mania — and the innocent, too, for that matter.

"I had twenty minutes before my train went," Miss Farrell was saying. "And I didn't want any tea. So I went after them and saw them go into the Tudor Arms, and then I went off to my train ..." She paused artfully. "Well, what happened there I couldn't say. And they *may* have parted company quite soon after, just as they *may* have met just by chance; I quite realise that. And I'd like to be able to believe it. I can't see that it does any good to believe the worst of people ... Be that as it may, I *happened* to have to ring Miss Post about something that evening, and the child said she was out. 'Oh, when will she be back?' I said. 'I don't think she's coming back to-night, Miss,' says the child." Miss Farrell nodded meaningly. She said, "Of course you can say what you like — men never understand these things anyway — but I call it downright criminal to leave that little thing alone in the house night after night. She's absolutely terrified and Valerie Post knows it. I don't know how many nights a week she sleeps out, and I wouldn't like to ask where she spends them. *Not* that it's much better for Ruby when she's at home. She is the most immoral young woman! The parties she gives! *Needless* to say, none of the local people are invited ever. So we can't say for certain just what does go on at them, but I believe that nobody knows beforehand who sleeps with whom or where." She grimaced at the idea. "And I have heard," she said in low shocked tones., "not that I believe it, I think it's just scandal myself, but they say that once they had a sort of lottery and just pulled the names out of a hat! Isn't it the most revolting thing you've ever heard? Of course Miss Post is one of those things so many young women seem to be to-day ... I never can remember the word when I want it ... a pretty poetical word ..."

"Nymphomaniac?" suggested Mr. Chaos.

"Yes, that's it. That's what she is," said the old woman unblushingly. She had enjoyed telling the tale, carried away by the artful wickedness of them, and she was certain that the detective had been quite absorbed by it. She broke off the edge of a scone and piled on it a chunk of the sticky blood-coloured preserve.

"What is Miss Post — I mean, what does she do? She's quite a young woman, isn't she?"

"She doesn't actually do anything now. She's a lady of leisure. I believe she was a mannequin or something once, but then she was left some money. I don't mean to say ... she was always a *lady*, of course."

Mr. Chaos remarked with faint irony that he could tell that.

"It's a dull sort of life for a girl, really. I can't think why she doesn't get married. I'm sure that's why she took on Ruby after the war — sheer loneliness. And then, having had her for six years already, she'd grown attached to her."

"Then you don't think, as I've heard it suggested, that she kept her on more out of regard for the labour shortage than consideration for the child?"

Miss Farrell looked offended. "What an idea! Whoever told you that? I'm sure it's not so. I'm sure she's genuinely devoted to the child."

"I'm glad to hear you say so. Although Miss Post hasn't adopted Ruby officially, has she?"

"Well, no. I quite see her objections to that. One wouldn't want to make a child of that type one's *own*, one's heir, would one? I shouldn't. I wish I knew who'd told you that. Of *course* she's not a servant. Besides, she's only fourteen, and small for her age. She helps in the house, naturally. And why not, pray? Very likely Miss Post is training her to go out to service when she's older. A very good idea."

Mr. Chaos looked dubious. "You may be correct in all you say, but surely you must agree that Miss Post is hardly a suitable guardian for a young child ... after all you've told me."

It seemed to him Miss Farrell flushed.

"You have to take into consideration that if she were in her own *milieu* she would probably be worse off, certainly no better; children of her class are brought up under most immoral conditions; nobody to blame, just general slum problems." She spoke with a pontifical air. She added with less assurance: "I'm sure we all did the best we could for the kiddies when they came. But it was no joke. There were thousands of them. And the complaints we had to deal with! I dare say you remember all that. Ah, well, those were the days!" she said with a hint of nostalgia for the dear lost days of the war, when even the meanest spinster was of value, when there was always something fresh to gossip about at camouflage parties (though, of course, one was always careful not to spread alarm and despondency), and then the sense of danger, of people hazarding their lives — oh, yes, those full rich days were gone!

Mr. Chaos, with quite other memories, said with bitter stress, "Those *were* the days!" He thanked Miss Farrell for her excellent tea and —

But Miss Farrell, partly from genuine nagging curiosity and partly from a desire to keep him with her a bit longer, ejaculated vivaciously, "How stupid of me! I know now who must have told you about Ruby Smith being no better than a servant. It must have been one of The Seekers. That sort of thing is quite typical. They're for ever making themselves out better than they are by blackening other people's characters, if you see what I mean. That's a thing I can't bear. It's so uncharitable. I mean, we're none of us saints, so why pretend to be?"

"You don't think they are saints?"

She gave her harsh rackety laugh. "Saints! I could tell you a few things about them, if I was given to scandal-mongering. But I haven't time for the sort of people who tattle about their neighbours. What I always say is, there should have been an eleventh commandment: 'Thou shalt mind your own business.'" Once again she gave her raucous laugh. If he *wanted* to know, that was a different matter, then it was her *duty* to tell him. Not that there was very much factual stuff. It turned out to be mainly a repetition of the kind of thing she had hinted at the funeral. True, most of it turned out to be concerned with sexual irregularities. It seemed to be much on her mind. On the other hand it was quite possibly true; there was no way of knowing. It was a fact that Miriam Fry was the daughter of a titled family and that she had had to break with them entirely in order to follow her star — Wesley Titmarsh. Miss Farrell indignantly considered her extraordinary devotion to the Master positively unhealthy. And what, she demanded fiercely, were strong young men like that William Brown and David McQueen doing so innocently mixed up in a odd galère like that? An idiotic, pointless life for young men. All very well for the old dodderer — what did they call him? — Brother Bernard.

Mr. Chaos picked up a book lying open face downwards in the inglenook. It was called *The Belle Romance*.

"Do you know who wrote this?" he said.

"That! Yes. Gay Herrick." Miss Farrell spoke shortly, displeased she should be discovered to wallow in this particularly sweet brand of trash. Not for worlds would she have admitted how much it meant to her.

"But do you know who Gay Herrick is?" persisted Mr. Chaos. It flustered her a lot to learn that it was Audrey Lewes. She had to reorientate herself visibly to reconcile one of her favourite authors with a person she despised and derided in a half-suspicious way. It quite put her off the books. She felt obscurely that she had been sold in some way. People had no right to hide behind anonymity. All the sweetness and sincerity of the books seemed false to her now, seemed *ruse* and pregnant with propaganda for her "cause." On the other hand, there were things in them, as she immediately pointed out to the inspector, which simply could not have been written without Experience; scenes of passion and childbirth.

Mr. Chaos forbore to ask how she, a respectable spinster, could affirm the truth of these scenes. He let that one pass, and agreed that Miss Lewes must be a dark horse.

"I should have guessed," she said scornfully, "for she generally puts a bit of faith-healing in her books." She said very seriously, "I'm dead against that, you know. A little kiddy here lost his life because that Titmarsh made the mother throw all the medicines away and bring him out into the garden. I call that murder," she said flatly. There had been a lot of feeling about it generally, and she had gone round to every one in the village and got them to sign a petition insisting that in future he should leave healing to the medically qualified. Quite a lot of people had signed, she said defiantly — about three hundred altogether. Dr. Blake had behaved most nobly and said the child would have died anyway; he had already told the mother that, and the most that Titmarsh's action could have done was to hasten the inevitable end.

"All the same, he has performed some miraculous cures, I believe."

"Pardon me," said Miss Farrell huffily, "to my mind that's blasphemy. I said as much once to the one they call the gloomy Dane, Mr. Carpenter. 'Why?' he said. Just like that. 'Even in your religion Jesus healed,' he said. Imagine that, if you can, comparing themselves with Jesus Christ! It's blasphemous! Then he wanted to know whether I thought the miracles were a divine dispensation. I said, Of course. I was furious. And he said, well, what did I think it meant when Jesus said, 'He that believeth on me the works that I do shall he do also; and greater works than these.'"

"What did he mean by that?" he asked.

She puffed through her nose righteously. "I simply refused to bandy words with him. I look on them as no better than heathens. I dare say a great many people would have felt resentful about that, but I hope I'm a good enough church-woman to pray for my enemies, even though I don't happen to think it necessary to put on a fancy get-up in order to do so. As I said to the vicar, 'This isn't the Middle Ages, so why dress up as if it were?' It's such rot. And then I'm convinced the whole thing's a colossal blind."

Here Mr. Chaos, not wishing to be told that The Sanctuary was the headquarters of a spy-ring or a gang of international jewel thieves, murmured plausible nonentities and took his departure.

On the whole, Miss Farrell was not dissatisfied with her afternoon. She had purged her mind nicely of its accumulated scandal. And although she had done most of the talking herself and the detective had been quieter and more canny than she expected or hoped, yet she had not done so badly. And if she had not acutally learnt much, there was plenty that she could invent if she chose to. But she rather thought that she would not choose; she rather thought it would be infinitely more tantalising to refrain from speech for once. She might murmur something to Alice; she would drop hints to Connie, she promised herself; but to Mrs. Hemming she would not utter one solitary word. It should be as though the afternoon adventure had never been. And if she were asked about it outright she would simply look blank, quite blank. And that would serve Mrs. Hemming right.

CHAPTER NINE - BROTHER AUDREY IS DISTURBED

It was quite dark by the time he left Wee Holme. Though it was a little out of his way, he walked back by the road that led to Valerie Post's house. He was interested by what he had been told about her and there were some questions he would like her to answer. But when he arrived at the house he changed his mind. Miss Post was occupied, and in the circumstances he decided against disturbing her. It was a rule of his never to antagonise a potential witness if he could possibly avoid it. And he deemed that an interruption now might very possibly embarrass her, which would be nearly as bad. He could see them outlined in a violent embrace; it was as if they were silently fighting with one another. Then, as he watched, Valerie Post struggled free, and he heard faintly through the open window her low, mocking laugh ...

He sighed and walked away. Another time would do as well. He left that subject and began to ruminate instead on Miss Farrell's conception of The Seekers' philosophy.

He heard footsteps behind him and presently David McQueen came striding vigorously by. It was easy to recognise him in the distinctive white habit, but Mr. Chaos must have been less noticeable in his customary suit of solemn blue, for McQueen passed him without a glance.

The bell rang for Collation just as Mr. Chaos arrived back. He washed his hands and joined them in the Refectory. Rollo and Joshua were carrying in the steaming plates full of vegetable soup. There was somehow an impromptu air about the room, about the table to-night, plain and rough though it habitually was. It was as if whoever attended to it had been called away in the middle. When they were seated it became apparent that two of their number were missing: Miriam Fry and Lucy. They waited a few minutes, and then Brother Rollo pronounced a blessing on their food.

Brother Bernard chose a book from the shelves, and holding it at arm's length, began to read aloud in the worn, rather shaky, voice of an old man. He selected first two passages from the Koran, Sura 81, "The

Folded Up," and Sura 55, "The Merciful." Mr. Chaos let the sweet trembling voice beat in vain against his ear, his attention watchfully concentrated on the others. Audrey pushed her soup away from her, as though the sight of it made her feel sick. McQueen gloomily, absently, dunked his bread in the bowl ... and went on dunking. Ella was fidgeting, glancing continually at the vacant places, patting her hair and touching her face with little nervous gestures. Only Brothers Rollo and Joshua seemed as placid as usual. Brother Bernard closed the book and took up a volume of Pascal ...

When the dull meal was over Mr. Chaos quietly retired to his room. He was engaged in the slow but necessary business of going through Titmarsh's papers. There were three sections of them more or less: His personal and private papers, consisting of letters and diaries; his manuscripts; and all the business connected with the farm — which was pretty considerable. All that last section was kept by McQueen in his role of secretary, and he explained the business affairs to the inspector. At present he was working his way through the personal papers, and one fact in particular struck his notice. He could find no trace of any correspondence between Titmarsh and Blizzard & Lake. Yet in the letter which had arrived by the morning post mention was distinctly made of previous letters. What had become of those letters? Had they perchance been removed from among the tumbled mass of papers on the table since the Master's death? Or had the Master himself taken pains to destroy them and so prevent them falling into other hands? Since everything else appeared to be present and correct, the latter view seemed the more likely.

And if that were so, what reason had Wesley Titmarsh to communicate secretly with a firm of consulting engineers? And why must it remain hidden from those with whom he dwelt in truth and love?

Half aware of a desire for movement and air in the hope that it would stimulate thought, Mr. Chaos moved across to the door that led into the garden, opened it and stepped out. A dim whitish figure slipped between the bushes. Mr. Chaos called "Who's there?" But there was no answer. He went towards the place where the person had disappeared. There was a gap in the hedge through which clearly the person could have, must have, gone. He pushed through the opening into the roadway. The moon was fumbling through the heavy clouds. The figure in white was running down the lane.

Mr. Chaos could run surprisingly fast and lightly for a man of his bulk. He said, "Stop a minute, if you please." And taking no chances, put out his hand and caught her by the arm. Her upper arm was slender in his grip, he noticed, but wirily muscular.

Audrey gasped: "It's all right. It's only me. What is it? You haven't — you haven't found her?" He could not see her expression in the dark but her voice was scared.

Mr. Chaos said, "Why did you run away from me just now?"

She peered up at him in the dim light.

"Run away? I didn't," she protested. "I'm looking for her. I can't think where she can be? It's so awfully unlike her to stay out." There was a strained note of hysteria rising in her voice. "You haven't found her." It was a statement this time rather than a question.

Mr. Chaos asked patiently who.

She tugged at his sleeve impatiently.

"Oh, don't you see?" she said with a kind of desperation at his stupidity and ignorance. "It's Miriam. No one has seen her since early morning."

"Oh, Miss Fry, is it? I wasn't sure who you meant. I thought it might be Mrs. Titmarsh you were worrying about."

"No. Lucy! What could happen to Lucy?" she said wonderingly.

"And what could happen to Miss Fry, then?"

Without warning she fell up against his shoulder and began to cry. Through her tears she blubbed out, "That's what I'm afraid of. I've looked everywhere for her. We all have. Why hasn't she come back? She'd never be out as long as this of her own free will. Why should she? You don't know Miriam."

"Come, come, Miss Lewes. What do you think has happened? Try and be clear. You aren't being helpful, you know. Do you imagine that Miss Fry is being detained somewhere against her will? Is that it?"

"Oh, no, nothing like that. Worse, much worse. I'm sorry, I am trying to be helpful. But it's difficult for me because you don't really know Miriam. Not many people do. She's very reserved, you see, but underneath she's ablaze with passion. It's frightening." She drew her sleeve across her eyes. "I don't want to betray her," she said slowly.

Mr. Chaos gently, uncallously, removed his shoulder.

"You mean, that Miss Fry loved Mr. Titmarsh?"

"Then you knew!" she exclaimed, her face illumined with sudden moonlight. She said in a hushed voice, "She adored him. She never showed it, of course. I don't know how *you* discovered it. I don't think any one else knew. If I found out, it was because I really do understand people, often better than they do themselves. It's my gift," she said modestly. "That's why my books are so popular, they say. But heavens!" she broke off in disgust, "you don't want me to talk about myself."

If you can possibly avoid it, begged Mr. Chaos silently.

"When Wesley died, one of the first things I thought of in all that panic and confusion was to wonder what Miriam would do when she heard of it. And I couldn't help being terribly glad that the poor soul wasn't there to see it."

"What do you think she would have done if she had been there?"

"It isn't what she would have done. But the shock would have been greater. It wasn't a pretty sight, you know. I don't mind telling you I dream of it every night. Five and six times a night. I dream; wake up; go to sleep, and dream of him again. I suppose we all do. She hasn't got that. She never saw him at all of course."

"And when she finally got back that night and you told her, what was her reaction?"

"Nothing," said Audrey tersely. "She was like a stone. We were all half-dead with weeping; but she never shed a tear."

"Unfeeling? Some people haven't so vivid an imagination as you."

"No, oh, no!" she protested. "It was horror and incredulity ... She *couldn't* break down. That's why all this time I've been watching her, I've been fearing that something like this would happen, that in her despair she would be driven to — to —" She could not bring herself to utter the dreaded word. Instead she looked up at the detective appealingly, as if he would say it for her and save her from dishonouring her friend.

"So it's suicide, is it?" said Mr. Chaos.

"Oh, God," moaned Audrey, her fists at her mouth. "Oh, God, I pray not. I've looked everywhere. I went down to the weir — and — and the reservoir over by Shipley way. I can't think of anywhere else," she murmured in an exhausted voice. "I can't think of anything else to do."

"Where were you running to when I caught you, then?"

She stammered chokingly. "I was going ... I had a horrid thought suddenly." Moonlight glittered on her tear-drowned eyes. "I thought as a last resort ... the railway line ..." she shuddered.

"Oh, I don't suppose it's as bad as that," said Mr. Chaos comfortingly. "But we had better go along and reassure ourselves." He looked down at her thoughtfully, kindly. "You need not come unless you like."

"Thank you," she said, with a becoming little air of dignity. "I don't particularly like. But I think I should, all the same." She put her pretty little hand on his dark sleeve as they walked along.

Mr. Chaos then remarked that no one but herself seemed particularly concerned about Miss Fry's absence. Audrey proffered a variety of explanations to account for that. They were worried, but they concealed it more successfully than she did; they were more stoical. Or they weren't so worried because they didn't delve so deeply into the inwardness of things, they were not so acutely observant of their fellows. Or, more simply and sublimely, they didn't worry because they trusted her to the ever-present care of Omnipotent Love, whereas she, Audrey, too often yielded to fallible human anxieties.

And yet she was not perturbed over Mrs. Titmarsh's absence, commented the detective. For one thing, Audrey explained, she had not been gone so long. And besides, Lucy was not at all an emotional sort of person, she did not feel things deeply. Mr. Chaos was a stranger among them, or he would doubtless have noticed that, of them all, she felt the Master's death less than any. For another thing, it was not so unusual for her to go away on her own affairs when she chose to. She was answerable to no one — yes, her husband, perhaps, but not to the group as a whole, as they all were with their appointed tasks. And in answer to the detective's question she suggested carelessly that she might be with Mr. Prescott, the head master of the Grammar School. They were rather friendly. She took an interest in the boys. Audrey did not think she would have gone out in public with him so soon after her husband's tragic death, but she might well be dining with him quietly at home.

"You don't like Mrs. Titmarsh, do you?" Mr. Chaos observed mildly.

"Of course I do," she said defensively. "Why should you think that? Ah, you are thinking of the other night, aren't you, when I had that sort of brainstorm'" She put her hands to her face. "It was *awful* of me, wasn't it? I suppose I shocked you. I don't know what came over me, after keeping it quiet all those long hard years. It was as if something snapped inside me. That's a terrible cliché, isn't it? But it was like that. I felt I had to strike and hurt somebody, really hurt them, to relieve my own anguish. I suppose you would say it was a combination of jealousy and shock."

"In fact, what you think Miss Fry has been feeling."

"Well, yes, I suppose so," she admitted reluctantly, not caring to share her precious sensibility, and also being enough of a psychologist to recognise that she had fallen into the trap of projecting her own sensations and emotions about a certain thing on to another person. "Something of the sort perhaps, but with *me* ..." She sighed. "I wanted ... it was terribly wrong of me, I know, but I wanted to smash that magic circle of respectable happiness from which suddenly I realised I was shut out for ever. I thought I wouldn't mind; I thought I'd got over it. Don't misunderstand me, Mr. Chaos; it wasn't Lucy I wanted to hurt, not Lucy herself, only what she represented to me at that instant. I *suppose* it upset her dreadfully," she said guiltily. "I don't know how I could have been so mean. She's never said anything to me about it, never asked me a word about it. I don't know whether she believes it or not."

"She believes it all right," Mr. Chaos assured her.

"Does she mind very much?" asked Audrey wistfully. "It was a very long time ago — if that is any extenuation — nearly twenty-eight years."

The clouds were like great pewter bowls edged with tarnished silver; and the trees, like inverted brooms, reached up to the lowering sky to brush them away. From time to time melancholy and cruel night noises broke the quiet. But Audrey, reliving the past, was unaware of the scene before her.

"It happened when my mother was on tour in South Africa," she began. "She was an actress. Not a very good one, I think, yet she had a certain beauty and something else — charm, perhaps. On his side it wasn't even a love affair. Just one of those casual inconsequential things. A passing fancy, for him. But it landed my mother with me. I'm not saying he knew, I don't think for a minute he did. She wasn't the sort of woman to tell, for one thing. Besides, he was already married; so what was the use? Poor darling! she managed somehow, but it was always a wretched struggle. It meant that I never had a decent chance.

"When I was old enough to know, Mother told me. No lamentations or blame; a plain story; but it turned me against him more effectively than if she had wept. The sordid injustice of it! I hated him! I used to think to myself, One day I'll ... I was always hungry as a child, there was never enough to eat, and I used to dream ..." She broke off and came out of the past to say impatiently, "Oh, what's the use of all that!" She said with a shade of weariness, "It never came to anything. After Mother died I contrived to get to England. I managed with some little trouble to track him down. Now, I thought, *this* is my moment! I was only about eighteen. It had never entered my wildest calculations that when I saw him I should love him. Wasn't that ridiculous? He conquered me effortlessly from the first moment, as he did so many other people, simply by love. He was so obviously good. You couldn't hate him; it was impossible. That was part of his wonderful universality. I was proud to be his daughter, after all. And I think," her voice trembled, "I think he loved me too. I think he would have been proud of me, I think he would have liked me for a daughter, if he had known."

"*If* he had known?"

Audrey said dully, "I never told him. When it came to it, I couldn't. I was afraid he might send me away. I kept it to myself. It was to be my secret always. And so long as he lived, you see ..." From a long way off shrilled the eerie scream of an engine.

"Then you have no claim on his will?"

"No, of course not, not really. It was a momentary lunacy, I told you. To be honest, I always wanted his manuscripts, even though I saw no prospects of getting them. It does seem so terrible to me that they are just mouldering away unseen. I may exaggerate their importance. They may not be any good. But they should be given to the world to judge. It isn't a question of money, *do* believe that; it's simply for the sake of his memory that I wanted them. I know I'm the only one who cares. It's because I'm a writer, you see, and I understand. A writer lives in his work. They none of them see that. It's like I said the other night: suppose Einstein's work had never been published simply because no one understood it! Oh, they may try to get the stuff published, but they won't take it seriously. And I feel I owe him that."

So either Mrs. Titmarsh had found out in some way that Audrey was her husband's illegitimate daughter, or she was lying when she said she knew about it. But before Mr. Chaos had time to decide which it was, they saw Miriam Fry rounding the bend.

Audrey flung out her arms when she saw her. "Oh, *darling*!" she cried and began to run forward. But Mr. Chaos, wary of emotional embraces, under cover of which messages could be swiftly whispered, quietly pulled her back.

In answer to Miss Fry's greeting, he called lightly, "Miss Lewes, here, thought you were dead. She was afraid you had killed yourself."

"Killed myself?" said Miss Fry incredulously. "Why on earth should you think I would do that? Audrey, how could you imagine ..."

Audrey said feebly, "I don't know ... I thought ... it was foolish of me, I suppose ..."

Miss Fry repeated, "But why *should* I? That's what I don't understand. Why should I?"

Mr. Chaos interpolated in the awkward silence smoothly, "Because of Mr. Titmarsh, you see."

Miss Fry stared from one to the other of them, frowning, trying to make the connection in her mind. Then she got it, and her mouth rucked back in an expression of disgust. She said in a pained voice, "Oh, how contemptible! How could you!" And she brushed past them to continue down the road towards The Sanctuary.

Having found her, there was nothing more for them to stay out for, and they turned and started after her. They caught her up and walked on either side of her in silence.

"I'm sorry," said Audrey. "I'm truly sorry, Miriam. Mr. Chaos will tell you how worried I was. I wouldn't have mentioned it otherwise."

Miss Fry gave a deep sigh. She said with a certain acidity, "It's not likely to alter the ultimate scheme of things, I quite realise that; but I should have been better pleased if you had had enough loyalty to me — to us all — to hold your tongue. I don't know how people can bring themselves to make mischief. I never could do such a thing, in any circumstances; it's quite contrary to my nature. But you are not to be blamed for projecting on to me your own wishes, Audrey."

Audrey shook her vehemently. "I didn't wish you were dead, Miriam, I swear I didn't."

"I never said that," said Miriam, patiently disengaging herself. "Never mind it, dear." She turned to the detective. "I don't have to give an account of my movements, do I? It was purely personal and I prefer that it should remain private."

"So long as it has nothing to do with the investigations," he said.

"I can't truthfully say that. And yet, so far it won't be of any use to you. I have my own ideas about this affair and I want to pursue them in my own way, if it's all the same to you."

Mr. Chaos gave her a look. "I never object to co-operation; but a lone hand, if that is what you intend to play, is risky for an amateur."

"I'm not afraid."

"The risk is not so much to yourself. The risk is that you may lose the murderer. Through some clumsiness of yours he may be put on his guard," he warned.

She smiled thinly. "I think not." She said with passionate determination, "If it's the last thing I ever do I'll get him, I'll get the devil who did it."

"You know who it is?"

The muscles stood out in her thin cheeks. "I *think* I know," she said. "It remains to be seen whether I am right."

*

They were all assembled in the Refectory the next morning for Pittance, with Lucy Titmarsh, as serene as ever, ladling out the slow porridge. William and Joshua were discussing the autumn sowing of some catch-crop in one of the fields. Mr. Chaos did not bother to attend to it, absorbed in his own thoughts.

Soon afterwards he set out. He had not gone very far when he heard someone calling him, a high-pitched wordless call. It was the woman Ella Blade. Her faded blonde hair was flying out of its imprisoning bun and blowing about her face. It was another day of savage north-westerly gales, and the wind tossed her words away from him. She was saying something and gesticulating. He went nearer. He put up his hands protestingly. "It's no use," he said, "I can't hear." But she did not come to meet him. She waited for him to come up to her.

Then she said, "I've remembered." Her light blue eyes looked frightened and excited at the same time. "You haven't seen it yet, have you? Look!" Again she gesticulated and, running backwards, said, "Come here. You can see better from here."

Mr. Chaos, a little surprised to see her so free from self-consciousness and hear her speaking to him so directly, obediently followed. From the slight eminence on which she stood it was possible to see over the hedge into the field beyond. The field was empty. The cold slanting light gleamed on the newly-turned fresh earth. In the centre of the field stood a scarecrow, one arm outstretched stiffly, the other flapping in violent windy gestures like an orator. From beneath his battered black hat long strands of bast streamed and fluttered in grotesque mimicry of Rapunzel. There was nothing else to see, so far as he could tell.

Brother Ella chirped excitedly, "Directly I saw it I remembered."

"Remembered what?"

She stared at him. "Why, I remember now what happened when the Master was shot. I told you; I heard the bang, and all the birds flew up in the air. Well, I ran downstairs and out into the garden. When I got down to the bottom where the stone wall runs along I could see David in the field and someone on the ground. Then I knew there had been an accident and I rushed up to see what I could do. And I saw him." She pressed her shabby hands together earnestly. Her voice choked in her throat. "I can't tell you how frightening it was. The blood was spouting up." Her face seemed to shrink at the thought of it. "David was standing there. 'There's been a terrible accident,' he said. 'I must see what I can do. Help me, Ella.' He began taking off his habit. (I'm telling you this now how I remember seeing it. But at the time I was paralysed with shock. I couldn't make it out. I couldn't understand. I moved mechanically.) David was bending over Wesley. He turned his head and said again, 'Help me, Ella! If you'd just move that thing away I could get to him better.' I just did what he told me without thinking. I picked up the scarecrow automatically — still sort of numb and uncomprehending — and carried it out of the way."

Mr. Chaos nodded intelligently. "Where to?"

"To the end of the field. I suppose if there had been no hedge to stop me I should just have gone on and on walking with it till I dropped. But I came to the hedge and stopped, because that was the end. I don't know what curious instinct made me thrust it deep down out of sight among the roots and leaves. I was beginning to have that frightening sensation of grey unreality that prefaces an attack. Everything becomes uncertain and impalpable, and yet there is a strange heaviness weighing you down. You can't judge distances properly and you feel as though you could put your hand clean through solid objects. You want to struggle free. It's as if you must, must, must leap out of your shrinking constricting skin. And sometimes there is a little bit of you that resists, that tries to cling tooth and nail to reality. I wanted to get back to David. I knew I had to somehow, though I couldn't remember why," she explained pitifully. "I think I did get back, but I don't remember. I don't remember any more now," she said wearily, exhausted with the emotional strain. Her pasty skin shone faintly with sweat, yet she tried bravely tp smile. She brushed the hair out of her eyes and tried to fasten it back. "I must go," she said. "I have a length of cloth to weave and I have not yet set up the loom." She smiled shyly at him. "Good-bye," she said.

"Thank you very much," said Mr. Chaos. "Thank you for coming to me so promptly when you did remember."

"Oh, don't thank me. It was nothing."

"On the contrary," said Mr. Chaos, staring at the scarecrow, so tall and lean and black. "Quite the contrary, I assure you." The scarecrow flapped his empty sleeve at him energetically, contemptuously: Oh, go away, my good fellow!

That's all very well, mused Mr. Chaos, and it's a nice step forward, but it's not enough. For however carefully she may have hidden it, it was no longer there when the police came to search for a weapon or they would have come across it. The field was gone over with a toothcomb, as the saying is, and the rest of the grounds were still being searched pretty thoroughly. Who, then, had taken it away? And where had it been hidden meanwhile?

There was no chance to ask them about this till Refection. Then he asked who had erected the scarecrow in the field.

"I did," said Joshua slowly. "It's new-sown and we 'ad to protect the young seeds from the birds. 'Ave we done wrong?"

"Who are 'we?'"

"Brother William an' I. That's raight, isn't it, loov?" he appealed to his good-humoured friend opposite.

William jerked himself out of his smiling trance. "Eh? What's that? I'm sorry; I wasn't paying attention."

"I 'elped you put up the scarecrow, didn't I?"

"That. Oh, yes. Why?"

"I wanted to know where you found it," Mr. Chaos cut in.

"Found it?" echoed William lethargically, with his good-natured dreamy smile. "Why, in the cobbling shed."

"When did you put it there? Do you remember?"

"Oh, *I* didn't put it there."

"No? Then how did you know it was there?"

"I didn't. We couldn't find it. Brother Bernard told me where it was."

CHAPTER TEN - MISS POST'S CURIOUS PHILOSOPHY

Entering Valerie Post's house after the days spent at The Sanctuary gave Mr. Chaos the most extraordinary sensation. The enormous armchairs sprawling with arms outstretched to welcome him to their warm laps like dummy mothers, the ruffled curtains, the thick pastel carpet, the soft hangings, the bowls of exquisitely arranged flowers diffusing their perfumes on the air, combined to strike him with a sense of delight in the beauty and luxury and to overpower him at the same time. It was marvellous and rich and original, but also there was much too much of it, so many objects stifled, the air cloyed. It made him fidgety. He had intimations of how Brother Rollo felt about possessions. It represented too much thought for so trivial an end.

"Nice of you to come. I wanted to see you. Though I suppose this is an official visit," said Miss Post. She was wearing a striped jersey frock, designed to display her figure artfully. She was not voluptuously made, but she was slender and seductive. She was the sort of woman it was impossible to imagine not perfectly groomed. Clearly she took pains with her appearance. Her shining ash-blonde hair swept in sleek waves off her ears. Her nails glittered. Her lashes were long and stiffly painted. Every inch of her face was carefully coloured. Yet the bitter autumn light could not flatter her skin. There were tired marks beneath her melancholy brown eyes, and the smile painted on her scarlet mouth was pathetic in its weariness.

He refused a drink, refused a cigarette. "How gloomy!" she remarked with a grimace. "You make me feel as though I'm going to be arrested. Isn't it true that it's against the code to accept hospitality from a person you're going to arrest?"

Mr. Chaos chuckled. He made some general remarks about his charming friendship with Ruby. Miss Post looked amused.

"She hasn't told me anything about it," she said. "See the jungle law of feminine instinct beginning to work. If you've got anything good and you want to keep it, keep it to yourself! I can't say she hasn't profited from what I've taught her." She laughed. "She's a good little kid, though, and very affectionate and faithful." It might have been a dog she was discussing. "Of course she's precocious, like all slum children, and I should never be surprised if she sprang a baby on me one day. What can you do? You can't be after them every minute of the day, can you? ... Have you any children? Are you married?"

Mr. Chaos thankfully declined the honour. There was a lot to be said, in his opinion, for The Seekers' ideal of celibacy.

Miss Post wrinkled her nose.

"I think it's a god-awful notion. What the hell's the use of this life to you if you aren't going to enjoy it? What have we got bodies for? And why passions? My philosophy is just the opposite of theirs, you see. I believe in living as hard as you damn well can and experiencing as much as you can in the few short years you're given. I think when you're dead you're probably dead for ever. And, anyway, even if I'm wrong, it's obviously senseless to try to plan for a future that lies so far ahead and which in any case you can know nothing about."

"That sounds good sense. I admit that your ideas sound more practical than theirs. But is it so really? Does your philosophy make for happiness, that's the point?"

"Oh, *happiness*!" she exclaimed, and tossed her cigarette end into the fire, expelling a stream of smoke from her lungs. "I don't believe in happiness. It's the great myth of humanity. I don't believe it exists, apart from the dreams we have of it now and again which makes it seem real, as though we had actually experienced it. Happiness is one of the hopes men live by, like immortality, and it's just about as much use as that."

"Yet you must admit that The Seekers are happy."

She clasped her hands about her slender knee, and her bracelets jangled. "I have to admit they say they are," she said drily. "But what sort of happiness can it amount to, I ask you? Better a live dog than a dead lion. I'd rather *use* my life to feel every moment of pain and pleasure than moulder in a corner like a cabbage and call that happiness and the best of life. I tell you what I think," she volunteered. "I think they're plain scared of life. That's all their big talk boils down to. They're scared of taking the raps," she nodded like a sage young monkey. She sprang out of the chair. "Christ! what a bloody conversation! Let's have a drink; come on."

She went to the cabinet in the corner of the room and began mixing drinks. Mr. Chaos watched her. She came back with the brimming glasses.

"Here's to — 'the case,'" she suggested. "How's it going, by the way? Found the culprit yet?"

"Yes," said Mr. Chaos, and watched her face come alive with interest.

"*No*! Who is it? Darling Inspector, do tell! I'll be as secret as the grave!"

Mr. Chaos turned down the corners of his mouth. "A friend of yours, I believe."

A flicker of fear quivered over her face for an instant. She said more guardedly, "That's more tantalising than ever. Don't torment me. It's dangerous." She gave him a sad flirtatious smile, and absently drank down the drink she had made for him which he had not touched.

She was mad to know, yet when he told her she did not believe him. He said with a casualness that was almost sinister, "Menzies."

She said incredulously, "Percy Menzies? Why, that's impossible! You've made a mistake. I'm sorry, but you must have done. Why on earth should Percy *want* to kill Mr. Titmarsh? The very idea's ludicrous. For one thing, he hasn't the brains, poor Percy simply hasn't the brains."

Mr. Chaos thought otherwise. There was a surprisingly strong case against him. He mentioned the notorious quarrel at the Meet and the past business in South Africa.

"Oh, that's old history," she cried impatiently.

"Good subject there for a grudge. Besides, that's only the motive. The real thing, the bad thing, is that Titmarsh was shot with his gun."

That wasn't so easy to laugh off, he could see.

"Someone else could have taken the gun, I suppose," she said at last. "It still doesn't follow that he was actually the one to fire the gun, does it? Does it?" she pleaded.

"No," he said fairly. "We make allowance for that. But he doesn't help himself at all. He doesn't say that someone else took the gun. He doesn't say anything — except to hurl abuse at me, which isn't very helpful. You see, he offered up a most feeble alibi in the first place. And we broke it at once. And he can give us nothing rational to put in its place. If he wasn't shooting Titmarsh at eleven o'clock the morning of the sixth, what was he doing, and where was he? That's what we want to know and what he is not able to tell us." His gentle searching eyes held hers. There was a curious similarity in their impenetrable brown sadness.

She stared back at him, thoughtfully, questioningly. "The morning of the sixth," her lips murmured. Absently she took out a cigarette, arid as the flame of the lighter wavered towards it, she suddenly jerked the cigarette from between her lips and let out a delighted yell of laughter. She flopped back into the chair and shook with laughter. She couldn't speak. Every time the gust subsided and she opened her mouth she was caught up in a fresh wave. The big scarlet clown's mouth was a triangle of gaiety, but, above it, the screwed-up eyes peering from the crinkles were as profoundly sad as ever.

She sat up at last and patted herself into sleekness again. "My God, im a wreck! I haven't laughed so much in years! It's my shocking memory, you see. Half-past five Wednesday or Rio de Janeiro, it's all the same to me. Poor old Menzies! My God, if I was a bit more of a bitch than I am I'd let you arrest him and have him tried at the Old Bailey, just for the hell of it. And then at the last moment up I'd trot as perky as you please and say, 'Begging your pardon, m'lud, but there's been some mistake. The prisoner couldn't have done it, not nohow. Contrariwise. For at eleven a.m. on the sixth of October the prisoner was in bed with me!' Uproar in Court! Can you imagine it! Lord, I wish I had the guts to do it. What a thrill for the old tabs!" She went on improvising hilariously. "And then, of course, the wicked old judge would pretend he hadn't understood, as judges always do. 'Kindly speak up, Miss Post. Where did you say the prisoner was on this occasion?' 'In the Tudor Arms, m'lud.' 'Tut-tut, I thought you said he was in *your* arms.' (To the clerk.) 'Scratch it out.' 'No, m'lud, that's quite correct. In my arms in The Tudor Arms.' Cue for song, and grand finale." The laughter began to fade out of her face. She stuck the cigarette between her lips again and Chaos leant forward to light it. She observed him through her lashes. "So that was what you came round for, was it? Anything else you'd like to know? I tell you," she added to the world in general, "privacy's a thing of the past. Ask, and it shall be given unto you. Go on."

"Nice of you to take it so well. Most people —"

"Would be embarrassed," Miss Post said for him. "But then I've no inhibitions so far as that's concerned. It's not even bravado. I simply don't give a damn and I can't for the life of me see anything to make such a fuss about ... Of course Percy knows that and that's what makes him so nervous."

"You were registered as Mr. and Mrs. Martin, weren't you?"

She arched her eyebrows.

"You seem to know all about it," she said caustically.

"Only the framework, as it were."

"So I should hope. All the same, it was pretty smart of you to get on to it at all, I consider. We used to cover our tracks pretty carefully. How did you get on to it? What gave us away?"

Mr. Chaos grinned maliciously.

"Miss Farrell. She saw you in the train with your suitcase. And then she *chanced* to see you coming out of the cinema with Menzies, and *happened* to be going in the same direction, so she followed you to the Tudor Arms."

Valerie Post stamped her heels venomously on the floor.

"I'm only surprised she let it go at that and didn't follow us upstairs. Damned old cow, I hope her guts rot! My one fear is that I may become a gloating old harpy like that when I grow old. I'd rather die!"

But Mr. Chaos was not particularly interested in Miss Post's future. It was her past that concerned him just then.

"It wasn't the first time you'd been away together then?"

"No. But the first time we'd stayed in Towcester. We always stayed in quiet little country inns where we weren't likely to run into anybody we knew. Of course we didn't do it very often — perhaps half a dozen times in all these years. We could only go off when his wife was away herself. And that didn't happen very often. Trust Mrs. Moneybags not to let him out of her sight, dear creature! I'm not saying we didn't snatch an hour now and again, but we had to be doubly careful about that. It's a very risky game when you both live in the same place. Not that I cared. *I* had nothing to lose."

"In that case, if you had no anxiety about your reputation or anything else, it seems to me that Menzies' chivalry was rather misplaced."

"Menzies' chivalry! What's that?" she asked sarcastically.

"Why, the fact that he shielded your good name even after I had warned him of the seriousness of his position."

She laughed again.

"How charming you are! So old-worldly! I like you so much. (I hope it doesn't embarrass you to hear me say so.) That wasn't chivalry, my dear, that was *funk*. He wasn't protecting me, he was protecting himself: make no mistake about that," she said, sardonically.

Mr. Chaos frowned.

"You're hard on him, aren't you? I can hardly believe that he is under his wife's thumb to that extent. Even if she really is quite unaware that her husband is consistently unfaithful to her, surely she would not take it as badly as all that if she did happen to find out. It might mean that she would cut off supplies for a time or threaten to divorce him. (I take it she has the moneybags.) But he seemed to me quite able to manage her, the little I saw of them together. I confess I can't for the life of me see how he could have preferred to take the risk of holding his tongue. If he had been arrested it would have had to come out in the end and then he would have been worse off than before. For obviously no one would let a rope be tied round his neck sooner than lose a rich wife. As you say, better a live dog than a dead lion." He shook his head. "No, I'm afraid the explanation of funk does not hold water."

"Oh, yes it does. You're a rotten policeman," said Valerie Post calmly. "You haven't got the hang of the thing. He's not afraid of Elsie. Who could be scared of that mouse? He winds her round his finger. She adores him. No, I'm the one he's frightened of." She giggled pleasingly. "He doesn't believe in my altruism. He knows I'm a danger but he just can't keep away. Isn't it sweet? I'm smarter than he is, and he knows it. He knows that I'm always a jump ahead of him and it makes him nervous, poor lamb. He's never sure what I'm going to do next, and he can't make out what I'm after. I think it's so modest of him to feel I couldn't possibly love him for himself alone," she chuckled.

"What is it he's scared of? Blackmail?"

"Worse than that." Valerie sucked in her lower lip in mock dismay. "He thinks I want to marry him. That's why he's so deadly determined not to let himself be compromised, for fear I should take advantage of him. He's convinced I'm only waiting for the opportunity. Of course if I went straight along and had it out with Elsie there's no doubt she'd be so furiously jealous that she'd simply refuse to divorce him out of spite. But if she found out in some devious way, and if she knew it was the last thing on God's earth that he wanted, she might divorce him in sudden rage. And then, you know, a simple type like that might easily find himself jockeyed into marrying me before he knew where he was," she said solemnly. "That would never do." She yawned widely and stretched her arms above her head. "My God, if he had any idea of how he bored me! He's fun to go to bed with now and again. But to have him there morning, noon, and night; to have to meet him for every meal; to have to endure his appalling monologues about himself ... Lord save me!" She made a little grimace and twinkled at the detective. "Still, I wouldn't have let him guess my true feelings for the world. It definitely added spice to a somewhat conventional situation to know his nervous dread was quite without foundation and to be able to give him sly digs sometimes to prick him up."

Mr. Chaos could not but smile at her.

"You're quite heartless, aren't you?"

"Oh, quite, I hope."

"What made the poor fellow — I can't help feeling a certain sympathy for him, caught in your cynical clutch! — what made him think you wanted to marry him? He's not such a wonderful catch, without his wife's money."

"I should say not! Oh, I don't know how he got the idea into his head. Perhaps, like all men, he thinks every woman must long to be married and hear the patter of tiny feet. Or maybe when I was feeling low some time I moaned of my hard and lonely lot. Or it could have been that I told him of a proposal I'd just received, or something like that. I don't remember now what put the idea into his head." She rose to her feet. "He'll learn his mistake soon enough now," she said abstractedly, glancing at herself in the mirror and smoothing her hands down her hips. "God, I'm as dry as a bone after all this talking! How about some tea?" She flicked a powder-puff over her forehead and ran a moistened finger along her thin eyebrows, staring at her reflection secretively. "Yes," she said complacently, "in a day or two he'll hear that I'm going to be married and that'll take the wind out of his sails."

"May I felicitate you!" murmured Mr. Chaos, rather taken aback. "And who is the happy man?"

"Harold Prescott," said Miss Post, crossing the room and opening the door. "Hallo!" she exclaimed sharply. "What are you doing, miss? Come here, if you please. Oh, no, you don't!" She leant forward and grabbed at something. She pulled Ruby into the room by her thick plait. "Eavesdropping, eh? How often have you been told ...?" Ruby, red-faced and sullen, hung her head stubbornly and refused to answer.

"How long have you been listening, eh?" She gave her a little shake. "What do you think of that, Inspector? You should tell her what happens to little girls who listen outside doors. This gentleman is a policeman, Ruby, so you'd better take care, or else you'll find yourself in the lock-up before you know where you are."

"Ruby!" Mr. Chaos called softly.

She half-turned towards him but kept her face averted. The light from the window glistened on a wet tear-track on her cheek. Her small teeth were biting down hard on her rosy lip. Obviously she was trying not to cry, not to show her evident humiliation. She refused to look at her erstwhile friend or come near him. Valerie Post gave her a little push. "All right," she said. "Run along with you, now, and make us some tea."

"Imp of Satan," remarked Miss Post, closing the door behind her. "It's lucky I've no children of my own; I can't keep even one little evacuee in order. I'm too soft with her, that's the trouble. I can't help it. Kids! It's over all too soon with them."

"So you're going to marry Mr. Prescott. He's the headmaster of the Grammar School, isn't he?"

"Well, yes, I rather thought it would be a good idea. Joking apart about Menzies and all that, I thought it would be a good thing for me to settle down. I'd like to have a better position than I have as a single woman. And though it's not a thing I care to think about, I'm not likely to have very many more chances. I'm — well, thirtyish," she admitted with a smile for the vanity of her feminine reluctance to tell her exact age. "And Harold is mad about me. Poor lamb, he thinks he hasn't a chance. He'll be crazy when I tell him."

"Tell him what?" asked Mr. Chaos with understandable curiosity.

She eyed him quizzically with raised eyebrows.

"When I tell him that I'm going to marry him. He doesn't know yet. You happen to be the first person I've told. Count yourself fortunate that you have a sympathetic way with you, I'm not habitually of a confiding nature."

Mr. Chaos smiled and hoped that they would both be very happy together.

Miss Post said, "Oh, God, don't let's talk about it. The idea's beginning to bore me already. Talking about anything too much in advance always turns me against it. Harold's only a little less dull than Percy. He happens to be better educated and I suppose that helps. And he's a type that's not come my way often. 'It makes a change!' as an old maid of mine used to say."

"You like the thrill of something unusual."

"Yes." She eyed him deliberately, and then turned away.

"I think I'd better go and see what the child's doing with that tea."

"Like David McQueen," continued Mr. Chaos.

She paused in the doorway to look at him. "You do know a lot, don't you?" she said, and it was impossible to tell whether it was admiration or sarcasm which dominated in her voice.

Left alone, Chaos wandered inquisitively round the room, touching things gently, lifting up ornaments and opening drawers. The baby grand behind the door was closed. It reminded Mr. Chaos of something. He lifted the lid and struck a few notes softly while he tried to remember what it was. He raised the seat of the stool: inside was a pile of music, mostly jazz rhapsodies and mock-modern trifles based on dance rhythms. There was a hand-written manuscript on top, untitled and unnamed as to its author. It was scored for piano in a very rough sort of notation, imprecise and difficult to read, as if it were a first draft dashed off at white heat at the piano, and written partly in pencil and partly in ink.

Mr. Chaos propped it on the music-rest and, standing awkwardly, knees bent and one foot on the soft pedal, fumbled out the opening chords. No, that was not right. D ... Here we go! E, that was meant to be ... Ah, yes, now he had the hang of it! (Of course, now he knew why it was vaguely familiar. It was the thing McQueen had played at the funeral. Yes, and McQueen had composed it himself. He had said so, hadn't he?) The four notes of the theme crept up the piano in the little cold arpeggios he remembered hearing before ... a sound of utter desolation ... (Yes, and then Miss Post had told him he must take his music away, it was a nuisance to her, or something of that sort. Obviously, then, it was here he had composed it. Understandably enough since they had no piano at The Sanctuary. No doubt, too, it had not been inconvenient at the time to Miss Post. And it rather accounted for her being on such friendly terms — one might almost say terms of intimacy with him.) And here — D — he was back at the theme again — E — in those smashing triumphal chords which sounded so — A — magnificent thundered forth on the organ with all the stops pulled out — D. He removed his foot from the pedal, and Miss Post opened the door and came in pushing a tea-trolley.

"I'm sorry I've been so long," she said, with tightened jaws. "That little wretch has run off somewhere. But this is altogether too much of a good thing. You just wait till she comes back. Milk?"

"And three sugars, please. You really should not have bothered."

"I wouldn't have, only I happened to want some tea myself," she said tartly.

Mr. Chaos said affably, discreetly changing the subject, as it were, "I've been looking at your music. You compose, I see."

"Not I. Cake, Inspector?" she said, still in that tone of restrained irritation.

"Oh, disappointing! I hoped we had a genius in our midst."

"You may have. If he is a genius, which I beg leave to doubt. But he's in your midst, if that's what you want."

"How jolly! I have a great admiration for musicians always. May I know who it is? It looked rather an interesting work, I thought, from my hasty glance at it."

"Yes? I'm no musician; I wouldn't know. One of your little pets over the way wrote it. David McQueen." She was ostentatiously bored.

"Did he, now? A young man of parts evidently. And dedicated to you, I presume, since you own the manuscript."

"You couldn't be more mistaken, my dear Inspector. That's not David's line at all. Don't you know he's one of the Celibate Seekers. He doesn't like women, and regards sex as only fit for animals." There was the sharpness of pain in her voice and her upper lip curled contemptuously.

"Oh, come, I know better than that," said Mr. Chaos archly.

"You may think you do but you don't," was her terse reply. "He has no use for me and I've no use for him; to me he's not a man at all. Our dislike is mutual. The manuscript is here simply because I told him ages ago that he could always come and tinkle on my piano if he felt in the mood for it. There isn't one he can use anywhere else, and I happened to know that he used to be a musician of sorts. And so he did come up once or twice. The last time he came up he composed that."

"Not the last time, surely," Mr. Chaos corrected her.

She turned her head, startled, to stare at him.

"I meant," she amended, "the last time he came to use the piano. Actually, if you're anxious about precision, he composed it on two successive evenings. The first time he came I was out. The next time I was in. But he evidently found me a disturbing influence, for he did not come again. And he left the music behind him."

"How long ago was all this?"

"Jesus, if I'd have known I was going to be called to account for every moment I'd have kept a diary! I don't know when it was. How can you expect me to remember things that are totally unimportant? It was some time before Titmarsh was killed and all this bother began, obviously."

"Yes, it would be, I suppose. But let's try and fix it a little more definitely, do you mind? Can you remember where you had gone the night he came and you were out?"

Valerie's languid lids opened a little wider.

"Why the sudden interest? Is it really of any importance?" But that was the sort of question that Mr. Chaos always discreetly refused to answer. "Well, let me see, where did I go?" she ruminated. And then she remembered. She had had two friends staying with her over the week-end and she had returned to town with them, done some shopping and gone out dancing with them in the evening. They had gone to a show first, a Coward first-night, so they could date it by that easily enough. It was either the eighteenth or nineteenth of September. That was the best she could do.

Mr. Chaos was properly grateful — for the hospitality and so on and so forth (meaning by that, her unabashed frankness), and now he really must go.

"It's been a pleasure," she said mockingly, as she helped him on with his overcoat. "You must come and see me again, and not on business next time," and her fingers were cool against the back of his neck.

"I will," said Mr. Chaos glibly; "I will. But I'm only a timid bachelor. You must promise not to seduce me."

She laughed, but her eyes were sad. She smoothed down her hips with that familiar gesture. "I take a pleasure in making myself out to be worse than I am."

"I know," said Mr. Chaos in his sympathetic voice. "If you can't get what you want, then pretend you never wanted the damn thing anyway. Isn't that it?"

He carried away the picture of her standing in the doorway, her monkey-face sad and puzzled, with an almost human look of perplexity. He was awfully sorry for her. Moments like these made him detest his profession, though he knew it to be merely a passing impulse of sentimentality. She wasn't nearly as self-confident as she pretended to be. And things were going to be much worse than she had any idea. It was a nasty business and she was going to be hurt quite a lot, he thought. He hoped her queer unsatisfactory philosophy would uphold her.

It had been dark for some hours but the moon had not yet risen. And as he walked along the rutted unlit lane, he could not but wonder with an amused chuckle what Harold Prescott would say when he found himself proposed to by that very unequivocal young woman. Not a nice position for any man; and if the man were already pledged ... It was perhaps a case of, how happy could he be with either, were t'other dear charmer away. And what of Mrs. Titmarsh, if she should learn of Valerie's proposal? How would she regard it?

There was no doubt but that there was a lot to be said for The Seekers' way of life, or at least their beliefs — even if they did not work out so ideally in practice. Love and sex caused more trouble than all the rest put together. Wasn't that the problem for most of them? There was Valerie. And Harold Prescott. And Mrs. Titmarsh. And poor thwarted Miriam Fry. And Wesley's illegitimate daughter with her struggles and tears. And the unlovely partnership of the Menzies ... Yes, it was a bad look-out.

The only snag about The Seekers' arrangements was that it did not allow for the continuation of the human race. And that was a pity, wasn't it? Or was it?

CHAPTER ELEVEN - SOMETHING IN THE CELLAR

As he approached The Sanctuary he could see people moving about in the long room they called the Wool Room. He could see them as they passed across the bare windows, obscuring momentarily the golden light beaming into the darkness and casting amber squares on the grass. There is always a fascination about watching people who think themselves unseen, a temptation which Mr. Chaos often found irresistible. Now he crept near to observe them.

Inside the lamplit room it was like a mediaeval illustration of a guild at work. In the foreground, seated quarter profile to the window, Ella Slade, spinster, was at the ancient original task. The muscles in her strong bare leg slid under the skin as her sandalled foot pressed rhythmically on the treadle. The wheel spun. The spiral of natural wool on the distaff diminished slowly. The thread passed between her thumb and forefinger, steadily, smoothly, twisting, twisting. To one side, Miriam and David McQueen were setting up the six-foot loom, sharing the tiresome fidgety task of fastening the warp to the framework, across which the weft is woven with the shuttle. Beyond them, Joshua Platt, the sleeves of his smock rolled up to the shoulder, was leaning over one of the big coppers, swirling the contents round and round with a big stick. His arms were stained with dye almost to the elbows. His face was set with the effort. Every now and again he stopped to wipe the steam off his pince-nez. Old Bernard was weaving on one of the smaller looms. To the watcher at the window the shuttle slid noiselessly back and forth and the loom slammed down without a sound. Only from old Bernard's face was absent the look of anxious concentration the others wore; he had his usual tranquil expression. As for William, he had his back to the window so Mr. Chaos was not in a position to judge. He was standing on a pair of steps, pegging a sopping cloth back and forth from yard to yard over a sink to catch the drips. Ella Slade's thread broke. And at that moment the bell rang out above them. The rhythm broke. They slowed down or moved away from what they were doing. It was half-past six and time for the evening meal.

In the dark corridor Ruby almost ran into him.

"Sorry," she said breathlessly. "I'm late."

"Hallo, young Ruby! I should just think you are!" He was about to warn her that her auntie was liable to be cross with her when she got back, but as soon as she heard his voice she pulled herself away from him. He caught her wrist: "Now then, what's up?" Silence. "Aren't we on speaking terms any longer?"

"Speaking!" she stuttered, in a voice choked with rage and disillusion. "Yah! Dirty copper!" She tried to free herself with unscrupulous nails. Her sense of decency was outraged; she had been betrayed. He had pretended to her that he was an ordinary man, that he was a special friend of hers, that he didn't know The Seekers. She had taken it as such a favour that he had come to the funeral with her. She had been flattered at his interest in her friends. And all the time it had been nothing but a cod. There wasn't a word of truth in it. He was a liar like all the rest. You couldn't believe any of 'em.

Impossible to describe with what fear and loathing young Ruby regarded policemen. They were her hereditary enemies. They were not angels of justice, or defenders of the peace, or benign guardians to Ruby of Bethnall Green. They were devils, instruments of social injustice (though she might not have used those words), lurking in dark lanes to cop you if you didn't watch out.

He had made a fool of her, and taken advantage of her. It was too much. Worse than that, she feared she had betrayed her friends in her vanity at being able to talk knowingly like a grown-up. Some of this she had got off her chest in a fit of contrition to Auntie Lucy, who had kindly absolved her from blame. She felt better about that now. But it did not make her feel any better or kindlier towards that bleeding copper.

"Now what have I done?" asked Mr. Chaos in a pained voice.

"Lemme go!" muttered Ruby, and wrenched herself free. Then homeward to a sulky supper, and after, lonely tears.

Mr. Chaos sighed at this comparatively early exhibition of feminine temperament, and joined the others at the long Refectory table. There was a pottage of red lentils. William's strange selection for the evening's reading was from Plato's *Apologia, The Trial and Death of Socrates*, and while he listened to the warm voice repeating the beautiful familiar words, Mr. Chaos found himself dreamily considering the question of ancient birthrights in remote biblical days. Something in the notion seemed to connect up with the case, but he could not quite fasten his mind on it. Wesley's will? Audrey and the manuscripts?

While he chased it, the reading ceased and William closed the book. Talking was permitted again. Not that they conversed much at meals, rather they murmured slight phrases to one another, as do people too well acquainted to need the prattling disguise of words. Mrs. Titmarsh was looking fatigued, lines of strain ran from her nostrils. She caught his eye on her and smiled. What had he been doing to her little protegée? she wanted to know.

"Ruby?" he said. "Why, nothing that I know of. I saw her just now and noticed that she was rather offish with me. What am I supposed to have done?"

"She felt injured because you had told her you weren't a policeman. I said she'd probably misunderstood you, but I don't think she was quite reconciled. I really do wish you hadn't said that, Mr. Chaos; we are having such a lot of trouble to convince her that grown-ups don't lie."

"I should think you were," said Mr. Chaos drily.

"She trusted you, you see," said Mrs. Titmarsh reproachfully.

"Well, I'm practically a stranger to her, so I don't suppose it's done much harm. The important thing is that she still trusts you."

"She's such a loyal little creature in her affections. She came rushing down here as soon as she heard, not because of her own hurt feelings, but because she was afraid I should be upset when I knew and she wanted to save me that if she could."

"Upset about what?" he asked curiously.

"Why, you know," said Mrs. Titmarsh calmly. "That Valerie is going to marry Harold Prescott."

Mr. Chaos then chanced to observe a curious phenomena: the blunt-fingered hand on the table beside him trembled imperceptibly and the blood seemed to drain out of the fingertips, leaving the nails a queer livid white. But when he spoke, McQueen's tone held only mild interest as he asked, "Is that really so?"

"So I understand. Mrs. Titmarsh, if I'm not being impertinent, why should it upset you to hear of this engagement?"

She smiled, and carved an apple carefully into quarters.

"It didn't. I'm delighted. But the child thought I might be — jealous, I suppose, because as everyone knows he's a very dear friend of mine. The way children think is most odd! It was quite difficult to make her believe that I did not mind."

"As you say, she takes it for granted that grown-ups lie."

Mrs. Titmarsh looked a little startled.

"I never told her in so many words that I wasn't a policeman. I made some jesting remark on the subject and she misunderstood. Don't you agree that often happens with children? You weren't really blaming *me* for lying, were you, Mrs. Titmarsh?" he said pleasantly. "Or rather, you were trying to extenuate your own sense of guilt, I think. It must have given you quite a turn when she disclosed her thoughts to you."

She said pitifully, "I never dreamed ... Poor little child ..." She got up from the table. Signal that the meal was over. The others got up and moved away. The conversation was at an end.

Later in the privacy of the dead man's cell-like chamber, the detective paced thoughtfully along its narrow length; five paces down and two across.

Now things were beginning to form something of a pattern. There was a moment when it was dangerous to try and fit things together, lest one should unconsciously form a theory and thereby lose one's freshness and clarity of vision. (A detective, Mr. Chaos considered, requires the "seeing eye" as much as a painter: that ability to see things untainted by pre-existing assumptions.) Equally, there was a moment when it was dangerous not to piece things together. To diagnose the exact moment required a certain habitude and a certain sensitivity. Chaos said it was a pricking in his thumbs. For him the moment was imminent.

Motive, he divined. And because he knew the motive he knew who had done it. Yes, but how was it done? He had the pieces in his hand, as it were, and he could not fit them together. He turned the pieces round and round in his mind ... the bullet ... the spade ... the bell that did not ring ... the fragments of moss found in the victim's wound. They all *had* to fit and he could not make them do so.

His mind, weary of its enforced concentration, began to slide away. There was old Bernard Drag and his fantastic story of not hearing or seeing what happened because he was wrapt in meditation. That was an odd tale. An odd old man, as suave as a Chinese philosopher. Perhaps he should approach him directly, ask him outright who had done it. Likely enough he knew, but with his peculiar way of seeing things was keeping it to himself. However, if he had as much regard for Truth as the others had, he would not prevaricate if he were asked outright. He never put himself forward in any way but you could tell at once that he was a member of the group who really counted. If Audrey left to-morrow probably no one would give a tuppeny damn, but this old man mattered, even though he did not pull his weight in physical labour. He mattered in the same way that Rollo Carpenter mattered, for instance. They belonged to the spiritual side of it and pulled the whole thing together. That must have been the role Wesley Titmarsh played when he was alive. Had someone been jealous of it, then?

He remembered the dream of the stone angel he had had the first night he came. The stone angel he had thought was Epstein's Lucifer, in the inconsequential way one does recognise things in dreams even though they bear little or no resemblance to the object in real life. But as the angel rushed downwards he had seen the face was not Lucifer's but David McQueen's. He had awoken in unreasonable fright. He remembered now that smiling face as it bore down on him, and the smile was David's smile — and Lucifer's. It was that inward secretive smile that betokened spiritual pride. And it was spiritual pride that proved the downfall of men and angels, in the beginning and ever after — one might almost say, world without end. Mr. Chaos endeavoured to shake off his gloomy cast of thought. After all, McQueen was young, if it had any reality outside his own imagination he would doubtless grow out of it.

From dreams it was scarcely a step to Joshua's vision. He smiled. Truth or lies, it was amusing in its naïvety. Somehow it hardly seemed to go with the character of the hard-bitten old swindler he knew. And yet if it were not so, what was his little game? What was he doing, what the devil was he doing in this galley? And had Titmarsh been aware of his past? It was curious, when you came to look at it, that Titmarsh had accepted him as a member because he did not really fit in with the religious brotherhood at all. For one thing, his beliefs were rank with the old theological doctrines. He must have had a very calvinistic upbringing as a child, and now the forgotten dregs were drifting to the surface, and he spoke with the fervour of the repentant sinner of Damnation, hell-fire, the blood of the Lamb, winged angels, crowns and harps, and all the outworn paraphernalia of salvation. The Seekers, on the other hand, were free and undogmatic, without specific creed or ritual, worshipping the Spirit in kind, needing neither tears nor blood, nor vicarious atonement to free them from sin. But how could Joshua Platt understand that? Mr. Chaos made a mental note to ask Rollo about him. *He* would know what had happened and why Titmarsh had taken him in.

An unusual type, Rollo. It was easier to imagine him as a kind of monk, living somewhere beyond this world, than as a wealthy man living in the lap of luxury, and an adoring husband and father. It was not so surprising, when you came to think of it, that his wife had run away from him. Mr. Chaos could picture without difficulty the pretty, gay society girl, years younger than her too rich, too passionate, too pampering husband. Of course she was bored because she had married without love, likely enough. And then, before things had a chance to get really stale, there was the baby. Something for her to love, something to draw off part of his overpowering love for her. They might have pulled through after all. But the baby died. Perhaps in such circumstances that she felt some personal guilt in the matter. In any case, whether from conscience, grief or revulsion, or a combination of all three, life with Rollo thereafter became intolerable to her. The first chance that came her way in the guise of some pretty boy, she ran off.

And he had gone nearly mad with grief, hadn't he? Was it any wonder; both his dam and chick lost in one swoop. A terrible wound that to a man's esteem; and a rich man, accustomed to the servile admiration outwardly directed at him but actually inspired by his possessions, would feel it more than most. Sometimes a wound like that never healed. Rollo had wrenched himself away from all memory of it; torn up his roots, scattered his belongings, driven himself into a new way of life. And had he succeeded, wondered Mr. Chaos.

Honestly, what would become of The Seekers as a group now that their Master was dead? Would it quietly fold up and all its members drift into fresh organisations? Or would Rollo contrive somehow to hold them together? So far it looked as if they intended to stay together, and certainly no allowance had been made for their disbanding in Wesley's will. What would happen to Mrs. Titmarsh if the thing did break up? What would happen to Abbot's Breach, for that matter, which Wesley had left to the organisation? To the organisation, not to any individual

Seekers by name. So once the organisation had ceased to exist it would revert to the status quo, presumably, and become Lucy's property as the widow and next of kin of the late owner.

Mr. Chaos yawned, stretched, scratched his ribs vigorously, got into bed and extinguished the light. To bed but not to sleep. He sighed and turned from one side to the other on his narrow cot. Dared he make an arrest? Dared he not make an arrest yet? Was he exaggerating the risk there was in playing for safety on his side? One more day, he promised himself, just one more day in which to make sure. To-morrow he would contact his old friend Professor Vitell. What Charles did not know about ballistics was likely to be a sealed chapter to everyone else.

The next day, early after Pittance, he went down to the village to make a phone call. There was someone in the phone-box, and as he drew near David flounced out with a face louring like a thundercloud. Chaos looked at him in surprise.

"Hallo, shirker," he cried affably. "Oughtn't you to be at work?"

David stared at him abstractedly a moment with his blue marble eyes. He looked worried. He flipped the hair back from his temples. "I should," he said. He knotted the red cord more tightly about his slim waist; looked as if he was going to confide something to the detective and then evidently thought better of it, shrugged his shoulders, and humped off.

Mr. Chaos watched him stomp down the road, a sturdy, self-contained little man, with something faintly pathetic about him, as small, very tough, little boys are sometimes pathetic.

"Is that you, Charles?" demanded Chaos when he got through. "It's me, dear boy, Chaos and old night. Are you busy at the moment? Because, if you've nothing on ... no, no, I speak figuratively not literally, don't be coarse ... if you can spare the time, then, I have a little problem which I think might interest you. It's one of those things like that silly joke, how high is a Chinaman? ... No, if you can come it must be to-day. There's a train at ten-five, gets you in at twelve-fifteen ... Good man!"

To look at Professor Vitell was less like a professor than any one you could imagine. He was enormously fat and untidily dressed, with a red face and quantities of wildly springing black hair. His hands were surprisingly small and delicate. Though he could hardly move without knocking something over inadvertently, his touch was as light as a butterfly's.

Outside the station he surveyed his rural surroundings without pleasure. "No taximeter-cabriolets?" he exclaimed indignantly.

"You are in the country now, dear boy," said Chaos pityingly.

"On your own head be it, then," said the professor. "Since you have not had the forethought or consideration to provide me with a conveyance, you will have to insinuate my unwieldy frame into an omnibus vehicle."

"No buses here, Charles."

"No taxis, no buses!" cried the professor, shocked out of his pedantry. "Do you mean I shall have to *walk*?"

"Not far," promised Chaos, dodging a floundering blow aimed at him.

"Damnable jackanapes!" snarled his friend. "You have lured me here under false pretences."

"But since you *are* here ..." And Mr. Chaos hauled him off, panting and protesting bitterly all the way, to the police station. They retired together into the inner room. Mr. Chaos sent the young constable down to The Black Dog for a dozen bottles of beer. There was nothing like beer for pacifying Vitell, for reviving him and sustaining him too. And it was fortunate that they had it, for they were working there from half-past twelve to half-past four.

At half-past four, Vitell leant back in his chair and removed his glasses to rub his eyes. The hard white electric light made his eyes ache.

"There you have it," he said with a wave of his pretty supple hand. "I don't think I can do anything more for you."

"I don't think you can. Thank you, Charles," said Mr. Chaos soberly.

"Not at all. A pleasure. Clever of you to have hit on it, in the first place. Are they all dead men?"

Chaos started. "Oh, the bottles! Yes, you've killed them all, I'm afraid. Come along now, or you'll miss your train."

Professor Vitell held the last bottle against the light and then put it sadly down. He fought his way into his coat sleeves grumbling inaudibly the while of frenzied peripatetics and aimless perambulations.

It was dark long before Mr. Chaos got back to The Sanctuary, of course, and The Seekers had come in from the fields and were at their various indoor tasks. He went from room to room looking for someone;

but in vain. As it was nearly time for the evening meal, he waited for the bell to sound which would call them from their labours.

But no bell sounded that night.

Instead, the night was torn up with a calico scream — the sexless inhuman cry of extreme pain or terror. It cut through the air with cruel shrillness again and again, coming nearer with each cry. It made the blood chill and the heart halt with fear.

Mr. Chaos stood in the centre of the hall listening for the direction of the sound. He heard footsteps, stumbling and tripping, and someone whimpering with each sobbing breath. Audrey ran forward blindly with hands outstretched and staring eyes. Her face was quite bloodless. She almost fell into his arms. She opened her white lips to speak. Her eyes rolled upwards, and her body became a dead-weight against him.

He laid her gently on the floor. Her drab habit was stained with dust and dirt, as though she had fallen somewhere filthy. People were coming now; doors opening and closing, feet clattering on the stairs, anxious voices calling, "What is it? What's happened?" seeing the man kneeling by the recumbent figure.

Without looking up, Chaos said curtly, "She's fainted. If someone will kindly bring some sal volatile or — better still — brandy."

There was no brandy, there was no sal volatile, they said, with a suggestion of embarrassment; they did not use such things.

"You'll find a flask in the upper left-hand pocket in the valise in my room," said Chaos. And when it came, poured a generous trickle between her teeth. She choked and gulped. The long black lashes moved against the white cheek. She looked up at the inverted faces staring down at her, in surprise and then fear and then stark terror. She struggled to sit up and tears spilled weakly out of her eyes.

"Well, all right. Cry," said Mr. Chaos, and put his arm round her shoulders.

Lucy knelt by her and patted her hands. "What is it, darling? What is it?"

"I don't want to cry," said Audrey, struggling to control the tears spilling faster and faster down her cheeks. She jerked out between the involuntary sobs: "I'd forgotten the apples for the table to-night ... I hurried down with the bowl ... and as I ran across the cellar ..." She broke off and flung the back of her hand against her mouth, as if to press back another shriek ... "I bumped into — into something hanging ... soft ... it swung away," she began to sob again, "It — it — was still — warm ... Oh, God!" Her voice rose higher and higher. "I felt the hand brush my face ..." A rim of white showed round her staring pupils. She tugged wildly at her dishevelled hair. "Soft and cold, it dangled in my face ..." She drew her chin in sharply, ducking away as if it were still before her. She was with them and not with them, narrating the horror and reliving it at the same time. She looked half-crazed with shock. "I was frightened; I *screamed*," she whispered. "I screamed and screamed ... and then at last I found myself running ..."

"You didn't see who it was?" asked Mr. Chaos softly.

She pulled in her lips and bit them — hard. She shook her head.

Mr. Chaos stood up. He screwed the top on his flask and slipped it into his pocket. He looked round at the others. They looked startled, apprehensive, uncertain. Besides Audrey there were only five of them present. His eye rested momentarily on William in speculation. He stared back at him, puzzled, his mouth a little open. Mr. Chaos turned away. He said, "Platt! I'll ask you to come with me, if you please."

Joshua said placatingly, "All raight, loov," and followed him in the direction of the cellar. Mr. Chaos had not been in the cellar before, since they had told him it was merely used as a storage chamber for root vegetables, hard fruits, cheeses and so forth.

A flight of steps like a ladder ran perpendicularly into the darkness. There was a rope rail at the side to cling to. The thin line of light from his torch fell downwards but did not reach the bottom. Mr. Chaos made a small grimace unseen, and ran down the steps backwards. He stood at the bottom scribbling a pattern of light against the dark. Then he saw him.

He was hanging in the middle of the room from the centre beam that divided the cellar into two parts with folding lattice doors. These were open and the body hung in the space between them.

It was not at all a pleasant sight. The white habit of The Seekers hung loose, ungirdled. Like a rag puppet the head lolled on the right shoulder in its jaunty tie of crimson rope. Absurd puppet, like a Russian toy in its belted blouse, coarse blue trousers, and limp sandalled feet with toes turned in! Grotesque doll, with the loose yellow hair falling into the blue marbles that served it for eyes, with its long bright tongue stuck so impudently in its face of purple felt!

At his feet lay fragments of broken pottery. To one side and a little behind him lay an empty apple crate on its side. From somewhere high above a voice called, "Shall I come down?"

In that brief moment of transition from normality to sudden death, Chaos had forgotten about Brother Joshua waiting cautiously above stairs. Now he called to him impatiently to come along and bring a light with him.

"There's a light down there, loov," said Platt in a faintly nervous voice as he descended. He crossed the cellar hastily, averting his gaze from the dummy swinging in the middle of the room by the dim illumination of the detective's torch. He struck a match. There was a faint hiss; and a greenish light flared noisily out of a gas-jet high in the wall.

Mr. Chaos sawed through the scarlet rope and the body dropped heavily against him. He staggered under its sudden weight, and together he and Joshua laid it on the stone-flagged floor. But it was no use. He was quite dead. Audrey was mistaken; he was no longer warm, though the body had not stiffened into the final rigidity of death.

Brother Joshua muttered plaintively over and over again, "Whatever did he do it for? ... Poor lad! ... Poor lad!"

Mr. Chaos said: "You will go to the police station. You will explain what has happened, and you will ask them to send the police surgeon at once." He glanced at his watch. "Hurry, please." He listened to him lumbering up the steps out of sight. Then he was alone. Except for the hissing of the gas, it was deathly quiet. Now that he was conscious of his thoughts again, Mr. Chaos found that there was a sickish sensation at the base of his stomach. With a feeling of unutterable depression crushing him, he realised that his deductions had been correct. He should not have wasted one more valuable day verifying them. He loathed above all things an untidy conclusion to a case. It gave him a feeling of guilt to see the dead boy lying there. As though he were to blame. And wasn't it best in the end, all things considered? To die now or in a year's time with all the long-drawn anxiety and misery of imprisonment and trial: which was best? Who would question his choice? He stared at the bits of pottery on the floor. That authenticated Audrey's story, he thought; that must be the bowl she had dropped in her fright. He heard someone coming down the stairs. It was Lucy Titmarsh.

"I had to come and see what the trouble was. Brother Joshua rushed past us without saying a word. We called, but he was in too much of a hurry to answer." She stopped speaking. She had seen the body on the ground. She ran forward and dropped on her knees beside him. She said in a strangled whisper: "It's David! What's happened? What has he done? Oh, God, what has he done?"

Not wishing to have any more hysteria or swoons to cope with, Mr. Chaos said drily, "It appears that he has killed himself."

She turned to stare at him with the blank affrighted gaze of a sleep-walker. "But why?" she queried dully.

But Mr. Chaos was examining the noose and either did not hear or did not choose to answer. The noose was made from the rough scarlet rope that girdled McQueen's own habit. He had fastened one end securely about the beam and made a running knot ... There was the frail wooden crate, which had borne his weight for the necessary moment before he kicked it away to step into eternity.

It might have been the impulse of a moment, or a deliberate decision. No way of telling, but Mr. Chaos inclined to think it was a sudden impulse of fear or of despair. Perhaps something had warned him of what was to come. Or maybe it seemed to him that he could no longer attain what he so desperately craved. Then it might well be that life no longer seemed worth living. Well, whatever it was, would probably never be known now, since he had left no last message as so many suicides obligingly did. He had chosen to put paid to his account and to leave the rest in silence.

Mrs. Titmarsh came towards him, tensely earnest.

"Why did he do it?" she said. "You've got to tell me why?"

Mr. Chaos put his finger to his lips. People were approaching. They trooped noisily down the steps, their feet resounding on the stone floor. They could hear Sergeant Bean, loquacious as ever, and the short dry answers of the doctor. Brother William escorted them in silence.

The light was not good in the cellar even when the gas was full on, but by its dull greenish illumination Brother William did not seem to twitch or change colour when he saw his friend dead before him. He had perhaps had time to orientate himself. Lucy went to him and he put his arm round her shoulders.

Sergeant Bean said cheerily, "Getting to be quite a little epidemic round here, as you might say ... Arrrumm! ..." He shook his head seriously. "You wanter watcher step. Y'know what they say: If you have two you must have three. There's bound to be another death."

"Sergeant!" said Mr. Chaos sharply. "Will you collect all the household in one room! The Refectory will be the best, I think. Any of them will tell you which it is. I want to ask them a few questions. Mrs. Titmarsh and Mr. Brown will be good enough to accompany you."

William looked at him curiously and then put his hand through Lucy's arm and drew her away. As they went, Mr. Chaos heard Lucy saying again, in that dazed incredulous voice, that she could not understand why he had done it. And he heard William answer, "My poor Lucy! My poor dear! You mustn't hate him too much! It was cowardly; but *we* may not judge him. He chose what was the better way out for himself. Perhaps the only way. He could no longer carry the burden of his guilt. Pity poor Judas, Lucy! He had killed the best man in the world and he had nothing left to live for."

CHAPTER TWELVE - OLD UMBRELLA'S LAPSE

While the doctor made his cursory examination, Mr. Chaos prowled round the cellar, raking the dark corners with his torch, staring abstractedly at the apple-racks and cheese-presses. To one side of the cellar was a narrow passageway, scarcely five feet high, with deep time-worn wheel-ruts in the ground. It was only a couple of yards long and led to big iron-bolted double doors. This was the entrance to the cellar from the lane outside. Mr. Chaos jerked back the heavy bolts: they were heavy but not stiff. The doors opened outward, letting in the sweet fresh night air. It was this way that the produce had been brought in to store since time immemorial.

"You can take him out through here. Easier than up those stairs," said Mr. Chaos to the doctor, his voice sounding hollow in the night. There was some half-formed thought floating through his brain which he could not arrest. There was something he had seen that had begun to suggest something quite different to him. It should have called up a train of associated ideas, but the thread had been broken — someone had spoken or something else had caught his eye, and he could not recapture the lost end. Maybe it was only a trivial notion, maybe it had nothing to do with the case at all but had some connection with his personal life; there was no way of telling; but it did not cease to fret him. It was this that made him move round and round the cellar trying to hit on the sight that should revive his memory. However, it was no use.

The ambulance panted quietly outside the cellar door. McQueen's body was carried out and lifted into it. There was something furtive about this silent slipping away, with no mourners to watch him go to his last home.

Mr. Chaos pulled-to the doors and slammed the bolts into place. One last look round ... Nothing ... He extinguished the gas. But as he walked upstairs in the dark he was again haunted by that puzzling sense of something wrong, out of place, out of key somehow ... He shook his head free from these pesty inconclusive thoughts and proceeded to the Refectory for the questioning.

They were all there; silent; hunched on chairs, leaning against the walls, or staring out of the windows. They seemed to be avoiding one another's eyes. There were tears; but they were quiet and stifled; this was not a matter for the free expression of natural grief. Suicide was something shameful. The keening was in the privacy of their own hearts.

As he looked at them he suddenly felt awfully tired, and he felt again the depression he had experienced in the cellar at the sight of the dead boy. He stood stiffly with his back to the wall and said, "I'm sorry about this. I didn't expect it. I need hardly say that if I could have prevented it I would. And now, I'm afraid I must ask you some questions. The sooner these routine matters are attended to the more likelihood there is of obtaining accurate answers. The first thing I want to find out is who saw him last."

There was an uneasy silence as his eyes turned curiously from one to the other. No one seemed to want to speak first. To start the ball rolling he said, "I myself saw McQueen this morning in the village. The time was about nine-thirty. I did not see him alive again. I presume some one of you must have seen him after that. If he was not seen at work, he came to Refection, I suppose?"

"Yes," said Mrs. Titmarsh, "he was there. But I didn't see him after."

Nor had any one else apparently. They had all gone about their several jobs, not paying any particular attention to one another. Chaos asked what McQueen should have been doing that afternoon. Brother William mentioned that he was supposed to sort and pack the apples for Miriam and Joshua to take on their next trip to town.

"So that he would have been in the cellar anyhow?"

"Yes."

"Should any one have been with him, helping?"

"No. It was work that he could quite well do alone. As a matter of fact it is the kind of light task we generally keep —" he coughed slightly and dropped his voice — "for Brother Bernard," he mumbled, indicating the old man in the corner.

"But he was fully occupied just now so David said he would do it, meaning to sandwich it in somehow among his other work."

"How long would it take him to do?"

"Oh, I don't know. Two or three hours perhaps. He was a quick worker. But he might not have intended to do it all to-day."

"Actually, he did not do any at all, did he?"

Brother Joshua licked his lips.

"Well, I suppose not. But to tell you the truth I didn't really notice. I was that appalled —"

Mr. Chaos assured them that there were only empty crates in the cellar and the apples had been neither graded nor packed. So much for that, he said. It might be, though, that he had not visited the cellar till later. In that case, where and what was he doing beforehand?

"You see," he said, "the doctor puts the time of death roughly between two and three hours ago. That's as near as he can get it at present. Even so, even if it is three hours ago, it leaves an awful lot of time unaccounted for between the end of Refection, when he was last seen alive by you all, and the moment in which he killed himself. Where was he? It is hardly possible that he was down in the cellar all that while, doing nothing."

William looked round at the others sorrowfully, as if apologising for what he had to say.

"Perhaps he was thinking about it. Perhaps he had to pluck up courage ... it was a very dreadful thing he had to do, wasn't it? Perhaps he just wanted somewhere where he could be alone and quiet to think it out uninterruptedly. He would know that no one was likely to go down there and disturb him."

Mr. Chaos said, "Do you mean to say there is no one of you who goes around and supervises the others? How can you be sure that the work is done then?"

"*Quis custodiet custodes?*" Rollo spoke for the first time.

"I beg your pardon?" said Mr. Chaos, who really had not caught the mumbled phrase.

Carpenter raised his head. The furrows were cut deeply in his sallow skin, and his eyes had sunk far back in his head, leaving two skull-like hollows. It was apparent that he had sustained a bad shock. He said, "We are not here to supervise one another. The only profit we seek from the work here is to our own souls. Should we prefer not to work — well!" he shrugged the rest away.

"No recriminations then if one should slack or not take on his fair share?"

Brother Rollo gave the ghost of his narrow wolfish smile.

"No recriminations."

"I see. So you don't know what McQueen was doing from after Refection to the time he killed himself?"

Brother Rollo stared at him piercingly without answering.

Mr. Chaos knew now of what those deep tragic eyes, those sunken cheeks and anguished mouth reminded him: the terrible Christ-crucifixions painted by Mantegna. The great clumsy hands crisping in his lap were disarming in their helpless strength like a peasant's.

"No," said Brother Rollo at last.

"Well, how was he at Refection? Did any one notice? Did he speak? Was he in a good mood? Did anything about him strike you as strange or unusual in any way?"

"He was quiet," said William eventually. "But he often was that. We subscribe to no conventions. We don't need to talk if we don't happen to feel like it."

"Quiet, but not unusually so. Did he address any remark to any of you, please? After all, we must imagine he had something on his mind," Mr. Chaos resumed. "A man does not commit suicide just like that." He snapped his fingers. "Particularly a religious man, a man interested above all things in the welfare of his soul — as Mr. Carpenter has just intimated. The actual deed may have been impulsive, but it is highly improbable that it was quite unpremeditated. The thought must have occurred to him before, perhaps often, although he always dismissed it. It may be that he had already made up his mind quite definitely on the point. He may have said, 'On such and such a day and in such and such a manner I will kill myself.' But it requires a remarkable degree of self-discipline to preserve one's customary poise before others. I'm not saying that McQueen could not have managed to bring it off. I don't think that for a moment. But I would like to know whether anything he said inclines you to one view more than another."

There was nothing much to tell, they still insisted. He had asked for bread to be passed to him, for cheese, for water. That was all. He had appeared distracted, morose; no, not *quite* his usual self and yet nothing surprising either.

Audrey said angrily to the others, "Why can't you speak the truth? What is there to hide? I don't understand!" She turned to the detective. She was still white and strained but she had recovered her equilibrium.

Considering her excitability and her emotional outlook, considering the performance she had put up in the hall, her recovery had been pretty rapid. Now she addressed herself to Mr. Chaos. "The fact is, his ill-humour didn't surprise us. If you prefer, I'll say it didn't surprise me. I rather expected it after last night." She looked at the others defiantly, as one who has done her duty.

"Last night? What happened then?" asked Mr. Chaos.

"You were there," said Audrey. "But naturally it wouldn't have meant anything to you — a stranger. I don't think Lucy knew either, or she'd never have said it right out like that. We never did know quite what it was he felt for her, but I knew he was bound to feel something when he heard that she was going to be married."

"You are talking of Miss Post, are you?"

"Who else?" said Audrey.

"You think he was in love with her?"

Audrey hesitated, and before she could answer Ella broke in impulsively: "Oh, no, dear. That's not true!"

Audrey put a hand on hers.

"Ella, darling, there are things you simply cannot understand. I'm not suggesting that he didn't fight against it."

"Oh, no, Audrey." Ella shook her head. She looked frightened. "He wasn't weak like that; David wasn't."

"Ella, darling, as I said before, you just *don't* understand. Weakness or strength doesn't come into it. It's something that happens in spite of yourself, deep down inside," — she clenched her fists beneath her breasts passionately. "He was young and healthy and times it was torture for him, *I* know. But he knew better than to give in. He knew it would destroy him if he did."

Without lifting her forehead from the window-pane, Miriam said, "Perhaps it did," in a dreary voice.

"Perhaps it did what?"

"Perhaps it did destroy him, as you suggest. Perhaps that's why he killed himself."

Audrey swung round affronted.

"How can you! He'd never do a thing like that. Why, that would be weak! I never meant that for a moment."

"You may not have meant it but it may still be true," said Miriam calmly.

"Oh, stop! Do stop!" Ella implored. "It's all so horrible!"

Mr. Chaos said gently, "Well, Miss Slade, why do you think he killed himself?"

She looked stupid, badgered. She said, "I don't know ... Perhaps it was a mistake. Perhaps he never meant to," imploringly.

"Do you really think that? Or is it merely what you want to think?"

"Don't torment her," said Lucy Titmarsh. "She's too sensitive to be able to tolerate it. Bully us if you must, but leave her alone."

Mr. Chaos said in surprise, "I hope I'm not bullying anybody; it is not my intention. Why should I? I only want to arrive at the truth. There'll have to be an inquest; you realise that. The clearer we can get things beforehand, the simpler the actual business becomes. The Coroner will inquire into his state of mind at the time. Naturally. They will have to decide why he took his own life."

"Temporarily unbalanced mind," Miriam was heard to murmur from her post by the window.

"You don't agree with that verdict? Miss Slade doesn't care to think he killed himself at all. Miss Lewes doesn't believe he killed himself for love. Has any one anything to suggest?"

William said sullenly, "Why do you torture us? You know better than we do."

"Why should you think that? Do you imagine that I am trying to provoke you into saying something you want to keep to yourself?"

The old man in the corner stirred from his tranquil pose. He opened his small bright eyes, remote, unblinking, heartless in their gaze like an animal's, and surveyed them benevolently.

"When thoughts clash there is confusion of wills," he pronounced. "If you want to understand the truth look for it. The truth is there, it needs only to be uncovered. To lose your heads and chatter and blame one another is worthless egotism. Don't resist the truth; accept it," he advocated in the quiet, cracked, old voice of moderation and common sense. "The boy is dead. That is the truth, you say. But I say, you turn things upside down and miss the truth. There is too much talk of death. Death is the negation of life, it is not a positive thing in itself. The world says Wesley is dead. We know he is as much alive as ever he was. But we must admit that something we have known has ceased to be manifest to us. He was wrenched away from us suddenly, without warning. And it seemed to us with our limited understanding a very terrible thing. As a result, grief, fear, dread, suspicion, anxiety invaded our pure consciousnesses. We became, as it were, subject to them. We were filled ceaselessly night and day with thoughts of violent death. Is it surprising that it became real to us, that we came to believe in death as a power, despite our long training in understanding it as it truly is in the scheme of things? We are the result of our thoughts. No one will deny that. So it was only to be expected that violence and agony of mind would continue to be present among us ... and they will continue among us until we can get rid of these thoughts about them. David now lies dead. That will not be the last tragedy you will experience if you continue to give power and reality to those negative emotions which have no power or reality of themselves. That is *why* David died, if you really want to know. Because you had all let loose the forces of evil. Stop picking over his dead bones. They can tell you nothing. Leave him in peace, and get about your business." The tired thin voice quavered to silence.

"It's true, you know, what he says. It's quite true. It is our own fault that this happened. It is stupid to try and find some other cause. You were right to pull us up, Bernard. Thank you, dear. One false step and it is so pitifully easy to go on walking in the same direction without realising we are on the wrong track. We are all guilty, but I am most to blame," said Rollo in his slow echoing voice, and it seemed as though his eyes were full of tears. "I —"

Audrey flopped on her knees beside him and took his big hands lovingly in hers.

"No, darling. Why do you blame yourself? It's not right."

Brother Rollo stared down at her mournfully. For a time he did not answer her, as if he were thinking what to say, and then he said, "Do you think if Wesley had been here this would have happened? Do we, too, cast all we have learnt aside because our Master is no longer with us, and go a-fishing, like those others long ago? Wesley trusted me to carry on in his absence. And I have not carried out his trust." He made a sour mouth, self-disgusted, and shut up.

Ella said, "Our hearts have been too disturbed. We have forgotten the truth. We must spend more time in earnest prayer. It is only by opening our minds to God in prayer that we shall learn the truth about our poor David."

Miriam turned wearily to the inspector.

"Please, may we go now? We've told you all we know. And we're very ..."

Alone, Mr. Chaos paced thoughtfully up and down the big room. No one had bothered to draw the curtains though it had been dark a long while. Here and there yellow stars of light shone out unevenly across the invisible fields. He drew the heavy handwoven drapes across the dark picture of the night.

Apart from Audrey's understandable little *crise* in the hall there had been no extravagant parade of grief for their dead comrade. They were red-eyed, shocked to silence by this double catastrophe, and perhaps they were ashamed of the way trouble had come to them for the second time. Murder was bad enough. Suicide was somehow much worse. That they should have occurred in their sacred little community naturally made it worse still. This would make people talk if they had not done so before. It certainly would do nothing to improve their reputation as holy, God-fearing healers. It meant two inquests in ten days. That in itself ... Yes, it was a rotten affair and it was no wonder that they were stunned by all its implications. Probably when all the fuss had died down they would move away from Market Keep and settle in some other locality where they would be unknown.

Mr. Chaos wondered whether McQueen had any relatives. He must ask the others and remind them that they should be informed. From the way McQueen had spoken to him, however, he very much doubted that there was any kin alive who cared twopence about him.

Mr. Chaos suddenly noticed that he was extremely hungry. It was nearly nine and they had not yet eaten. The table was partly laid. But after that grim interruption no one had thought of food, or perhaps it seemed to them heartless to eat when one of their number lay newly dead in such horrid circumstances. However they might feel, Mr. Chaos had no such compunction. There was bread on the table and a jar of honey. And with this Mr. Chaos was as contented as a bear. He roamed about the room chewing a great slice of home-made bread thickly coated with honey; he'd as lief have a meal of that sort any day. He liked the freedom and space and simplicity. For a few moments he dismissed the case from his thoughts, crouching before the bookcase, poking the titles towards the light with his forefinger.

Here a book had been thrust carelessly away lengthways across the top of the books. He pulled it out to put it back right side up on its shelf. It was bound in plain cloth, unadorned with title or author. It opened in his hand almost in the middle where a card had been slipped in to keep the place. The book contained — according to the words at the head of the page — the Yoga Sutras of Patanjali. Who Patanjali was or what his Yoga Sutras were, Mr. Chaos had not the least idea. He read:

"Non-attachment is freedom from longing for all objects of desire, either earthly or traditional, either here or hereafter."

The marker fell to the ground. It was a plain white visiting card. He stooped to pick it up and saw that the obverse side was engraved in copperplate —

J. CORDOVA, M.E., A.R.S.M.

Mining Engineer, translated Mr. Chaos. And Associate of the Royal School of Mines. Now if that was not interesting, he would like to know what was. He whistled faintly an unrecognisable tune between his teeth. He slipped the card back in its place and the book in his pocket. True, the card might have been there some time, it might be ages since any one had looked at that book. But the card looked fresh and un-dogeared, and it was not really very likely that the book would have been left lying the wrong way round for very many days. It was more probable that someone had slipped the book there in a hurry.

To-day, he remembered suddenly, was the thirteenth, and it was on that date that Blizzard & Lake's representative was due to call. It did not then require a great leap of the imagination to connect Mr. Cordova and Blizzard & Lake's representative as one and the same person. Mr. Chaos recollected David issuing from the call-box that very morning with thunderous face. Well, was there any connection? He could not verify that to-night anyhow.

What he could do, though, was to try and find out who had last been reading the Yoga Sutras of Patanjali. If he could find out that it would help a lot.

The next day the doctor's report came in. It confirmed that death was caused by strangulation. It placed the time of death nearer to three hours before the time it was discovered. That is to say, death must have occurred between three and three-thirty p.m. There was one other point mentioned, and that was that the right elbow of the deceased was severely bruised and some of the small bones fractured. The injury had occurred while he was alive and might have been sustained by a bad fall on a hard surface, except that there were no other marks elsewhere on the body such as you might expect to find if he had fallen.

That might not be as important as at first appeared, Mr. Chaos reminded himself impartially.

At that moment he saw a slender figure hurry past his window with bent head. He tapped and she looked round. He could hardly repress a start of astonishment; she looked so different from the smooth and glittering figure that usually represented Valerie Post to the world. He opened the garden door and pulled her in out of the rain.

"My dear," he said, "my dear girl, what is it?"

She was an ugly, wizened, sick old creature. She could have been any age. She was huddled into an old coat, and she had not even stopped long enough to put on a pair of shoes. She was wearing what had lately been a pair of blue brocade mules trimmed with ostrich feathers: now they were sopped through with wet and the feathers draggled in wet brown streaks over the edge. Her stockings were splashed in mud to the ankles. It was almost incredible that she could have run along those rough puddled roads in such frail rickety footgear. She had tied round her hair carelessly a scarlet bandana, and its gaiety contrasted shockingly with her drawn unkempt face. She had dashed some powder unevenly on her cheeks and the bright lipstick smeared across her mouth with a shaky hand was evidence of her agitation. She shuddered spasmodically.

He made her sit down and take off her soaked slippers. He rubbed her numb fingers. He said, "Now, what is it?" in his most sympathetic voice.

"I-I-I've come ... I've j-j-just ... Where —?" her teeth chattered hopelessly. Her monkey eyes gazed at his in mute appeal. He poured some neat brandy into his tooth-mug and handed it to her. She clutched it gratefully, with both paws curving to hold it, and spilled it quickly down her throat. A semblance of life crept into her eyes and skin. She gave one more convulsive shiver and handed back the empty mug.

She got a grip on herself after that. She forced her face into an impassive mask and pulled up the collar of her coat and thrust her hands deep into the pockets with an effort at rakish swagger.

She gave him a quick upward glance.

"I came as soon as I heard. Mrs. Moley, my daily woman, told me when she came this morning," she said in a low voice. "I can't tell you —" Her eyes filled with tears and she broke off. "Where is he? May I see him?"

"McQueen? No, I'm afraid you can't see him. He isn't here."

"Not here? Then —?" Some bright emotion flashed across her face for an instant at the unspoken question.

Mr. Chaos shook his head.

"I'm sorry if you misunderstood me," he said gently. "McQueen lies in the mortuary."

She looked sick.

"For a moment I thought ... Then it's true! He killed himself. When Mrs. Moley told me I couldn't believe it. I never thought he meant that. I'm rotten but I'm not as bad as that. I wanted to — oh, I don't know what I wanted or what I hoped for now," she cried. "But, God, I'd give twenty years of my life —!"

Mr. Chaos said apologetically, "I'm sorry I can't make out what you're talking about. Could you be a little more explicit?"

Her voice was harsh. "Sure! It's plain as the nose on your face." She stood up abruptly and stood with her back to him, staring blankly out of the window at the rain-washed landscape. "If you can understand unvarnished fact, here's the truth of the matter. I killed that boy!"

Mr. Chaos made no comment and she turned to look at him.

"You don't believe me," she sneered. "You think I'm being melodramatic and seizing the situation to dramatise myself."

"A little, perhaps," said Mr. Chaos mildly.

Valerie said bitterly, "I assure you I am as much responsible for his death as if I had stabbed him with my own hands."

"Do you know how he killed himself?"

Flummoxed by this inconsequentially, she stared, stammered, "What? ... No ... of course not."

"I thought perhaps you imagined he had stabbed himself."

She put her face in her hands and rocked slightly to and fro.

"I'm sorry," he said. "I'm sorry." He patted her shoulder.

She raised her ravaged head at last to glare at him bleak-eyed.

"I wanted David. I don't know what it was that appealed to me so much. Perhaps his youth and freshness, though actually he was only a year or two younger than I. But there was something unusual about him, a strength that attracted me. And there was something that repelled just as much; a dominant streak of hardness that I loathed and at the same time wanted to overcome. Perhaps if he had not resisted me so determinedly I would have lost interest. As it was, he was so insolent to me whenever he got the chance that I made up my mind I'd brea down his resistance. He was going to sweat for every insult he had handed me.

"I set out to make him." She glanced at him sideways, viciously. "Well, what's so surprising about that? Women hunt no less than men, but their methods of attach differ. Thackeray knew quite well what he was talking about when he said that any woman who hadn't a positive hump could get any man she wanted. I'm not unattractive when I put myself out. And I didn't expect it to be very difficult. David was no saint — with that sensual chin and those stubby, passionate hands.

"No, he was no saint. But he had an iron self-control. He wanted me desperately, I knew, but his will rode his desire. That excited me. I delighted in his moral strength and was all the more determined to master it." She was talking aloud, unconscious of her listener. A sly smile curled her ill-rouged mouth. "It was the game I knew, the game I loved best. What made it so amusing was that he refused to play. Although he never said so, he was perfectly well aware that I was trying to seduce him. And he hated me for it. And I — I — loved him." The words faded into a sigh. "How do these things happen? Without rhyme or reason one falls in love, and generally, by some jest of the gods, it seems to be with the most unsuitable person. I knew it would never work, even in the most favourable circumstances it *could* never work. But love is beyond logic. God knows, I thought I was hard-bitten, but I swear that if he had asked me to marry him I would have done so like a shot. Unfortunately for me, he never did. No, not unfortunately really. I've enough sense to know it would have been hell after the first month. We had nothing in common. And he feared and despised me. Still, I wanted him; and I tormented him.

"When I found out that he needed a piano to compose, I offered him the use of mine, as you know. He accepted, on the understanding that he would come only when I was out so that he would not feel he was disturbing me. The truth was, of course, that he did not intend that I should disturb him. And when I came back he fled, like Joseph, never to return." She laughed dryly at the recollection.

"But he did come back, didn't he?" said Mr. Chaos. "I saw him with you the other evening."

"When?"

"I passed by your house. You were standing by the window in his arms. There did not seem to be anything shy about him just then."

"He wasn't shy. I had lured him up on the pretext of fetching his manuscript back. And he knew it was only a pretext. He held back at first, but when he did walk into the trap finally it was with his eyes wide open. He left without his music all the same." Her light mechanical voice came to a stop. She began to groan with her head in her arms, savouring to the full now the bitterness of those unfulfilled moments of passion. Never again would she experience that harsh struggling embrace. "What a bitch I've been," Chaos heard her mutter. "What a bitch ... I drove him to it."

She pulled off her bandana scarf and shook free her tousled hair, as though she was stifling in the prison of her memories.

"Dreadful things he said to me then. He told me how he hated me. He loathed me because I had so nearly won. He said he hoped so long as he lived never to see my face again. He cursed me. He frightened me. I was scared and sore and angry, and yet I could hardly believe I had lost. And when you came along I saw my chance, and I told you that I was going to marry Harold, knowing perfectly well that you would come back here and tell them, and he would hear of it. I knew how that would hurt him. I wanted to hurt him. I wanted to make him feel sick. I meant him to think I'd only been playing with him. I hoped he'd believe then that I'd never loved him, that it was all part of the game of pretence. I knew that whatever his reason argued, his body would feel the cruel sting of humiliation; just as I had felt it when he turned from me.

"If he had but known, it was the end for me, it was my way of throwing up the sponge. I meant never to trouble him again. One savage wound in payment of all the wounds he had inflicted on me. How was I to dream he was so near capitulating? How could I guess that it was love he fought against, not me? Or that in frustration and despair he would kill himself? How could I know?" she cried.

The detective's brown eyes were profoundly sad.

"You believe David McQueen killed himself because he learnt you were going to marry Harold Prescott, is that it? You feel that it was only when he learnt that he had lost you that he found he loved you?" He sighed deeply, not caring for what he had to say. He was so kindly by nature that the least form of brutality was offensive to him. "You know, Miss Post," he began, "you were quite right just now when you said that love blinds you to reason and logic. The heart always knows the truth but the mind refuses to accept it. I'm afraid your violent passion for McQueen has muddled your clear unpitying brain. And then this shock on top of it ... If you could get your head above this confusing mist of desire you would see that David was the last man in the world to kill himself from unrequited love, or thwarted passion, or anything of that sort. He had not a very loving nature. Like most artists, he was self-absorbed. And he was self-sufficient; his egotism did not need bolstering up from without with pettings and admiration. Also he was hardy, and I would judge his rare bouts of sensuality to have been brief and unconnected with his everyday life by threads of tenderness or gaiety (without which there is no saving grace). His body felt the shock of physical outrage when he heard you were going to be married; the blood drained away from his fingertips when he learned another man would possess your body, but believe me, his cold mind and unflinching heart were totally unmoved. Bluntly, it was not for love of you, or hate of you, or anything to do with you, that David killed himself."

His words seemed to strip her of everything that went to make up her brave, defiant, reckless personality. It was a mortal blow. Her face was quite grey. Her fingers scrabbled for support on the window-sill. It seemed there was nothing left to her now. She felt stupid and ridiculous, she could see dimly the absurdity of her self-deception, but she did not care.

"Why?" she muttered at last, the rouge standing out in ugly smears upon her bloodless lips. "What other reason had he to kill himself?" she stumbled out, dreading to hear some mention of another name, to hear of some other person in his life of whom she knew nothing.

Mr. Chaos opened the palms of his hands.

"I don't know," he confessed.

"Then why should I believe you?" she demanded. "What do you know about it? What do you know of his inner life and the motives that swayed him?"

"Not much," admitted Mr. Chaos deprecatingly. "But then his inner motives did not have very much to do with it, anyway. It so happens that David McQueen did not commit suicide. *He was murdered*!" He said: "Sit down! Did I startle you? I'm sorry."

"*Murdered*!" she repeated incredulously. "Then why did they say he had killed himself?"

"It was meant to look like suicide, you see. He was supposed to have hanged himself. There were other possible motives besides love. I need not go into that now. He was strangled and then hung up by the cord from his own habit. The rope was carefully arranged over the actual marks of strangulation, so that it should appear they had been caused by the pressure of the rope; I may say that in itself struck me as a little odd. The rope is excessively rough and hairy, and from my experience of suicides they nearly always like to make themselves as comfortable as possible in their last moments. I have never known any one put his head in a gas oven without first placing a cushion conveniently for his neck. And I have often come across people who have hanged themselves by means of a soft silk handkerchief. And people who take poison naturally take the least painful kind they can procure. It is simply a curious psychological factor, this last act of self-pity. And McQueen, I noticed, had a sensitive skin which was chafed even by wool. It was not very likely that even in the stress of the last moments that the coarse rope would not cause the reluctant flesh to shrink.

"But there was something else that bothered me for quite a while. There was something definitely wrong down there in the cellar. It was dark; pitch dark. Now if it was still daylight when he killed himself and he left the outer entrance doors open, it would have been light enough for him to see. *But* — that could not have happened because the cellar doors were closed and bolted from the inside. He could hardly have hanged himself and then come down and closed the doors. On the other hand, the doors might have been closed anyway and the cellar illuminated by the gas-jet. But how and when did he extinguish the gas? There you have the same problem repeated. The only alternative is that he hanged himself in the dark, and that I flatly decline to believe. It is not only against nature, it is practically impossible.

"What conclusion are we forced to arrive at then? He did not kill himself in the dark; and he could not have killed himself in the light: *ergo*, he did not kill himself at all. He was killed." He picked up the little ruined slippers. "I don't know how we're going to send you back in these," he remarked lightly. "You'll have to borrow a pair from Audrey or Mrs. Titmarsh. They're about the nearest to your size."

But Valerie was not listening. She sat hunched on the edge of her chair, a ragged sort of woman with scarcely the energy to repudiate grief, trying to pull herself together, to summon up a façade with which to meet this new variation of horror. Her lips shaped the name "David" but no sound came.

Mr. Chaos held out his cigarette case. Her long trembling fingers had some difficulty in freeing one from its tight nest. But it was with some relief, the relief of finding something stable and familiar again, that she stuck it between her dejected lips. Her lashes, by the flame of his lighter, cast long weary shadows on her pale cheeks. She inhaled deeply and expelled the smoke in little puffs as she spoke.

"Why was he killed?" she asked dully.

"Perhaps for the same reason that Wesley Titmarsh was."

"You mean, the same person killed them both?"

But Mr. Chaos was cautious. The first crime was premeditated; he was not so certain about the second.

She said slowly, "But that means that it is someone — here."

"Why?"

"Doesn't it? I can see that someone might have a grudge or something against Wesley, but surely not against them both. That must be some private —" She broke off unhappily.

"It may be so, but it doesn't strictly follow. We mustn't bind ourselves down to that idea. It may have been intended to give that impression. And I think the fact that he killed himself was supposed to give us the idea that he was the guilty person, that he had killed Titmarsh and then hanged himself because, because — oh, because he couldn't stand the burden on his conscience any longer, or something of that sort."

"But he wasn't killed simply for that," she pleaded. "No one but a madman would kill for so little reason."

"No. I dare say he knew too much. He may have threatened to tell, or he may still have been unaware of the importance of what he knew. Once the murderer got to hear of it, his number was up." As he said this, he remembered Miriam standing in the moonlight and saying, 'I'm not afraid.' And he had answered, 'The risk is not so much to yourself. The risk is that you may lose the murderer. You may carelessly put him on his guard.' Perhaps she had done that very thing, and David McQueen had paid the price of her clumsiness.

He found a pair of shoes for Valerie Post and walked her home. She was in no state to go alone. And he had a phone call to make in the town.

He found Ruby in the kitchen dabbling gruesome-looking slices of liver in flour.

He said, "Ruby, your aunt would like a cup of tea, I think. She isn't feeling very grand."

"Coo!" she said. "You're tellin' me!" She held her fingers under the tap for a minute and then filled the kettle. She banged it down on the stove, and turned to him eagerly, all her recent distrust of him apparently overcome. "Here!" she said huskily. "Is it true that he done himself in?"

"If you refer to Mr. McQueen, you hateful little ghoul, no, he has not done himself in."

"Oh!" she said, not attempting to disguise her disappointment. "Ole Moley said he had."

"Old Moley was mistaken. Which should teach you not to believe all you hear."

She was disconsolate and muttered vengefully of the fuss they all made about nothing. There was Aunt Lucy, who was not to be trusted after all with her stupid jokes. And all that stuff about not saying this and not saying the other. And lies all the time just like other people. And pretence. It made her sick. Why couldn't grown-ups say what they meant? And Umberella, the soppy thing —

"What's umbrella got to do with it?" demanded Mr. Chaos quizzically.

Oh, she was another. Old Umber Ella, that's what they called her. The potty one. They knew all about her. She taught once in the council school. She was soft all right. Ole scaredy-cat! They didn't half used to have a lark with her, 'n' she never tole on them. Too scared, was Ruby's guess. Like the other day: she had met her on the way back from Bidlington and old Umber Ella had gone all silly and made her promise not to mention that she had met her. She'd get into trouble, she said, because she was supposed to be on duty, in case she was needed. There was some private business that she had to see to, she told Ruby, and she didn't want them to know about it.

"Cor!" exclaimed Ruby impatiently. "No one'd ever think she was a grown-up and could do what she liked. Fancy caring about a kid sneaking on her! 'Course I wasn't going to anyway," she said virtuously, quite oblivious of the fact that she had just given her secret away.

What was this duty she had shirked? Did Ruby know?

Oh, yes, she was the one who was supposed to stay in the house in case any one called.

"When was this — in the afternoon?" asked Mr. Chaos, metaphorically sitting up.

"Yes. 'Bout free-thirty when she was coming home."

"So yesterday afternoon —"

"No, not yesterday," corrected Ruby. "The day before."

"The day before!" He frowned at her. "It can't have been. It's impossible. You must be mistaken."

She said pettishly, "Well, I'm not, so there!"

He stared blankly. Then a faint incredulous beam lighted his eye and he said eagerly, "Ruby, could you swear it was the day before yesterday?"

She said, "Hey! you're hurting!" and rubbed her arm ruefully. Yes, she was absolutely positive.

In that case, he mused, stroking his jaw ... His imagination seized eagerly on this new fact, and twisting it this way and that at last forced it into the vacant space in his mental jigsaw puzzle ... So that was how it was! he thought incredulously. How was it I didn't think of it before? And even now, if it were not for Ruby —

"You're my good lass," he said enthusiastically. "I must go now; but I'll come back. And then we'll go places. We'll hit the high spots in Towcester, shall we; what do you say? That's a promise, and we'll seal it with a kiss." He bent and touched her forehead with his lips.

Her first kiss (except for that silly kid, Dicky Green, and he didn't count!). So this was love at last!

Ruby, emancipated, feeling ten feet high and as desirable as Loretta Young, watched him go, vowing in her heart that she would wait for him — for ever, if need be.

CHAPTER THIRTEEN - ADDENDUM TO THE ABBOT'S BREACH DOSSIER

The following notes are my personal record of the case. An attempt, solely for my own benefit, to describe certain factors that are outside the bounds of a dossier. A dossier must keep strictly to facts; the evidence collated thus consists of timetables, statements, clues, exhibits, and so forth; but there is a world of material which has no place in it but which is none the less valuable to the student of crime. These notes will not only elucidate (I hope) certain points which could never be understood from the dossier alone, but will illustrate how the crime was solved.

To begin with, I was called to the case when it was already several days old. Nothing was the same as it had been at the time the crime was committed. The people concerned had had time to reorientate themselves. Clues had been obliterated. Important facts forgotten. Lies prepared. Obviously it makes all the difference if you are on the spot almost at once, before things have been altered, and you are able to get a fresh and accurate impression of the witnesses' reactions.

There was one bright spot about this case though: the main witnesses were supposed always to speak the truth (which is certainly more than can be said of the average run of people), and if they adhered to the truth, or even to what they believed to be the truth, it should make things considerably easier.

The first curious thing that struck me about the crime (apart from the fact that it should have occurred at all among a group of people dwelling together freely in holy poverty and love) was that it had taken place in full view of half a dozen people. So my first question was, Was the locale deliberate? And if it was deliberate, what was the significance of it? The alternative was that the crime was unpremeditated. But the more I looked at it the more apparent it was that it must have been thought out in advance. For one thing, one important thing, was that while he was shot in the open, before witnesses, he was shot unseen; the murderer contrived to be invisible. Plainly this was not mere chance. In fact, I could not see how he was shot at all. And for a long time *how* remained the important question for me.

Titmarsh's watch was out of order, running first fast then slow. That might have been a lucky chance for the murderer, but on the day he was killed his watch was slow and the regulator had been pushed all the way back to the minus side, so that it *should* run slow. Surely that was more than a coincidence. Put that with the fact that the bell that summoned them habitually to their various duties — for this brief occasion was silent — and at once you get a glimpse of how suspiciously convenient it was for the murderer.

Titmarsh must not know the time. So the bell which should have called him across the fields did not ring. It was necessary to the murderer that The Seekers should be quietly in their cells facing the field where the crime was scheduled to take place. Therefore Titmarsh must be prevented from arriving on the scene too soon. He could be waylaid, but that might mean an accomplice would need to be found. Safer to alter his watch, or cause him to alter it by making him imagine it was running unreliably fast, so that the murderer would have ten or fifteen minutes' grace. The murderer must be working to an exact time-table, and the murder had to take place at a certain moment. Either because the method of killing was a time-sprung trap, or to provide an alibi, or possibly both.

Well, there was the stage set, and that was how I roughly saw it then. All I had to go on were their testimonies of what they had seen and heard. Taking that they were all speaking the truth in so far as they apprehended it, their versions varied quite considerably. That they were indefinite and confused was understandable enough. Accidents and all deeds of violence occur with such incredible rapidity that the eyes cannot correctly analyse what has happened, any more than the ear can distinguish the different sounds made by an orchestra playing one chord. A man is seen to put his hand in his pocket; there is a flash; a report; another man falls; and we say that we saw him shot by the first man. Actually we saw no such thing, and for all we know to the contrary the first man may have been feeling in his pocket for his handkerchief. Add to that the confusion of the senses caused by shock, and you get some idea of the ineptitude and worthlessness of most testimony. In this instance, then, I was not dismayed by their vagueness (though McQueen's was remarkably clear), but one or two points struck me.

What accounted for a great deal of their variations was the thick autumnal mist which hung over the country that morning. Hardly any one mentioned it or realised its significance. In fact it made a lot of difference. Most observant people have noticed how fog or mist distorts not only vision but hearing too. Places become unrecognisable, however familiar, perspectives alter, dimensions change. Things are enlarged through mist and at the same time appear from their blurry outlines to be farther away than they actually are. From lack of usage the eye cannot rectify these incalculable changes, and accepts in some stupefaction the sight of things supernaturally large. The same thing occurs with sound.

So we had Ella Slade, who saw the startled birds fly up and some of them — like vultures, she said — come flapping slowly towards her. It was the mist that made them appear so ominously large. Undoubtedly they were common rooks, which are very numerous in the tall trees which surround the house. Miss Slade was confused by the suddenness of it, did not trouble to ask herself why these huge unknown birds should suddenly appear, or, being a countrywoman, she would very likely have realised that it was caused by the atmosphere. As it was, it merely added to her nervous excitement. The same with William Brown, only it was the sound distortion he suffered from. Miss Lewes was the one who came nearest to describing it accurately. But her eye was attracted to something she thought she had never seen before. Her description of it was so unlikely that none of the others could believe her; they dismissed it, apparently as a hallucinatory image caused by shock. Miss Lewes firmly believed that she had seen Titmarsh shot, although there was absolutely nothing to show that a living person had been there.

Yet she was right. But I did not know that till later.

What I asked myself then was, What were they meant to see? Was Miss Lewes supposed to have seen what she did see, or was that an unlucky accident for the murderer? Why were they meant to see their beloved Master killed, I wondered. But perhaps that was only a part of the plan. There may have been something more to it than that. Suppose it was really to provide an alibi for somebody? Was that why that particular hour had been chosen for the crime? A time when they would be all under one another's eye, so to speak, and yet not too closely so. The only other times during the day when they were able to account for one another was at communal prayer or meal-times. But then they were all together and it would not be possible for one to absent himself without the others remarking it. And more difficult still would it have been to get Titmarsh out of the way. No, obviously the most suitable time, so far as an alibi was concerned, was during the period they called Solitary Meditation. But I also realised with some misgiving that if that deduction were correct it meant that the murderer was one of this happy little band of pilgrims, and I was fully aware just how unlikely that was. Why should any of them want to kill their Master? He was no tyrant. They were all free. There were no awkward ties between them, so far as I knew, and they owed one another nothing but love. What possible motive ... ?

At somewhere about this point I was forced by the very grim unsolvability of *how* to turn to *why*. In other words, I left method for the moment to try to puzzle out motive.

The first and most obvious link-up was the business of Percival Menzies, the rehash of the old quarrel, the recent passage-at-arms between them, the proximity of the two estates, and last but foremost, the important and unshakable evidence of the bullet fired from Menzies' own gun. Well, Menzies had a fine unbreakable alibi, in spite of things looking so black against him. Yet on second thoughts I rather wondered whether that alibi was not a little too secure. He might not have pulled the trigger himself, but he might have set someone to do it, or he might have contrived some trap whereby Wesley would shoot himself. I could not forget that Wesley had crossed the field to pick up a spade. Pure chance? Perhaps. But I remembered a curious twist of wire round the neck of the handle, just above the blade. Was that quite without significance? Above all, there was the gun. Yet I wondered whether any one who had the ingenuity to fix such a careful alibi would be so stupid as to use his own weapon.

Still, someone might have got hold of it without his knowledge. And there was the strange affair of Audrey Lewes, who suddenly broke out to the effect that she was Titmarsh's illegitimate daughter. She had kept it from them for about ten years; so obviously her sole reason for coming out with it then was so as to claim as her inheritance her father's manuscripts. Of course she put over a sob-story about it. That was her way. It was plain she still felt resentful about it, however, and it may have been partly the desire to wound and humiliate Titmarsh's wife that had made her bring it out then. It would add to it that I, a stranger, was there.

There too was a kind of explanation of why she was the only person to have seen this mysterious figure, tall and thin and clad in black, standing beside Titmarsh. In that case, the others would be right in their surmise, and it would have no other existence save in her imagination, except that she would have purposely conjured it up and not involuntarily. Perhaps she hoped that she could impress her image of it so firmly in their minds that they would also think they had seen it. But it had not worked out like that.

Well, there was some kind of a motive; that she wanted to get hold of these manuscripts; though I did not really think she had the peculiar type of brain or mode of thought to have planned or carried out a crime of this character. It was not a typically female crime, by any means. And I did not believe a woman had conceived it.

But there was someone who had a sound motive and also the ability. Here was a love affair carried out with all discretion. Apparently no one knew anything about it except for the chance observances of a child who had watched them unnoticed. Perhaps, like Caesar's wife, Mrs. Titmarsh was above suspicion. It is not difficult for Caesar's wife to be above suspicion if she is a quiet, homely, unglamorous little woman, past her middle age; and if her lover is the head master of the local school and ten or more years younger than her, there is still less ground for gossip. But the child in innocent affection had followed them about, watching and listening, and had arrived at her conclusions without any conventional sense of shame. That was just the way it happened to be and it seemed quite natural to her. She tattled of it glibly to me, and I took it as it was presented.

It appeared that Mrs. Titmarsh had been wife only in name for a considerable number of years. That in itself was not abnormal of course, but Mrs. Titmarsh might have felt she was unfairly deprived of her maternal rights. She had always longed for children; that was common knowledge. It was too late for her to remedy that now, but as head master's wife at least she would have other people's children to care for. Nor would it be the first time a woman had fallen desperately in love with a man younger than herself. There was motive enough and they might have planned the crime between them. The child, Ruby Smith, said she had heard them planning to get rid of him, and that Mrs. Titmarsh had promised her that when she married Prescott she should come and live with them.

Yes, it would have been possible, I am sure, to build up quite a good case on those foundations. Good police evidence perhaps, but psychologically invalid. Knowing the people, I was just about as certain as could be that in fact none of it had occurred just like that. I did not believe Lucy Titmarsh was in love with any one. She was too serene. She could never have been a passionate woman; it was in affection that her emotions had outlet. I judged her to have had a very deep and unselfish affection for her husband, and if it had been at all thwarted — which was likely enough — well, that was no more than many a woman married to a genius has had to bear (for Wesley Titmarsh must have been a type of genius). True, it was her great disappointment that she had no children, but she did not blame any one but herself for that. With the result, that she sublimated her maternal instincts in seeing to the welfare of children in general. It was this that she had in common with Prescott, of course. He used to come and discuss his problems with her and ask her advice. The woman's point of view. He knew she took a keen and practical interest in Child Guidance and Psychology and so on. It came about that she began to advise him on other matters beside the scholastic ones. He brought to her his more personal problems. To his dismay he found himself in love with Valerie Post. It hinted at ironic tragedy. He could see quite well that she was not suitable for a head master's wife and he tried his best to put the idea of her out of his head. The trouble was that Miss Post did not take him seriously. She was willing enough to have an affair with him, if that was what he wanted, but the idea of marriage simply made her laugh in his face. That stung him cruelly. From having been "prepared" to marry her as a generous sacrifice, he found himself struggling against the sweeping longing that he had to have her at any price. He used to talk out his sore heart to Lucy Titmarsh. She soothed and encouraged him. And it was on one of these occasions that he wryly remarked how different things would have been if he was married to her. She, of course, laughed and said it was too late now to rectify that. The child heard it and misunderstood, that was all. Just as she misunderstood what they were talking about when she heard Mrs. Titmarsh tell Harold Prescott that there was only one thing for it: he must get rid of him. They were discussing one of the masters whose behaviour was not all it should be. It was no good hanging about and waiting for things to right themselves, Mrs. Titmarsh said firmly; he must go. Naturally, when they found Ruby had heard, as they thought, they made her promise not to tell any one, for it would make things very awkward if it chanced to come to the master's ears before he knew of it officially. Of course when she alluded to Ruby as his future stepchild she was thinking of her position as Valerie's ward. Unfortunately, it is as hard for adults to understand the way a child's mind works as it is for a child to understand an adult. How was Mrs. Titmarsh to know that Ruby was utterly serious when she asked if she might come and live with them if Mrs. Titmarsh married Mr. Prescott? Of course she said yes, thinking it was a joke; to her it was as if she said, Yes, when the moon becomes green cheese; to the child it was as if she had said, Yes, in the near future, perhaps next month, we shall all be together and live happily ever after. The whole thing was a stupid mistake: and it was a cruel disillusionment for Ruby when she found out the truth, the evening she had gone to warn Aunt Lucy of Prescott's supposed infidelity.

No, the secret of the crime lay in the character of the murdered man. I was sure of that. Motives of revenge and ambition? Well, Audrey Lewes was the most likely one in that direction, so far as I knew. There were no possessions, no inheritance. He was a man who despised possessions and who taught his followers to despise them too. He knew that the greater your stake in worldly goods the less time you have to spare for the things of the spirit. It takes a great deal of thought and energy to acquire and maintain riches of any kind, because if you don't look after them when you've got them they soon disappear. To men like Titmarsh and Carpenter it seemed the most absolute waste of time to spend your days worrying about how to get rich when whatever you get has got to be left behind for someone else to enjoy or squander. Vanity of vanities. They preferred to put their energies to perfecting their immortal souls, believing in the eternal "now." I add Carpenter's name to Titmarsh's because I am sure his experience of wealth had really sickened him: he had learnt the futility of possessions, how they degrade a man by making him measure his importance in terms of his wealth. Only a man who genuinely felt overburdened with all his senseless and beautiful demanding objects would have thrown them all away as Carpenter did.

There was the quotation from Emerson: "I no longer wish to meet a good I do not earn, for example, to find a pot of buried gold, knowing that it brings with it new burdens..." Yes, I remembered that and how it was under-scored, when I opened the letter from the firm of Consulting Engineers, Blizzard & Lake. With what object could he be having a secret correspondence with consulting engineers? I say secret advisedly, because although they referred to earlier correspondence I could find no trace of it among his papers. Either he had hidden it or it had been removed after his death by someone else. Then I learnt that there was the remains of an ancient mine not very far away, a pit that had proved unworkable many years since. That knowledge; the lump of coal that served as a rough and not very efficient paperweight; and a telephone conversation with Blizzard & Lake did something to put me on the right track.

That first evening at The Sanctuary, Rollo Carpenter mentioned that he had had five loads of soil dropped on Screw Acres. On the surface there was nothing in that remark to cause the tension I felt in the atmosphere. Add up all those small, insignificant items and what is the sum? This was my answer, anyway. By chance, when deep-ploughing Screw Acres (bad land, as its name implied), the plough had turned up a coal seam. It is not uncommon to find these outcroppings of surface coal; at least, it is fairly uncommon but not by any means unique. Sometimes it leads to a really rich seam, sometimes it is just a chance streak.

McQueen was the lucky one who turned it up. Naturally it excited him. It did not require the blood of a gambler to be thrilled by that. He told the Master of course. And the Master told Carpenter. It was a little council of three to decide what was to be done. But there was never any doubt of the outcome. The Master was interested — as he would have been interested in a goldfinch's nest, just one of the many wonders of the world which had chanced to come his way. Carpenter, a more sentimentally minded man, to whom coal was spelt in terms of exploitation and human suffering, was probably even less interested. And McQueen was flung back on himself with a thud. He was young, a different generation from the other two, and he had had a very different view of life. He could not see the matter as they did. Quite simply, he thought this lucky chance should be exploited. I would not suggest that they quarrelled about it. But I am of the opnion that McQueen put forward some very strong arguments on his side, for clearly Titmarsh was worried about the right and the wrong of it. McQueen may have suggested that it was throwing God's gifts back in His face, or leaving the talent buried in the ground. Carpenter never gave the matter a second thought, his views were quite positive. But Titmarsh *must* have been arguing it out with himself as he read his Emerson, and finding what seemed to him the perfect answer, which at least coincided exactly with what he felt himself; he underlined it in triumph to show to his dear David the next day. Well, he showed it, and that was that. There was no arguing beyond that point, because Titmarsh's word was final.

Inwardly, McQueen *was* a ravening wolf. The life he was leading was not what he really wanted, however much he might kid himself it was. It was better than the past. It had security, affection, honour, importance, and so on. But it was not enough for him. Within his cold crushed heart he longed to repay his past debts of humiliation and contempt. He wanted to repay in kind all the people who had made him suffer, and all those fools who had not appreciated his true worth. He was still secretly ambitious for the glories he had never known. He could not but feel he would be better able to despise wealth if he had a surfeit of it.

Here was his first chance. And it seemed to him that one man only stood in his way. I cannot, of course, pretend to know of his struggles with himself or how long they lasted. But he could not have decided to kill his benefactor without some heart burnings, I suppose. Having once made up his mind that he must gain possession of the coal-field there was nothing else for it, though. He knew the contents of the will. With Wesley out of the way he would have a free hand. Rollo's opposition would not count and as for the others — He might not sell the land of course, but as executor he had the authority to let out part of it if he choose. And that was what he proposed doing, renting the mine to a firm of mine-managers, on the advice of Blizzard & Lake's expert, if it proved a suitable proposition. Titmarsh had already had Blizzard & Lake's consulting specialist down to see whether it was worth the fuss David was making over it. (This was after he had taken the trouble to read up all about it in the Towcester records.) The expert advised an opencast, which should prove an interesting proposition.

Well, there was a motive for murder, in outline.

His method must have taken some time to plan; it was not the sort of plot that was likely to spring fully-fledged into a man's brain. What he wanted was to kill in some way that would provide him with an alibi. That was probably his first consideration.

The trouble with murder is that nothing comes out quite as it is planned: there are always unforeseen occurrences. No murderer ever realises that at the time he plans a murder, if he did he would never attempt it. All the same, McQueen was very lucky: he had one or two pieces of real good fortune. One was the weather. That fog helped a lot. It made everything strange and eerie. There was no moon the night before; he must have waited for that.

The crime appeared thus just as he wanted. A man shot point-blank at close range in the middle of a three-acre field with no one in sight. There were witnesses to that who had seen him alive, walking across the field, and then saw him fall dead. And McQueen was with them, in a room between two others, no doubt of that.

So far, so good.

The very first bloomer he made was in his testimony. He had it all off pat, there was no indecision or hesitation there, he knew exactly what had happened. That was his undoing. He knew because he had planned it, not because he had seen it. He thought he didn't need to see it, but he described too exactly what should have happened. He didn't mention the mist. He wanted to be sure that someone gave an accurate account; it must be certain that Wesley had crossed the field alone and then been shot. But he could not afford to wait and see it happen. He wanted to be down those stairs the minute the shot was fired. He *had* to be first on the scene. Suspicious? He had to take that risk.

He must have had a very bad moment when he saw that his victim was not dead. He would naturally suppose that at that range a soft lead bullet like that would kill him outright. But it was not a human hand which pulled the trigger, and inaccuracies are unavoidable. Still, he could see in that first frightened examination that there was no risk of Titmarsh recovering from such a wound, and very little risk that he would regain consciousness either. Not that he could afford to take chances about that. He had to keep them all at bay as much as possible, by means of sympathy, errands and orders, or any other method that seemed appropriate to him. He dared not let them come too near. He dared not let them try to do anything for him. Anyhow, he wanted everything left just as it was for the police to see. He had not taken all those pains to prepare the terrain for nothing.

Having more or less decided that the murderer must be one of The Seekers, the thing that bothered me most was the weapon. There was not a shadow of doubt that it had been fired from Menzies' rifle, and yet that meant that not only had the murderer to have the right of entry to his house and easy acess to his gun, but he had also to run the risk after the crime of replacing it. Well, that was most unlikely, for The Seekers were barely on speaking terms with the Menzies. The only possible connection I could see was somehow via Valerie Post, who was friendly with them both.

And then McQueen brought up the business of his old shotgun. I knew he must have raked it up from somewhere, because it had not been in that cupboard when I first arrived. Was his story genuine? Or was it something that he dared not keep hidden any longer, and, remembering Poe's Purloined Letter, thought the safest thing was to hand it over all innocently to the police. Where else could he hide it safely? It's not so easy to get rid of a big weapon like that. I would not swear that what he did was foolish. It might have been safe enough if Ella Slade had not miraculously remembered what she had so inconveniently forgotten through her epileptic fit.

It was seeing the scarecrow that brought it all back to her. And when I saw it, I too began to understand. For one thing, as it leaned there so rakishly in its rusty black with its empty sleeve flapping, I had a sort of vision of what it was that Audrey Lewes had glimpsed through the mist. It was this lean, black, still figure, arm outstretched sideways, like a duellist, pointing at Titmarsh.

It was the bullet that flummoxed me still, till I remembered testing it at the police station and I realised that any one could do as much. Still, David's weapon was a shotgun, after all. I couldn't quite reconcile the two facts. But Professor Vitell could — and did.

Yes, firing a bullet into the sand-pit in the yard of the police station made me see that any one could have done as much. All the murderer had to do was to hang about the rifle-range up on the hills sometime when there was shooting going on, and then when no one was around dig a spent bullet out of the sand-butt on either side of the target. Then it would show by the marks of rifling on it that it had been fired with a rifle. It was sheer chance that the bullet he picked was fired from Menzies' gun.

It was perhaps only then while he was loitering at the rifle-range that the full beauty of his plan came to him. If a man was killed by a bullet, no one would ever think it had been fired from a shotgun. And David had a shotgun. The first maxim of every murderer should be: Use what you have to hand; distrust all plans which require new weapons.

The bullet was carefully wrapped in moss and inserted in the barrel of the shotgun. One moonless night the shotgun would replace the wooden arm of the scarecrow which stood in the middle of the field to scare the rooks away. The scarecrow stood a little higher than the average man, and his level arm slanted breastward. The hammer of the shotgun was raised and tied back with a fine wire. A spade was plunged deep into the ground about three feet away, at such an angle that it could be pulled out only from one direction. The other end of the wire was fastened to the base of the neck just above the blade. Unless you knew the wire was there you would never notice it. Now, the moment the spade was pulled out of the earth, the wire slackened and released the hammer ... and the bullet sped to its last lodgment in the victim's head or breast. In this instance it lodged somewhere between the two just where the neck joins the breast, and in the force of its velocity brought some fragments of moss with it.

It could hardly have been simpler. He had only to tease Wesley into believing his watch was consistently playing him false, by altering the other clocks. A trick as old as Time. On the day itself he climbed the bell-tower and hitched the rope to one side. By a fortunate concatenation of circumstances William was on duty that day as bell-ringer, and he knew that William would never have the nerve to go up and investigate for himself. Even if William had not been the one on duty, he would have found some other way of preventing the bell from ringing. As Wesley came back he was certain to see the spade lying forgotten in the field, and having seen it, he was equally certain to go and fetch it in. He was not the man to tolerate tools being ill-used. So he picked up the spade and —

The minute he put his hand on the spade, David tore downstairs. He did not dare to unfasten the wire lest someone should see him. But it only took a second to bend down and snip it close to the spade handle. The length of wire released coiled up like a spring into the scarecrow's shabby coat. When he saw Ella he had an inspiration and got her to cart the tiresome thing away, anywhere out of sight, out of the way of inquisitive eyes, to be dealt with later at his leisure. (And at some time he tossed the ragged figure into a corner of the barn and slipped the shotgun into the cupboard for me to find.) Even if Ella talked about it later or it was discovered, he would not be blamed, for by then no one would see its significance.

Well, all that sequence was very unpleasant for him, but it was not to last long and he had but to grit his teeth and endure it. I don't suppose he cared to have me on the premises either, nosing around.

Having got as far as this I had still got nowhere, I had virtually no proof. Yes, I could prove that Titmarsh had been killed like that, but I would need something more direct to prove McQueen had done it before I could arrest him without making a fool of myself. Somehow those facts had to be tied on to him. As they stood now they fitted any one — except for the minor factor of motive. Motive alone is not enough in a court of law.

Then *I* had a bit of luck for a change. I chanced across the requiem he had composed for Titmarsh at Miss Post's. When I heard it played on the church organ at the funeral I thought it was rather an impressive piece of work. So when I found it at Miss Post's I propped it up on the piano to fumble it out for myself. I nearly leapt out of my skin at the shock of my discovery ... *The theme was based on the four letters D.E.A.D.* And it had been written some three weeks before Wesley Titmarsh met his end! It must, in fact, have been written in a state of jubilation after the perfecting of his plan. It needed something like that to send him into the white heat of composition. DEAD, DEAD, DEAD, he was crying in his excitement. No wonder it ended in that magnificent shout of triumph. It would never have dawned on him how he was giving himself away. Ah, well, there's no accounting for the origins of inspiration!

There wasn't much doubt in my mind that I had it now. There remained one or two points that wanted tidying up. I like everything to be orderly and shipshape, so I cleared those up first. It was, perhaps, a mistake. In hesitation I was lost. When I came to arrest him, McQueen was dead.

It was to appear to be a suicide. But the murderer had made a couple of glaring errors. What jolted me badly was the thought that I must have gone wrong somewhere in my deductions. It seemed to me McQueen must be innocent after all, and the murderer had killed him because in some way he had become a danger to him. It did occur to me, but it seemed most unlikely, that someone knew McQueen was guilty, despaired of him being brought to justice, and decided to take the law into his own hands. It could be, but I didn't believe it. Ordinary citizens do not take the law into their own hands or even wish to. Murder for gain *is* one thing, but murder simply that justice may be done — No. People don't risk their necks for such impersonal abstractions.

I have mentioned already that the facts as they stood with my interpretation of them would fit almost any of The Seekers. But where was I to start from this time? What threads had I to guide me now?

There was Mr. Cordova's card. David coming out of the telephone booth that morning with his furious sullen face. Brother Ella's absence from door-duty the previous day, the twelfth. Somehow these things were all connected, I was sure. Why I could not *see* it was because I had it fixed in my mind that Blizzard & Lake's representative was to call on the thirteenth. While I held that idea nothing made sense.

Directly I contacted Blizzard & Lake they checked up on it and found that their representative was wanted overseas on a job and had had to rush through his appointments so as not to break the contract. He got down to Market Keep on the twelfth. He had no time to let them know in advance and just had to chance it that he would find somebody in. Of course Blizzard & Lake's representative *was* Mr. Cordova.

If things had gone right he should have seen Ella Slade, who would have fetched the one person who wanted to see him and whom he wanted to see: David McQueen. But Brother Ella had sneaked out to see her relatives because they were bothering her to return. And Mr. Cordova saw somebody else; somebody who did not fetch McQueen to him. So the next morning, when David went down to telephone to Blizzard & Lake to inquire what time their representative was likely to come, he was told that he had already been the day before. No wonder he looked black when he came out of the booth; astonishment had taken hold of him.

That queer little extract from the Yoga Sutras, or whatever they were called, in the book where I found the visiting card, was so typical of one of The Seekers that he might as well have written his name at the bottom.

"Non-attachment is freedom from longing for all objects of desire, either earthly or traditional, either here or hereafter."

Only one person really felt that with all his heart and soul I knew, apart from the old man, Bernard Drag — and he had already attained that state. But it was not that alone which put me on the track. As soon as I knew what had happened I knew whom Mr. Cordova had seen. There was only one other person who knew about the prospective coal-mining venture, who would have had the wit to know what he was talking about, who had an excellent reason for getting Cordova off the scene before he had a chance of meeting David.

When I went to get him he was waiting for me in his cell-like room. I could see he knew what I had come for. He looked up and gave me his faint remote smile when I came in with the constable. His words, however, were totally unexpected.

"I was wrong," he said. "The guilty soul cries out for justice. Freedom is intolerable. It was when God set Cain, the murderer, free that he lost his defiance and cried despairingly that his punishment was greater than he could bear. We reap what we sow; and punishment assuages suffering."

He held out towards me his great, bony, trembling hands. (There are moments when my job is frankly detestable.) I said: " Rollo Carpenter, I arrest you for the murder of David McQueen. And I warn you that anything you say will be taken down and may be used in evidence ..."

He smiled dimly.

"That's all right," he said. "I want to make a statement."

I advised him to wait for his solicitor before he said anything. But he did not seem to care about that at all. He plumped straight out for his guilt. I think he had no wish to be saved. Not then, at any rate. I think he was a heartbroken man if ever there was one.

Actually, when I had had his account of what had happened, it seemed to me he stood a fair chance of getting off on a charge of manslaughter. The bad point was that he had tried to conceal the crime. The good point was that he genuinely had not the least idea that McQueen was Titmarsh's murderer. So it was not revenge.

I append his statement.

APPENDIX
ROLLO CARPENTER'S STATEMENT

On the afternoon of the twelfth, about two-thirty as near as I can remember, I was crossing the hall when I saw someone standing in the porch. It was not my business to attend to visitors, but it seemed only courteous to ask if I could help him, especially as I knew he had seen me. I went over to him and he handed me his card. It did not convey anything to me. I said, "What is it you want?" And he told me he came from Blizzard & Lake. So I told him we had decided definitely that we were not going to do anything about it. We were going to leave things as they were. He seemed rather surprised at that and said he'd been asked especially to call by Mr. Titmarsh. I said, "But don't you know, Mr. Titmarsh is no longer with us. He passed beyond us a week ago." He looked very confused at that and murmured something about dates which I did not understand till later. I got rid of him. I thanked him for coming and sent him away. Then I went on with the job and thought no more of it.

The next day Brother David came to me and said he wanted to speak to me privately. He said, "We'll go down in the cellar. No one will disturb us there. You can say you're going to help me pack the fruit for market." I said all right.

He closed the door at the top of the steps. The doors leading into the lane were open. He said, "You saw Cordova when he called yesterday, didn't you?" I said, "Was that his name? Yes." He said, "May I ask why you took it upon yourself to send him away?" I saw with surprise that he was angry. I had never seen David angry before. "I supposed there had been some mistake," I said. "There was no mistake," he snarled, "*I* sent for him."

I said, "But, my dear David, whatever for? Why didn't you tell me?" All those stupid sort of things. But he did not bother to answer me. He was pulling-to the great doors and shutting out the daylight. He said furiously, "Light the light, damn it! We don't want every one to see us quarrelling."

I said again, "David, whatever is the matter? We're not quarrelling!" But it seems we were. He laughed unpleasantly and said, "Get this into your head!" And he told me then that he meant to use the coal that he believed ran under our land. I was horrified. It was almost the Master's last decision that we should not do this. I said, "David, you can't." He said, "I can and I will." No one should stop him, he declared. I said firmly I would stop him if it was the last thing I ever did. I don't believe in being weak about such things. It was dead against all the principles of our brotherhood, and if necessary I would take it to law to defend what I knew the Master would have me defend. Wesley trusted me to look after the spiritual welfare of the Brothers and I meant to carry out my trust.

It is so easy for anger to call forth anger. I'm afraid I let myself get rather heated over it. I was, to tell the truth, disgusted and astounded at David's attitude. Here was someone we trusted implicitly. The very fact of his rage told me he knew it was wrong. At last I tried to pull myself together and I said, "Well, I shall not stay here to argue with you. The first thing I am going to do is to tell the others and warn them against you. We have the power to turn you out of our assembly, you know, by a majority vote!" Stupid of me to tell him; I see that now, but at the time it seemed only honest.

He did not like that at all. He went deadly pale. And just as I moved towards the stairs the light behind him glittered on something he held in his hand. He was coming for me with a knife! I thought he must be mad. I called to him loudly to try to bring him back to himself. But I couldn't rouse him, and in self-defence I caught his wrist and banged his elbow as hard as I could against the wall. He gave a half-stifled shriek and dropped the knife. I had hurt him. He doubled up and clutched his arm. I thought he was going to faint. But as I bent over him to apologise and help him he sprang at me. It seems so incredible, and so unlike our quiet David, even now I can hardly believe it. I tried to keep him back, to hold him still. I had the advantage of him in height and weight. I held him off by the throat. What else could I do? He struggled for me, purple in the face. And then he stopped fighting. And I let go of him and he fell to the ground. He was dead. I had killed him. You know, I couldn't believe it. I was horrified. And then I was afraid. I picked him up but I couldn't revive him. I suppose I ought to have given the alarm at once. But I lost my head. What a cowardly fool I was! I thought I could make it look like suicide. I thought — I don't know what I thought ...

I took the cord off his habit and strung him up with it, so that it hid the marks my fingers had made on his neck. I put a crate beside him, to look as if he had kicked it over. Then I turned out the light because I didn't want any one to see him. I wanted him to remain hidden for ever. If I could have got rid of him altogether I would have. I hated the sight of my guilt.

They have told me that he killed the Master. I understand now. So much is clear that was obscure before. Poor David! He was not strong enough to withstand the temptation of sudden riches and power. He believed that they would give him something he otherwise lacked. He believed ultimately in the supreme importance of his own desires and will. To have yielded to violence so as to achieve his own ends must have seemed to him tantamount to destroying an antagonistic Fate. That would have been his strongest moment. Afterwards he must have known he was lost — one way or another, sooner or later, doomed. For violence begets violence. I pray these responsive actions of hatred and fear are ended now with my deed.

When Brother Bernard spoke that evening after David's body was discovered, I understood quite well what he meant, and I realised that I should never be able to go through with it. I was too aware of my guilt. I hadn't the strength of conviction necessary to carry it off. I was afraid. I waited, sick at heart, for you to come to me, and I secretly hoped that it would not be long. It is done; and I am weary; I long for expiation.

Read through, sworn to, and signed,
ROLLO CARPENTER.
15th October, 19 —